*The darkness he fights is matched only by the
darkness he holds inside.*

The taskmaster swung the cleaver through the musky air. Ryder watched as the blade glistened in the lanternlight. This scarred, shirtless creature seemed to be enjoying himself. He had a whip in one hand, a cleaver in the other, and was swinging them both like a child might wave its toys. It made Ryder's stomach turn. What sort of man would revel in such torment? What sort of life could have led a man to stoop to such a place? He was barely more than an animal.

Ryder stared down at the chains on his arms and legs. They were trying to turn him into an animal as well. He looked back at the taskmaster. He was still flailing around with his whip and cleaver. The taskmaster's chest and forehead were beginning to shine from sweat. That would be Ryder's challenge here. He could never let himself become like this man, never let them take from him the only thing he had left: his humanity.

*Jess Lebow tells a thrilling tale of honor, betrayal,
and vengeance, filled with the unbroken spirit
found only in the souls of*

FORGOTTEN REALMS®

THE FIGHTERS

Master of Chains
Jess Lebow

Son of Thunder
Murray J. D. Leeder

Ghostwalker
Erik Scott de Bie

Bladesinger
Keith Francis Strohm

Also by Jess Lebow

Magic: The Gathering™
The Darksteel Eye

Legend of the Five Rings™
Wind of War

Dungeons & Dragons™
Return of the Damned

FORGOTTEN REALMS®

THE FIGHTERS

MASTER OF CHAINS

JESS LEBOW

The Fighters
Master of Chains

Cover art by Raymond Swanland
First Printing: September 2005
Library of Congress Catalog Card Number: 2004116885

9 8 7 6 5 4 3 2

ISBN-10: 0-7869-3800-5
ISBN-13: 978-0-7869-3800-1
620-96990740-001 EN

U.S., CANADA,	EUROPEAN HEADQUARTERS
ASIA, PACIFIC, & LATIN AMERICA	Hasbro UK Ltd
Wizards of the Coast, Inc.	Caswell Way
P.O. Box 707	Newport, Gwent NP9 0YH
Renton, WA 98057-0707	GREAT BRITAIN
+1-800-324-6496	Please keep this address for your records

Visit our web site at **www.wizards.com**

Dedication

To SC. Hi, and hi. The best I've written for the best I've ever known. You make me happy. For being the princess.

Acknowledgements

Above all, thanks must go to my editor, Susan Morris. Your hard work and insights were a tremendous help, and this wouldn't have been half the book without you. I'd also like to thank:

Connie Beetlestone for tirelessly reading the rough draft but mostly for her enthusiasm. (You helped me get through the rough spots.)

Jay Adams for being a great sounding board for ideas.

Philip Athans, just because he's so cool.

Steve Whitman, for being brilliant.

Phil Tasca, for also being brilliant.

And last but not least, the baristas at the 1st and Pike SBC, for putting up with me while I wrote the whole dang thing.

Young Lord Purdun stepped around a ruined tombstone and pulled his sword from its sheath.

"Quiet now," Purdun said.

"What is this place?" asked Menrick.

"From the looks of it, I'd say it's the entrance
to a family tomb." Purdun pushed aside the
dried, thorny vines covering the façade of the
stone building with the tip of his blade. The dark,
dead plants made a light grinding noise as they
slid across the decrepit, withered stone.

"Well, well," said Lord Purdun. "What do we
have here?"

Unlike the rest of the tomb, cracked and worn
smooth from hundreds of years of rain and the
elements, the stone underneath the hanging
vines was a slick, polished black that shone like
a mirror. Carved into its surface were hundreds

of tiny figures. Each of them had been crafted down to the most minute detail.

"Help me clear away the vines so we can get a better look."

Menrick stepped up beside the young lord, and the two of them together cut down the dead vegetation.

A rectangular slab of jet black stone covered most of the front of the tomb. At the center of the wall an archway cut the slab in two. It looked to be outlining what must have been the entrance to the tomb, but the one-time doorway was now bricked up.

Menrick bent close to the stone, examining the carvings. "It appears to be obsidian."

Lord Purdun ran his hands across the smooth, black stone. "This is remarkable. It looks to have been carved within the last tenday." He took a step back and scanned the path leading up to the tomb. "But there isn't so much as a single footprint or chip of stone. No one has visited this place for years."

"My lord, the stone is likely enchanted," said Menrick. "Judging from these carvings, whoever rests here left behind a lot of mourners."

Purdun turned his attention back to the carvings. The figures were mostly human, though there were some dwarves, elves, and what appeared to be half-orcs depicted in the scene as well. All of them were looking toward a large ziggurat in the distance with a lone figure standing atop it. The figure was of a woman, wearing a cape with a thick collar. She held over her head a large box. Beams of energy or light radiated from the box, and the woman's eyes gazed upon it in obvious adoration.

Carved in the middle of the box was a strange rune. It looked like two entwined threes, twisted and gnarled, reaching toward the ground—a bodiless, headless spider ready to sink its clawed legs into an unsuspecting victim.

On both sides of the archway, the scene was repeated in

exact detail. Same woman, same box, and same strange, twisted rune.

"Look at this." Menrick ran his hand over the edge of the arch. "Oh my."

Purdun took a step closer. A jagged, rather chaotic pattern was inscribed around the archway. It reminded Purdun of the golden illumination on the pages of one of his favorite books, back in the manor library.

"What am I looking at? This pattern?"

Menrick nodded.

"Yes, that's very exciting," said Purdun, shaking his head. "Whoever crafted this stone had a real flare for decoration."

"This isn't decoration, my lord. It's an invocation."

"A spell?"

Menrick nodded again, not taking his eyes off the carvings. "The spell that opens this doorway."

Purdun squinted his eyes. "Why would a sealed doorway require an invocation to be opened?" The characters were so tiny, he couldn't discern where one ended and the next began. "I don't recognize the language."

Menrick took a step back and crossed his arms over his chest. "That's because it's Infernal."

"Infernal?"

Menrick looked down his long nose at his young master. "Yes, Infernal. And I don't know why the door would need an invocation to be opened, but if I had to hazard a guess, I'd say it wasn't a door that was meant to be opened more than once."

"I don't understand."

"The invocation likely summons a spirit or phantasm," explained Menrick, "some creature from another realm who can destroy the enchantment that guards this portal."

Purdun smiled. "You're saying this isn't a tomb—it's a vault, a treasure trove."

Menrick cocked his head, a stern look on his face.

"Well, I don't know, but . . . I would say it is quite likely. But I do not think it would—"

Purdun cut him off. "Can you open this door?"

"My lord, I really must protest—"

"Can you or can you not open this door?" demanded the young lord.

Menrick stood silent for a moment, then nodded. "Yes, my lord. I can."

Purdun stepped aside. "Then open it."

"My lord—"

"Open it."

Menrick bowed his head. "As you wish."

The old wizard pushed back the sleeves of his white robe and fished around inside his pack, eventually pulling a handful of scrolls from the cluttered sack. Unrolling them one at a time, he scanned the text until he located the correct passage.

Menrick cleared his throat then began reading. He spoke softly at first. So softly that Purdun could barely hear him. But slowly his voice rose in volume, until eventually Menrick was shouting. Lord Purdun still didn't understand the words his manservant spoke, but the sounds he made were familiar. They had the same tenor and pitch as words Purdun himself used every day.

Menrick fell silent. The runes inscribed so tightly around the edge of the archway began to glow a pale green and the pattern changed shape, transforming from a jumble of lines and curves into recognizable letters and words.

"Thank you," said Purdun. Then it was his turn to read.

> *Handmaidens of Lolth*
> *Ghouls of Baphomet*
> *Harbingers of death and despair*
> *Bring forth the suffering*

Release the shackles of night
Bear down the walls of Dis
Evade the hunters,
The Bebilith, the Retriever, the Vrock

Come now from your places of darkness
As once you were born from good
Return now to do thy bidding

Flaming Balor in the bowels of the Abyss
Accept mine invitation
From the pit I command of you
Tanar'ri come forth

Purdun finished intoning the last word and the ground began to rumble. Rolling waves of earth washed through the ruined cemetery like the wake of a ship slapping up against the shore. Headstones crumbled. Partially collapsed mausoleums moaned under the assault as if the dead themselves were lamenting this intrusion. Trees shook, birds scattered, and both the young lord and his companion were tossed from their feet by the shaking ground.

A hole opened in the dirt just in front of the old tomb. It was rimmed in the same pale green light as the runes inscribed on the archway. A thick gas spilled out, covering the ground like fog. Then the earth went still. All was quiet except for a scraping noise that grew louder and louder.

Purdun swallowed hard, unable to take his gaze off the glowing pit.

The foggy gas swirled, disturbed from the inside. A shadow filled the cloud, nearly blocking out the green glow. And out of the shadow a hideous beast emerged.

"Glabrezu," whispered Menrick. His voice sounded far away, strangled, as if he had tried to hold back the foul word, but it had been pulled forcibly from his lips.

The demon's skin creaked as it stretched and moved across piles of muscle. Standing almost three times the height of a man, the creature turned its massive bulk, shifting its entire body to look at Purdun and Menrick. Its eyes, glowing with the color of rotting flesh, were little more than withered and wrinkled husks. They seemed ready to fall from the demon's oversized eye sockets, attached by stretched, desiccated tendons that looked more frail than a thin strip of vellum.

Its head was like that of a dog's. Long, sharp, dripping fangs protruded from under a blackened lip that ran the length of its pointed snout. It snarled at the two men, revealing two more jagged rows of teeth behind rotting, pockmarked gums.

Lord Purdun got to his feet and drew his sword. He took a step forward, but Merrick's hand on his calf held him back.

"This is a fight we cannot win," said the wizard. Menrick pushed his chin in the direction of the demon. "And this creature is bound to us."

"Bound to us?" Purdun shook his head. "This is a beast of the Abyss. How is it bound to us?"

"The invocation," explained Menrick. "Its words bind the creature as well as summon it." He looked at the young lord. "This beast is here to open this door. Nothing more."

As if the glabrezu heard and understood Menrick's words, the demon turned toward the mausoleum and placed its four hands—two ending in jagged claws, two in crablike pincers—on the sides of the archway. A spark of green energy jumped from the stone into the creature, and the beast let out a wail. Purdun had to cover his ears against the agonizing sound.

The carved obsidian wall began to glow yellow-green— all of it except for the lines of power coming out of the box, suspended in the air by the worshiped woman at the top of both carvings. This light was a ghostly blue-white.

The tiny carved humans, dwarves, and elves in the relief pictures began to shift and move. They raised their hands to the sky, milling around each other as if they were alive. They moved with a purpose, executing some sort of ancient dance or mass summoning ritual. Then, as a group, the entire throng on both sides dropped to their knees, bowing down before the glowing woman at the top of the two daises. The box she held over her head rotated and the lines of energy shooting out of it cast a pale white light over all the worshiping subjects below. Shadows rippled and moved over the collected group as they raised their hands then dropped their foreheads to the ground.

"May Ilmater protect us," whispered Purdun.

Two glowing white boxes, held aloft by two identical carvings of the heavily robed woman, stopped rotating. Their beams of white light lifted off the wall and fell upon the demon. The beast clenched its claws and pincers, crushing handfuls of obsidian in its powerful grip and opening its mouth as if to scream.

But no sound came out.

The light danced over its flesh, illuminating parts that had likely not left darkness for thousands of years. The demon, its mouth still agape, its eyes raised to the heavens as if praying to the gods to save it from such torture, began to tremble. Its whole body shook and blue-white light began to pour from cracks in its flesh. The glow grew until it encompassed the creature's entire body. Then in a flash of brilliant light, the demon exploded.

Lord Purdun threw his arm over his face, covering his eyes from the intense glare. Despite the shield of skin and bone, the light penetrated Purdun's flesh. He could see the red blood coursing through his veins, the bones holding his body upright, and the muscles that made him move. A shiver went down his spine.

The light vanished, and Purdun's arm went dark. Cautiously uncovering his face, the young lord nudged

Menrick with his elbow. "It's safe."

Both men stared in awe at the mausoleum. The carved figures had gone still. The adored woman stood stoically holding her rune-inscribed artifact, unmoving. The glowing lights, the shadowy hole, and the demon were gone. All that was left in their place was a blackened circle on the ground where the glabrezu had stood and an open archway leading into the mausoleum.

Purdun looked to Menrick. "Shall we?"

Menrick got to his feet. "This is a bad idea."

Ignoring his manservant, Purdun crossed through the archway into the inky darkness. Two steps across the threshold, the hallway burst into light. Purdun dropped into a defensive stance, bearing his blade before him, prepared to fend off any unseen attacks.

But nothing came.

Eerie torchlight cast shadows into the cracks in the walls and along the flagstones of the floor. A single torch hung at about head height from a sconce. It did its best to push back the oppressive darkness, illuminating a small circle before the door. It was enough to see by, but little more.

"Isn't that nice," quipped Purdun. "Whoever built this tomb thought of everything." The young lord straightened himself and pulled the torch from its sconce.

"My lord," said Menrick, "I have a bad feeling about this."

"Nonsense." Purdun lifted the torch to extend its reach. "We had to summon a demon just to get in. Nothing and no one has been inside here for hundreds of years. What could happen?"

"I can think of many things," replied the wizard.

"You worry too much." Purdun pointed the torch down the hall. "Come on."

They continued deeper into the mausoleum. With each step the crackling circle of yellow light revealed more of the tomb, one brick at a time. Behind them their footprints were swallowed by the shadows. The hallway continued on for some time, the surroundings changing little. Only the cut of the stones and the accumulation of dust gave any indication that they were making progress. Finally, the floor tilted down, becoming a set of descending stairs.

With little more than a glance over his shoulder at Menrick, Lord Purdun headed deeper into the tomb.

"Stay close." As he descended, the air grew heavy. Gone was the fresh, flowing breeze on the banks of the Deepwash. In its place were the stale, last breaths of the dead.

The dust on the ground grew thicker and their surroundings colder as they descended. When Purdun finally stepped off the last stair, he found himself in a large, open room.

The young lord thrust the torch out into the darkness. The wavering, shadowy edges of several rectangular polished-stone structures materialized in the dim light. Their sides reflected the glow, scattering the torchlight.

Purdun stepped forward and, sheathing his sword, placed his hand on top of one of the structures. The rectangular box was seemingly carved right out of the stone of the floor.

"Sarcophagi," he whispered. Moving closer to the center of the room, he waved the torch slowly from side to side, trying to take it all in. In long, straight rows, with just enough space between them for a man to walk, the sarcophagi filled the space from wall to wall.

"There must be over a hundred people buried here."

In the middle of the room, perched above the others on a stepped dais, sat a larger, gem-encrusted coffin. The rubies and sapphires sparked brilliantly even in the faded orange light of Purdun's torch.

"You see that," said the young lord. "I told you this was a treasure trove."

"My . . . my lord," stuttered the wizard. "This tomb is not empty. It is unwise to disturb the dead."

Purdun smiled. "Do not worry. They will not miss what we take." He patted his manservant on the shoulder then bounded to the top of the dais to get a closer look at the coffin.

Unlike the bland, rectangular stone boxes along the floor, the coffin was carved and embellished to resemble a human woman. No detail had been spared to make it look as if it were in fact a princess who had just been laid down for a final rest. She was dressed in what appeared to be a long, flowing blue gown rimmed with silver accents and gemstone inlays. Long black hair spilled over her shoulders and ran along her pale, resting arms. And on her lapel was the same twisted rune that had adorned the artifacts on the front of the mausoleum. The woman's eyes were closed, but the carving was so remarkably detailed it looked as though she might open them at any moment.

Purdun moved quietly up to the head of the coffin. He was gripped by the feeling that any sudden movement might wake the sleeping beauty, and he would be scolded like an impetuous, thoughtless child. He placed his hand gently against the side of the woman's pale cheek, but instead of the soft warmth of human flesh, he felt the cold solidity of wood. Startled by the contrary sensation, the young lord knocked on the woman's hair with his knuckles. It made the familiar deep, hollow sound of a wooden coffin.

Menrick stepped up on the dais. "My lord, we should not be here." He grabbed Purdun by the shoulder and spun him away from the coffin. "It is not unheard of for the dead to rise again. We have seen it here in Ahlarkham many times." His voice quivered as he spoke. Looking around the room, he took in the rows of sarcophagi. "The invocation may have triggered spells that will awaken them. We should not be here if that happens."

Purdun took another look at the carved beauty beside him. "I . . . I. . . ." He felt compelled to touch her in the flesh, to see what was under the carved wood. He struggled with the feeling. It was like an itch that he just had to scratch. Placing both hands on the lid of the coffin, he lifted.

"No, my lord!" Menrick lunged, trying to stay Purdun's hand. But it was too late.

The wooden box creaked as it opened, and Lord Purdun looked down on a resting woman. Her long black hair and porcelain skin matched perfectly the carving on the lid of the coffin. Her arms were folded over her chest, and her lips were turned up at the corners, as if she were in the midst of a pleasant dream.

"She's beautiful," said Purdun. He reached in to touch her hair. Unlike the coffin he'd touched before, her hair was soft and supple—the way he wanted it to feel. Running his hand down her cheek, he felt his heart sink. "She's very cold."

"She's dead, my lord," replied Menrick.

Purdun shook his head. He was gripped with a deep desire. "No. She can't be. I don't want her to be." Though he knew it to be false, he felt he'd known this woman his entire life. He started to feel sympathy for her, all alone, deep within the bowels of that musty, awful place. "I want her to wake up. To take her away from here." He leaned down to put his face close to hers.

Her beauty was entrancing.

As if granting the young lord's wish, the woman slowly opened her eyes. They were a deep jade green, and they stared up lovingly at Purdun.

"What devilry is this," shouted Menrick. The wizard tried to push the young lord aside. "We must flee."

But Purdun stood firm.

The woman sat up, and Purdun leaned back to give her room. A smile crossed her lips as she gazed at the young lord, and he felt his heart jump within his chest.

Her eyes seemed to dig right into him, as if she could read his thoughts and know his desires. The feeling was more exciting and terrifying than anything the young man had ever experienced.

Their eyes remained locked for a moment more, then Purdun had to look away. He didn't want to, but her beauty was too much for him to bear. He felt as if he would wither if he continued to look.

Menrick shoved Purdun again. The young lord was off balance, and he had to take a step back to gather himself. In that brief instant, the old wizard stepped into the gap and drew a dagger. Lifting it, he shouted the words to a quick spell. Purdun didn't recognize them all, but the last four he did.

". . . the bane of the unliving."

Menrick's dagger began to glow with a blue-white light. The mage wasted no time in bringing it down on the woman with both hands, impaling its tip in her shoulder.

"What are you doing!" shouted Purdun. He grabbed the wizard's hands, but Menrick leaned into his dagger, forcing it deeper into the wound.

The woman reeled from the blow, but no blood poured from the wound. She flailed, her arms swinging wildly. One of them hit Purdun in the gut. The woman's arm had the strength of ten men, and the blow knocked the young lord backward off the dais. He landed on his back and the room grew darker as the torch clattered to the floor next to him.

With her other arm, the pale woman grabbed Menrick by the neck and lifted him off the ground.

"Who dares wake Shyressa?" The woman spoke her words with a quiet hiss, as if forming them without the help of air.

She shook the wizard. The empty blackness surrounding the woman began to shimmer and move, lighting the room in a dim purple glow. Her smooth, porcelain cheeks withered and turned gray. Her paper-thin skin shriveled, pressing tight against her cheekbones and pulling away from her gums to reveal long, sharp fangs. Her lustrous blue-black hair slipped away, leaving in its place random clumps of graying straw clinging to a cracked, purplish scalp The flowing gowns that had covered her soft, curved body became tattered and worn, leaving nothing more than a torn, hole-filled rag hanging from her bony frame. Her beauty and youth drifted away, leaving in their place a hard, hideous visage.

Purdun leaped to his feet, drew his sword, and charged up the dais. The woman held Menrick off the ground with one hand, and with her other she slapped at the oncoming lord. Her sharpened claws caught Purdun on the left side of his face and once again he was sent flying. His sword skidded across the dusty floor, and he landed hard on his back between two stone sarcophagi, the wind knocked from his lungs.

Seeming to float, Shyressa stood up inside her coffin, keeping her one-handed hold on Menrick's throat. Her claws dug in deeply and blood ran down his neck, staining the collar of his white robes. The old wizard's eyes were closed, and he struggled against her grip, scratching at her hand with his fingers. His lips moved feverishly, as if he were trying to coax the air into his lungs by talking to it.

Shyressa reached up and pulled Menrick's dagger from her shoulder. It left a deep wound, but had apparently hit nothing vital. Tossing it to the ground, she glared up at the wizard in her grip.

"You will pay for that." She shook him again.

Menrick looked like a child's toy, his legs flopping as if they had no bones while he dangled from the withered woman's grasp. He struggled, letting out a coughing, gurgling sound. Then his body seemed to relax, and he opened his eyes. His hands lit up with yellow-white fire, and five glowing orbs of energy, each a different color, appeared circling his head. With a nod, the wizard sent the orbiting projectiles flying down on Shyressa.

The crypt lit up from the impact, the mix of colors sending hideously deformed shadows out to all corners of the room. The decrepit woman let out a hissing scream as the spells splashed over her skin.

Turning as best as he could, Menrick looked down on Purdun, who was still struggling to regain his breath.

"Run . . . my lord," Menrick spat out in a strangled voice. His eyes seemed to bulge in his head.

Shyressa shook her head, obviously hurt and angered by the wizard's attack. Her withered skin smoked where it had been struck and tattered bits of it fell from her face, revealing the stark white bone beneath. She let out an angry hiss and drew Menrick to her open mouth.

"No," coughed out Purdun.

Biting down on Menrick's neck with her massive fangs, Shyressa shook her face back and forth, tearing away the fresh flesh like a wild animal devouring its prey. The old wizard's body went stiff as he let out an anguished wail. Blood flooded down Shyressa's cheeks, spattering her hunched shoulders and the ragged remains of her dress.

Menrick shook for a moment longer, his body twitching in agony. Then his head slumped to one side, and he stopped struggling.

Menrick was gone.

Purdun felt his whole body tingle then go numb. Only by sheer force of will did he manage to pick himself up off the ground and grasp hold of the torch. Leaving his sword where it lay, the young lord turned away from the still-smoldering Shyressa and the body of his dead manservant and bolted for the stairs.

Lord Purdun ran with all of his might, skipping steps on the way up. The musty air burned his lungs as he drove his legs on, trying desperately to escape the damned tomb.

Finally, with a last burst of speed, Purdun forced himself out of the stairway, down the hall, and out the door into the sunlight. As soon as his foot touched the ground outside, the archway slammed closed. The smooth, polished stone that had been destroyed by the demon returned, leaving in its place a perfect replacement.

With only a single glance back, the young lord continued to run. Menrick, his mentor and confidant, was dead. Purdun had enough of that tomb for a lifetime. He wanted to put the whole episode as far behind him as humanly possible.

Deep inside the crypt, Shyressa pulled her teeth from the weeping neck of the wizard. Stepping down off the dais, she lowered his limp body to the ground beside one of the stone sarcophagi. Then she picked up the discarded blade lying on the floor. Examining the hilt, she read the inscription on it.

"Well, well," said Shyressa. "Lord Purdun." A smile crossed her weathered, now magically burned lips. "I think we shall meet again one day." Turning to survey the room, she lifted her hands into the air. "Rise, my children."

A loud grinding sound filled the chamber as the stone lids on all the sarcophagi began to slide away.

Ryder ran his hand over Samira's soft black hair. He felt her arms tighten around his middle.

"Don't go," she said.

He returned her squeeze. "I must."

Samira looked up at him, her beautiful blue eyes filling with tears. "Then promise me you'll return. Promise me that you're not going to get yourself killed doing something foolish."

Ryder smiled. She loved him. She loved him dearly, but knowing that only strengthened his resolve.

"I promise you, Samira, I will return to you." Though it pained him to do so, he pushed her gently away. "I will be back before nightfall." Then, grabbing his belt and sheath from the table, Ryder kissed his wife goodbye and stepped out the door into the afternoon sunshine.

"Close the bar behind me, and don't let anyone in until I get back," he said over his shoulder.

He could hear the extra-heavy crossbeam slide into place behind him as he crossed the dirt road. On the other side, Liam was leaning against a heavy tree, his arms folded on his chest.

Ryder clasped him on the arm as he approached. "You ready, little brother?"

Liam slapped the hilt of the sword dangling from his belt. "Ready."

Ryder nodded, satisfied. "Then let's go meet the others."

Liam knelt in the bushes alongside the well-traveled dirt road running west from Zerith Hold, Lord Purdun's fortress in Duhlnarim, through Furrowsrich village and out of Ahlarkham. Six other men knelt beside him, including his brother. They were waiting for a carriage that was reportedly leaving the Hold with a diplomatic letter bound for High Watcher Laxaella Bronshield, the still-mourning baroness of Tanistan. Liam and the others intended to make sure that letter never reached its destination.

Liam, Ryder, and the rest of the Crimson Awl had made significant headway in the past few months against Lord Purdun's elite guard. The last thing they needed was for Lady Bronshield to add her might to that of Purdun's. The Awl would worry about one barony at a time, starting right here at home. But to do that, they had to make sure the neighboring lords didn't broaden the scope of the fight too soon. That was why they were all here, to stop Purdun's request for aid from getting through to Tanistan.

In the near distance, Liam heard the telltale sound of horse hooves and rough wooden wheels rolling over the packed earth.

His brother must have heard it too. "This is it," said Ryder. "You all know your jobs. There should only be two guards. If we're swift about this, nobody needs to get hurt."

Liam looked over the other men. Locals, all of them. They nodded at Ryder's instructions. All of them, that is, except Kharl.

The young man, the son of a local merchant, had never been on one of the raids before. He hadn't heard a word Ryder said. His eyes were focused on the road and his right hand gripped the hilt of his long sword so tightly his knuckles were turning white. A line of sweat had started to form along the edge of his golden blond hair, and he looked a little pale. Liam could have sworn he was shaking.

Ryder must have noticed it too. "Don't worry," he said, smiling at Kharl. "You won't even have to use your sword."

Kharl nodded hesitantly. "But what if they give us trouble?"

Ryder shrugged. "Then I suppose you'll get the opportunity to use your sword after all."

Kharl shook his head. "No. I mean, what if they don't give us the letter? What do we do then?"

Jarl, a great big bear of a man with a tattoo of a mermaid on each forearm, spoke up. "We take it from them, lad."

The other men nodded their agreement.

"But . . ." Kharl stuttered. "But . . . do we . . . ?"

Ryder put his hand on the young man's shoulder. "Kharl, I won't ask you to kill anyone in cold blood, if that's what you're asking."

Kharl nodded, his shoulders relaxing a bit.

"But if things do get out of hand, you may have to defend yourself." Ryder suddenly got serious. "If that happens, if you find yourself in the position where it's your life or his—" Ryder looked up at each of the other men, his eyes lingering on Liam a moment longer than the rest, then back at Kharl— "Then I expect you to kill that man dead. I won't be losing anyone on this raid. Is that understood?"

Kharl nodded, and the other men grunted their assent.

"Good." Ryder chuckled, and the moment of seriousness passed. "You know, Kharl, you can do me a favor."

"Really? What?"

"Your mother makes the best beef stew in all of Erlkazar. When you get back, see if you can't get her to make a pot and invite Samira and me over for dinner."

The worry on Kharl's face faded. "All right, Ryder. I'll do that."

Liam shook his head. His brother had always had a way with people. "Hey, Kharl."

The blond man leaned back to look at Liam. "Yeah?"

"I want some of that stew too."

Kharl threw his arms out wide. "You're all invited."

The sound of horses and wheels grew louder as it came around the bend, transforming into a well-appointed carriage pulled by a pair of majestic-looking horses draped in the livery of Lord Purdun. The coach wasn't in any hurry. The doors were painted with the familiar shield-and-double-crossed-sword crest that turned Liam's stomach every time he saw it. It was the official seal of Lord Purdun, the owner and master of the land on which all of Liam's family and friends lived and had to pay taxes for.

Just as Ryder had said, there were only two guards and the driver. Whoever rode inside was concealed by velvet drapes covering the windows. Liam imagined the occupant was some corpulent, bloated diplomat with a double chin and greasy fingers. Who better to deliver a letter of alliance from the bastard Lord Purdun to one of the other regional barons?

The carriage drew near, and Ryder rose onto the balls

of his feet, still hidden from the road by the tall brush. He held his hands to his face and whispered to Liam, "Before you can truly move forward, you have to be willing to live with the consequences."

Then Ryder smiled and looked at the other men. "It's time to give it to old Firefist." He dropped into a deep crouch, then sprang out of the bush. "Now!" he shouted, pulling his long sword from its sheath as he came down in front of the carriage.

Liam didn't hesitate. He was the second of the eight men to reach the road and draw his weapon, taking his position beside his brother.

As Liam had expected, the horses were startled by the sudden appearance of armed men on the road. They bucked, and the driver had to struggle to keep control of them.

"Halt!" shouted Ryder, holding his palm out to the coach.

The other men leaped out of their hiding spots—two more up front, the final four behind, boxing in the coach on the packed dirt road.

The guards on top of the carriage had to hold on to the seat to avoid being tossed from their perch. But as the horses came to a stop, they stood up and drew their weapons.

"Don't be foolish," shouted Ryder. "We're eight. You're only two. Just drop your weapons and give us the letter you carry, and there will be no need for you to be harmed."

Liam wished he were as eloquent as his older brother. No wasted effort, no beating around the bush, just the facts, plain and simple.

The guards stood motionless, still gripping their swords. They looked far more relaxed than Liam thought they should. Hells, they looked more relaxed than he felt.

"I said 'drop your weapons!' " shouted Ryder. He

stepped to the side of the carriage, the afternoon sun glinting on his polished blade.

The guards looked at each other, then tossed their weapons to the ground.

"The letter is inside," said one of the guards, lifting his hands into the air. "The countess carries it. Please don't harm her. We're responsible for her safety."

Ryder glanced back at Liam, a smirk on his face. Then he nodded. Without a word, Liam followed his brother to the side of the carriage.

Ryder knocked on the wooden door with the hilt of his sword. The heavy pounding scratched the paint, marring the jade green and royal blue of Lord Purdun's crest.

The door remained closed.

Liam spared a glance back at Kharl. The young man was shifting his weight from side to side, but he kept his gaze squarely on the two guards, his sword drawn, just as he'd been instructed to do. Tonight, in the pub, the young man would be telling stories of his own bravery, and the nervousness he felt now would be nothing but a distant memory.

Ryder knocked on the door again. "We seek only the letter you carry," he said. "Surrender it, and you will not be harmed."

Still the door remained shut.

Ryder's simple smile faded and was replaced with a look of serious contemplation. It was a dangerous look. Liam had seen it many times—whenever his older brother didn't get his way. Liam had feared that look since they were both little boys. It meant Ryder had reached his limit. It meant he no longer intended to play nice.

"Countess, this will be your last warning," said Ryder. "You have until the count of three to come out and give us that letter, or we *will* come in."

Liam gripped his sword. This was not the way they had hoped it would go.

"One . . ."

Time seemed to slow down. Liam could hear his heart pound in his chest. They had known this was a possibility, but nobody wanted this to get rough.

"Two . . ."

The door burst open and slapped against the wall of the carriage. Right behind it poured out a half-dozen of Lord Purdun's guards. Six more jumped out the door on the opposite side.

Ryder's sword came up and parried the first guard's blow as he backpedaled away from the carriage. "It's a trap!"

The other men jumped into action.

Liam stepped up beside his brother, stopping Ryder's retreat. The two of them lunged forward.

Unable to stop the onrush, the guard's eyes went wide. He managed to bash aside Liam's blade, but he was too slow to catch Liam's brother's. The tip of Ryder's long sword found a crease in the man's half-plate and sank into the flesh below. Twisting sideways, the guardsman pulled himself off the blade like a piece of skewered beef, dropping his sword and giving way to the five armored men behind him.

The baron's elite guards encircled the brothers, three training their swords on Ryder, and two on Liam. Liam spun around, placing his back against Ryder's. This wasn't the first time they had fought like this. Liam hoped it wouldn't be their last. Both men began turning a slow circle, holding their attackers back at sword point.

Standing there in the middle of a ring of armed soldiers, the eye in the middle of an oncoming storm, Liam caught sight of Kharl. The young man was battling the two carriage guards. They had regained their dropped swords and had locked the young man into combat. One was circling around to the side, attempting to pin Kharl between them. For a relatively inexperienced fighter, Kharl was holding his own. He parried a blow from each side, then took a large step back, keeping the guards from flanking him. Despite the young man's terrific effort, he was still losing ground. He was in a fight he couldn't win. He just didn't realize it yet.

Liam scanned the area, hoping someone else could get to Kharl before it was too late, but the other men were busy with guards of their own. Counting the carriage drivers, there were fourteen armed elite guardsmen to eight freedom fighters. Kharl was on his own.

If the men they fought were just hired toughs, this wouldn't be an issue. Liam would put anyone in the Crimson Awl up against two local thugs. It would be no contest. But the baron's elite guards were trained soldiers. They had good weapons and the best armor—and they knew how to win a fight.

The sound of Ryder's sword bashing aside a guard's blade brought Liam back to the fight at hand.

A pair of soldiers rushed the brothers, one on each side. Ryder stepped left, Liam right. They moved together like a multi-headed creature sharing a single spine. Their blades moved in perfect harmony, striking out at different foes. Liam didn't need to see what his brother was doing. They had been practicing this style of fighting since they were young.

❧ ❧ ❧ ❧ ❧

Liam held a tree branch tightly in both hands. It was his eighth birthday. As a present, his uncle had made him a toy wooden sword. That sword was now in the hands of Tyler, the local bully.

Liam could feel his brother's back against his as they turned a slow circle, looking out at Tyler and his three friends.

"Don't worry, Liam," reassured Ryder, also with a branch in his hands. "I'm a good fighter, so you will be too."

Liam nodded his head. If his big brother said it, it must be true. "All right."

"Hey, Liam," taunted Tyler. "You want this?" He shook the toy sword in Liam's face.

Liam's chest burned with hate.

"Don't fall for it, Liam," directed Ryder. "Let them make the first move."

"What? Are you scared?" Tyler laughed. "Too afraid to come get your little toy from me?"

Liam gripped the branch tighter in his hands. He wanted so badly to swing it, to bring it down on Tyler's head and make him give back his birthday present. But more than anything, Liam trusted his older brother.

"What's the matter, Tyler?" taunted Ryder. "You've got us outnumbered. Looks like you're the one who is scared."

Tyler lifted Liam's wooden sword over his head. "I'll show you who's scared." Then he came running right at Ryder.

The three other young thugs followed the bully's lead and came rushing in.

Liam felt something in the pit of his stomach clench, then he lost control. His arms reacted without his willing them to. He watched as the branch swung wildly from side to side. The whole thing didn't seem real. He wasn't in control, and he didn't know the outcome. All he knew for sure was that his brother's back against his was the most reassuring feeling in the whole world.

From behind him Liam heard a loud crack, and just like that the whole thing was over. The young punks retreated, not wanting to get hit by a flailing branch. Liam stopped swinging when they took a step back. Then he followed their gazes over his shoulder.

Tyler lay on the ground, blood pouring from his nose, Liam's sword on the ground beside him.

"I'll take that," said Ryder. He picked up the birthday gift. The branch he held in his other hand was broken in two.

Ryder turned and grabbed Liam by the shoulder. "Come on," he said. "I think they have had enough."

✥ ✥ ✥ ✥ ✥

Liam's blade danced, parrying blows. He could feel his brother's back against his own. Despite their teamwork, the guards they fought were not going to fall for any cheap tricks. They came in at the same time, thrusting in short bursts, trying to overpower the brothers. They kept Liam off balance, never giving him an opening. It was all he could do to defend himself.

The guard to his left feinted high then went low. Liam brought his sword down, smashing the attack to the dirt. The other guard came in high. Liam dodged to the side, bringing his sword up in a long arc and bashing away his opponent's blade with a flourish. The two elite guardsmen took a step back, regained their composure, then lunged together. Liam snapped the forte of his blade around in a short circle, catching the tips of both blades with his and flinging them toward the sky. Had there been only one attacker, Liam would have lunged for a riposte. As it was, he'd be opening himself up to one of the two guards, so he held tight. He wouldn't fall for the ploy. He could hear Ryder's voice inside his head, "Let them make the first mistake."

This back and forth dragged on for what seemed like an eternity. The guards would rush, and Liam would fight them back, threaten a bit, and make them retreat. Then they would return with a different strategy.

Liam could feel Ryder step, lunge, retreat, parry, then lunge again. From the pattern, he could tell that his brother was fairing similarly with his three. Defense was one thing, but there was no way they were going to win the fight if they didn't make some headway soon.

"In the name of Lord Purdun, surrender now, and you won't be harmed," shouted one of the guardsmen.

"Never," replied Ryder.

Behind him, Liam could feel his brother pick up the pace.

Just hearing Purdun's name made Liam's blood run hot with anger. He moved quicker, matching Ryder.

The guardsmen came in again. Liam dodged both blows in swift order.

Then he made his first mistake.

Stepping away from his brother, he lunged, sticking the tip of his long sword into the hip of the soldier on his right. The man wailed and stepped back, but the other guardsman took advantage of the opening, swinging his sword at Liam's exposed middle.

Liam retreated, bashing aside the first attack, but the soldier pressed his advantage, swinging his sword again. The second blow slipped past Liam's guard, catching him in the shoulder. His chain mail tunic took the brunt of the attack, but the tip ran up under the short sleeves, cutting a shallow wound into his arm. Liam hissed at the pain, pulling sideways and away from his brother.

Ryder spun around, knowing his little brother had been hit. "Liam!"

Liam pulled his arm in toward his side, trying to minimize the pain, but in doing so, opened up his back. Two of the guardsmen lunged at the same time, taking advantage of his exposed body. Liam swung down with his right hand, trying to parry, but his wounded arm slowed him down.

Both blades came in, slipping past his defense.

Liam tightened his gut, preparing for pain. Out of the corner of his eye he caught sight of Ryder's sword. It came out of nowhere, a silvery flash that caught one guardsman across the forearm and slapped aside the other's blade. With his off hand, Ryder shoved Liam out of the circle.

Liam stumbled forward, crashing into the guard he'd already injured. The two of them fell to the ground. Liam tucked his sword up tight against his body as they tumbled across the dirt. When they came to a stop, he rolled forward with all of his might, pushing away from the soldier. He somersaulted twice then leaped to his feet, twenty paces from where he had begun. The guard's heavier armor had weighed him down, and he struggled to get up from his back like an upside-down turtle.

"Run, Liam!"

Liam looked back at his brother. Ryder was surrounded by four guards with no one watching his back. He turned a quick circle, brandishing his blade to keep the guardsmen at bay.

Liam took two steps toward his brother.

"Watch out," shouted Ryder.

Liam looked down just in time to see the injured guardsman on the ground swing at his ankles. He leaped into the air, jumping over the blade. Coming down on the prone soldier, he drove the tip of his long sword through the man's helm, pinning his head to the ground.

Putting his boot on the fallen soldier's shoulder, Liam pulled his weapon from the ruined skull then turned to help his brother. Ryder lunged at one guard just as another lunged at him. His blade hit its mark, driving deep into the soldier's neck. But the guardsman's blade also struck home, slicing Ryder across the belly.

"Ryder!" Liam broke into a run.

Ryder dropped to one knee, his left arm holding his stomach, his hand covered in blood. He gazed down at the wound in his belly then up at Liam. He looked so sad, so scared, like a lost child. Liam had never seen his brother like that, and it sent a shiver down his spine.

Liam skidded to a stop.

"Run, Liam," said Ryder, his voice raspy and strained. He pointed away from the carriage with his chin. "Go." Then he turned his attention back to Lord Purdun's elite guardsmen.

Liam was frozen in place, unable to move. He just stood there, watching his brother's blood spill to the ground.

Ryder couldn't stand, but he held the remaining three guardsmen at bay from his knees. He swung his long sword in a wide arc, then jabbed at them with the sharp tip. Each strike was accompanied by another splash of Ryder's blood. The ground was painted with the stuff.

The guards took a large step back, and Ryder turned to look at Liam.

"Look after Samira. Tell her I love her."

With Ryder's attention turned away, the biggest of the three guardsmen charged forward.

The blood in Liam's veins ran cold. "Ryder, look out!"

"Run, Liam." Ryder turned and brought his blade up into the guard's gut.

The big man let out a screech as he impaled himself. Ryder held the hilt of his sword as best as he could, but the guardsman in all his armor was just too heavy, and the soldier fell forward, smothering Ryder.

For a moment, every inch of Liam's body tingled. It was as if he were trying to fight against the forward movement of time, and it tore at his skin. This was the moment in which he would lose his brother. This was the moment of his greatest failure, and he desperately wanted to go back, to stop everything before this instant, to replay the moments of his life over and over again, always stopping before he reached this part.

Four more soldiers came around the back of the carriage.

Liam stood there stunned, the fibers of his body struggling to keep him rooted in time—but it was no use. This was a fight he could not win.

The other guards wasted no time, charging in, stabbing at Ryder's prone body. Liam winced, the wounds of his brother stinging doubly for Liam. He wished desperately that it could be him lying there on the ground. He wished he could trade places with his brother, take his place under the killing blows of the guardsmen.

His face grew hot, and he began to see red. This trap was yet further proof of the treachery of Lord Purdun.

Liam's lip curled up into a sneer. His body was steeled by the hatred and pain now coursing through his body. The baron would pay for this. But first, his guardsmen would all be sent to Hell. Liam lifted his sword.

"Liam . . ." came a strangled voice.

It was Kharl. The young man was still alive, but he was bleeding from a large wound in his side.

"Liam, please help me."

Liam looked back at Ryder. His brother had stopped moving. He lay on the ground, his torso bent back over his heels and his hand still clutching the hilt of his sword. The big guardsman lay on top of him, impaled on the tip of his blade. The fury that had momentarily taken hold of Liam suddenly fled. His hatred turned to sadness, and his arms felt tired and weak.

"I'll tell her," he said. "I'll make sure she knows."

With what little strength remained in his body, Liam turned away from his brother and helped Kharl up from the ground. With the young man's arm over his shoulder, Liam took off into the forest, leaving the carriage and the bodies of the other six men behind.

CHAPTER 2

Kharl groaned as his weight settled against a large tree. He was bleeding from a jagged cut down the right side of his ribcage and a puncture wound in his thigh.

Liam peered out around the tree, watching for Lord Purdun's guardsmen, but the only things behind them were more trees and the memories of what had just happened.

"Who else?"

Liam looked down at Kharl. "What?"

"Who else escaped?"

Liam shook his head. "Just us."

Kharl lowered his head, his chin touching his chest, and sobbed. "I knew it. I knew this was a bad idea."

Liam shook his head. "Someone set us up. They knew about our plans."

Kharl ignored him. "What were we thinking? How can we ever beat Purdun? All this revolution, all this freedom for the people of Duhlnarim, is just going to get us killed." Kharl slid down the tree to the ground, his chest quivering and his sobs cutting off his words. "Damn . . . Purdun . . . Damn . . . Ryder . . . Damn . . . you Liam . . ."

Liam dropped into a crouch, grabbing Kharl by the shoulders and looking him in the eyes. "Pull yourself together." He shook the young man. "I know you're scared, but pull yourself together. Ryder is dead, all right. Do you hear me? Dead!" He let go of Kharl. "And I won't have you damning him now."

Kharl lowered his eyes, covering his face with his hands as he continued to cry. "I don't want to do this anymore. I just want this to be over."

Liam wanted to comfort the young man, but the image of his brother collapsing under the falling guardsman played over in his mind. The heavy pang of guilt that he felt over not being able to save him pushed to the surface. The pain inside welled up and began to boil, a deep ache that grew from the very center of his chest and spread out to squeeze his stomach, arms, and throat. It threatened to strangle him, and for a moment, Liam wished it would.

He stood up, shouting at Kharl. "You knew what you were getting into. You knew the consequences."

The young man looked shocked. He stopped crying, stunned at Liam's quick turn.

"Ryder knew it too. He knew this could happen, and he chose to go through with it anyway."

Kharl looked to the ground, remaining quiet.

Liam stared down at the young man for a long time, not saying a word. Then, finally, "What you do with the rest of your life is up to you. But I'll continue to fight Purdun until they pry my sword from my cold, dead hand." He turned away from Kharl and headed through

Furrowsrich village toward his brother's house. "I will not let Ryder's sacrifice be in vain."

Liam knocked on the heavy wooden door. He didn't know what he was going to say. He didn't know how to make the news any easier. Hells, he was in shock himself. Not long ago he'd left his brother's dead body lying under a dying guardsman.

Samira opened the door. She smiled, looking relieved. "Liam." She wrapped her arms around him in a warm hug. "Thank the gods you made it back safely."

Liam felt his heart sink into his belly. Nothing could have made what he had to say any harder.

Except that.

He tried to raise his arms to return the embrace, but they rebelled against him. Nothing would work the way it was supposed to. He stood motionless, stiff as a board, with his brother's wife's arms around him.

Samira must have felt it because she pushed herself away in a hurry. "Where's Ryder?"

Tears welled up in his eyes.

"Liam," she said, the high pitch of desperation entering her voice, "*where* is Ryder?"

"He's gone." Liam began to sob just like Kharl had sitting under the tree. "He fell trying to give me a chance to escape."

"No." Her voice pleaded with him. "No. No. No. He's not gone. He can't be gone." She gripped his arms and shook him. "Tell me where he is. Tell me he's coming back."

Liam stared at the dirt in front of the doorway. He couldn't look Samira in the eye. Instead, he watched his tears as they fell to the ground.

"I'm sorry," he said. He gathered the courage to look up at his brother's widow. She was trying to hold herself together, but her face was dark, streaked with the lines of pain that he felt deep inside. "Ryder is dead."

Liam watched as her last bit of strength fled. Samira's anguish overtook her entire face, and her knees went weak. Liam caught her before she hit the ground, and she collapsed into him, her head falling to his shoulder.

Liam held her up, squeezing her sobbing body against his. She was so soft, so clean, and so without fault. He felt dirty and ruined, as if the events of the day had somehow changed him, made him less of an honest man and more of an evil one. Her pain only served to amplify his own. It was his fault his brother had been killed. It was his fault Samira was now alone.

He stood there in the doorway for a moment longer, trying to let the wave of sorrow and guilt wash over and pass.

It never did.

Liam took Samira inside, closing the door behind him.

"What happened?"

Liam looked up from his load. "Mother? What are you doing here?"

The gray-haired woman stood up from the kitchen table where she had been sitting. "I came to talk to Samira about Ryder's birthday," she said in a huff, crossing the room to lay her hand on Samira's forehead. "What happened? And where's Ryder?"

Liam carried Samira across the room and placed her on the bed. She clung to his neck, continuing to sob.

His mother grabbed him by the arm. "Liam, answer me. What happened?"

Liam disentangled himself from his brother's widow and turned to look down on his aging mother. He remembered what she had looked like when he was a child. Her curly locks had been a beautiful auburn. Her skin had been smooth and tan. Now, though, her bushel of hair was a salt-and-pepper gray, and her skin had bunched up in folds and wrinkles, transforming into a soft, pale whiteness.

"Liam." She shook him. "Liam. What's wrong with you?"

Liam looked her in the eyes. The same sadness that had consumed him upon seeing Samira at the door welled up again.

"Ryder's gone."

"I know that," she said, miffed. "But when is he going to be back?"

Liam put his arms around her. "He's not coming back, mother. Ryder is dead."

"What? Dead?" His mother shook her head. "What are you talking about? He can't be dead. Where is he?" She squeezed his arm tighter. "Stop fooling around and tell me what's going on here."

Liam took a deep breath. "Ryder and I ambushed a carriage today . . . a carriage from Zerith Hold." Liam stuttered a bit, not really wanting to recount the story. He already knew his mother's reaction. "It was . . . it was one of Lord Purdun's carriages. We were only after a letter, a treaty that was to be signed by High Watcher Laxaella Bronshield, the Baroness of Tanistan. But the carriage was a setup. We were attacked by more than a dozen of Purdun's elite guards."

"But why?" His mother held her hands to her face.

"Ryder and I are . . . were part of the local resistance."

His mother let go of his arms. "The Crimson Awl? All those stories about bandits robbing Lord Purdun's coaches and mercenaries roaming around attacking his guardsmen . . . that was you? Liam, why?"

"Because we had to," said Liam. "Lord Purdun is an evil, evil man. He takes our crops, taxes our livelihoods, and imposes unfair laws." Liam had endured arguments with his mother on the topic before. They had never seen eye to eye. "But more importantly, he was in the process of putting together a treaty that could have ruined everything we've worked for, perhaps irrevocably." Liam took a breath, holding up his hand to keep his place, making sure his mother didn't butt in, as she was wont to do.

"The Awl is not a large organization," he continued. "We are all farmers or craftsmen. We don't have the means to fight a large-scale war. We've made progress against Baron Purdun and his guardsmen. Their numbers dwindle, and they have trouble recruiting new members. The people of Ahlarkham believe in what we are fighting for, and they refuse to help Purdun keep us down. But if Tanistan sent men as well, all of the work we have done would be lost. All our sacrifices would have been in vain."

"And what about Ryder's sacrifice? Did he know about all of this?" his mother demanded.

Liam nodded. "Ryder was our leader. The organizer. He planned most of the raids, and I helped him."

His mother suddenly got angry. "What has Lord Purdun ever done to you?" She hit him across the chest. "You and your foolish notions of right and wrong. How many times has your father told you to keep your nose out of the baron's business? Now look at what you've gone and done. You've gotten your brother killed, haven't you? And we'll never get him back." She began to cry. "This is all your fault, Liam. All your fault."

"No it's not, Angeline."

Liam turned around to see Samira sitting up on the bed. Her eyes were wet with tears, but some of the color had returned to her cheeks.

"Ryder knew what he was getting himself into." Samira stood up and placed her hand on Liam's shoulder, standing beside him in defense. "He knew the risks just as well as Liam did."

"How can you say that, Samira?" said the matriarch through her sobs. "Your husband is dead."

"I know that, Angeline."

"Do you not grieve?"

Samira wiped the tears from her eyes, the pain on her face turning visibly to anger. "How dare you say that to me. Of course I do. And so does Liam."

Liam felt a calmness wash through him. Somehow, Samira could forgive him for what he could not forgive himself. How could she do that? Samira was an angel. That must be it. No other creature on the plane could have such love in her heart. No other creature would be able to see through her grief and not condemn the brother who lived for the death of the one who did not.

Angeline stared at Samira for a long moment, seemingly piecing together the words she had just heard. Then she turned to her youngest son, now her only son.

"And what of the rest of us?" she asked, glaring at Liam. "Samira may forgive you for Ryder's death, but your foolish little game has now put us all at risk."

Liam shook his head. "How?"

"Do you think those guards are blind? Do you think Purdun is stupid?" Angeline threw her hands in the air. "As soon as he realizes even one of you got away, he'll send his men out looking." She stepped up right into Liam's face. "And when they come looking, they will be looking for you. And when they find you, we will all be in jeopardy."

Liam put his hands to his head, rubbing his temples. He hadn't thought of that. "What do you want me to do? You want me to march to Zerith Hold and turn myself in?"

Angeline opened her mouth, but Samira cut her off.

"No. Absolutely not." She stared at Angeline until the older woman looked away, then she turned to gaze at Liam. "We've lost enough of our family for one day, I think."

A tense silence filled the house, broken only by the crackling of the fire.

Liam watched his mother, not knowing what to say to her.

She watched him back, a stern look of disapproval on her face. Then the anger in her eyes faded, replaced by sadness, and she wrapped her arms around him. "You're right," she said, sobbing again. "I'm sorry, Liam. I'm sorry."

CHAPTER 3

Two hooded figures stood before the mausoleum in the ruins of the cemetery outside Dajaan. A jagged hole in the ground slowly closed, taking with it the eerie green glow, the thick wisps of fog, and the demon the two men had summoned. All that remained was an open archway and a dark passage leading deep into the stone structure.

One of the men removed his hood, revealing a young half-elf with graying hair, ashen skin, and a long scaly ridge running from the back of his head down his neck and into his heavy robe. He wore a golden torque with five large oval rubies laid into its surface—the traditional symbol of power for the baron of Impresk.

"I hope you're right about this," said the bejeweled man.

The still-hooded man nodded. "I assure you, Lord Tammsel, the tomb offers all that you desire and more." He bowed and held his open palm out, as if offering the baron the tomb's entrance as a gift.

The half-elf eyed the darkened opening to the mausoleum. Then, adjusting his grip on his axe, he stepped forward and into the darkness. As he crossed the threshold, a torch came to life, filling the entrance with a thin, flickering light.

The hooded man took the torch from its sconce. "This way, my lord," he said, indicating a flight of stairs leading down deeper into the tomb.

The two men followed the low light down the dusty stairway. At the bottom they stepped out into a large room filled wall to wall with stone sarcophagi. The lids on all of them were ajar.

Baron Tammsel stepped up to an empty sarcophagus. Not even the bones of the occupants remained.

"It looks as though we are too late," said the baron. "This tomb has already been raided."

"We are not petty thieves, my lord," assured the hooded man. He walked farther in, heading for a raised platform in the middle of the room. "We are here for a much greater purpose."

The half-elf wearily followed his companion to the center of the room. There, atop a stepped dais, sat a beautiful coffin carved in the shape of a human woman.

The hooded man took all of the steps in a single bound and lifted the torch, casting a weak circle of light over the entire coffin. The baron scanned the room, seemingly very uncomfortable in the bowels of the tomb.

"The wisdom you seek lies inside this coffin," said the hooded man.

The baron shook his head. "Something is not right here." He squinted, peering into the far reaches of the room. But even with his keen eyesight, the darkness ran out too far for him to see all the way across. "I sense we are being watched." He turned a slow circle, still searching for something. "This is a place of great evil." He spun back to face his companion. "I do not know why you brought me here, but I no longer believe your stories of steel dragons and scrolls of ancient wisdom."

Baron Tammsel backed down the steps, away from the dais, keeping his eyes on the other man. "I am leaving now."

The hooded figure shook his head. "No, Lord Tammsel. You are not."

The half-elf spun around, breaking into a run toward the stairs. The shadows on the walls began to shift, taking shape. Moving with a preternatural speed that far outpaced the swift half-elf, they blocked the exit.

Lord Tammsel skidded to a stop, the dust on the floor rising into the air. The shapes before him were not made of shadow. They had only been using the darkness to conceal their presence. They hissed at him and moved closer. In the fading light Lord Tammsel could see their tattered flesh and jutting fangs.

"Vampires," he said.

Backing up, he turned to see that the coffin on the dais lay open, and a female human—or what had once been a female human, now skeletal and decayed—stood beside the hooded man and looked down at Tammsel with great interest. Arrayed around the steps, several dozen slavering thralls clawed at the air, hissing and exposing their fangs.

Lord Tammsel let out a low growl. Dropping his axe, he pulled his arms out of his long sleeves, revealing two sets of powerful dragon claws. With a quick slash, the half-elf, half-dragon tore away his robes, exposing the elven chain beneath.

"I know not what treachery this is," growled the baron, "but I assure you, I will not go down without a fight."

The woman on the dais laughed, a sound like teeth chattering together. "You were right, Montauk," she said, placing her hand on the hooded man's shoulder. "He is full of fight."

The man pulled back his cowl. His pale skin seemed even paler so deep in the mausoleum. And his hair, tied back in a ponytail, looked like a slithering snake, writhing over his back in the flickering torchlight. He smiled. "You are too kind, my mistress."

Lord Tammsel growled again, a deep rolling sound from within his chest. His eyes narrowed. Then he charged the door and the stairs leading out of the tomb.

The entire room seemed to lose air as the vampires and their spawn let out a collective hiss. They gathered in a tight group in front of the door and closed in behind him from the dais. The half-dragon, half-elf baron leaped into the air and came down in the middle of the vampires' blockade.

The tips of his outstretched hands ripped into the first spawn in his path. The creature let out a wail as it was torn in half, shredded by Lord Tammsel's powerful claws. He turned on another, ripping its head from its shoulders with a single swat.

His enemies attacked back. A fist slammed into his shoulder, spinning Tammsel to one side. The blow temporarily dazed him, but he managed to shake it off, bringing his hand up in time to block another fist meant for his jaw. A pair of teeth bit down on his arm. Jerking away, the baron lifted the vampire off its feet, its fangs still clenched against his elven chain.

With a mighty roar, Tammsel hurled the undead from his arm, sending it flying into half a dozen of its brethren. They fell to the floor in a hissing pile of fangs and claws. He'd managed to make a small opening, and he took advantage of it, stepping toward the fallen foes and into the gap.

One step closer to the door, Lord Tammsel fought on. Grabbing hold of a vampire spawn with both hands, he pulled the creature toward him and sank his teeth into its face. Shaking his head, the Baron of Impresk bit the spawn's face right off its head and the spawn fell away, unable to see.

With a satisfied purr, Tammsel spat the rotting flesh from his mouth and came on guard again. He took another step, closing in on the door. His life was nearly saved. The prize of freedom he sought was near, and it filled him with new strength.

There were only a handful of undead between him and the doorway. Taking in a deep breath, the half-silver dragon shook his head back and forth, blowing out all of the air in his lungs. A gust of super cold spread out, catching a half-dozen vampire spawn in a maelstrom of freezing breath. The bile and mellifluent fluids that held them together turned to ice. Their slumping skin turned hard and fell from their bones. Collectively the quickly freezing beasts let out a wail, then they went silent, either stopping in their tracks or falling frozen to the ground.

Without hesitation, Tammsel dived into the new gap, moving within just a few steps of the way out. He reached for the next in his way, but something caught him from behind and spun him around. Looking back at the dais, the baron could see the circle of undead closing in. The vampires he had knocked down were already back on their feet.

They seized him, clasping his arms, legs, shoulders, and head. Though he struggled, the undead piled on. Their hands scratched at his skin. Their fangs clanked against his armor. Slowly the tomb disappeared from his view, replaced with dead gray flesh and shadow.

The onslaught was more than the baron could take, and he sank to his knees. Twisting under the pile, he gritted his teeth and growled, struggling for one more look at the door. He reached, his claws grasping around in the stale crypt air. His fist shook as his body was pummeled, over and over again, until he finally stopped moving. His hand fell limp to the floor.

The pile of spawn climbed off his corpse, leaving the older, more deserving vampires to lap up the fresh blood.

Montauk looked down on the former Baron of Impresk, a smile on his face. "Goodbye, Tammsel."

The woman standing next to him placed her hand on his shoulder. "I trust his replacement has been put into place."

Montauk turned toward the woman, bowing. "Yes, Mistress Shyressa. Our man has assumed his identity and taken control of Impresk. He's been ruling the barony for more than a tenday now, and everything goes according to plan."

Shyressa nodded her approval. "Well done." She lifted a sack of gold from inside one of her sleeves and handed it to the ponytailed man. "For your good work."

Montauk took the sack and bowed once again. "Thank you, my lady."

The vampires on the floor were tearing large chunks of the dead baron's flesh from his bones and throwing them to their spawn. The half-elf, half-dragon's blood covered the flagstones and the faces of the undead surrounding his corpse.

Shyressa smiled as she looked upon the carnage. "How many of the other barons of Erlkazar do we need to replace before we have them all?"

At this, Montauk balked. Casting his eyes to the ground, he cleared his throat. "There is only one, my lady."

Shyressa's smile faded. "And who would that be?"

Montauk steeled himself to deliver the news. "The baron Lord Purdun, my lady."

Shyressa touched her shoulder, remembering the wound she had suffered when last she had encountered Baron Purdun of Ahlarkham. "And?"

"And everything is on schedule."

The vampire mistress glared at the human standing beside her coffin. "That is what your predecessor said five years ago."

"Yes, my lady," replied Montauk.

"Perhaps it is time I took a personal interest in finalizing our plans."

"Mistress, please," begged Montauk, "allow me the time to complete the plan I have already set in motion."

"Where are you now, Montauk? How close are you?"

It was Montauk's turn to smile. "It won't be long," he said. "Already I have arranged to personally take control of the Crimson Awl. A well-timed tip to the elite guard has effectively beheaded the organization, leaving the climate right for me to move in and take power." Montauk rubbed his hands together. "If we cannot replace Baron Purdun with one of our own agents, we will discredit and overthrow him by organizing the peasants against him. I will become the new hero of the people, giving them back the land and cutting their taxes.

"Once Purdun's been removed from his position, the farmers will want me to be their new leader. To keep the peace, we will have the other barons of Erlkazar, who are all under our control, petition the king to appoint me as the new baron of Ahlarkham." He took a deep breath, his smile widening.

"And once we have control," Montauk continued, "we can begin our plans of secession. Each of the five baronies in turn will remove itself from Erlkazar, forming independent countries. After that, it's only a small matter of starting a war over territory, and the entire region will be in turmoil."

Shyressa nodded. "I do not want to deprive you of your fun. Still—" the ancient vampire waved her hands over her body, conjuring a blood-red cloak that covered her lithe frame— "I think I'll come along to see for myself just how well this plan is coming together."

Montauk bowed again. "As you wish, my lady."

She stepped down off the dais, coming up behind one of the spawn feasting on the remains of Lord Tammsel. "Let's bring a little gift for Lord Purdun." She reached down and stroked the hair of the undead man before her.

The minion looked up at his mistress, blood covering his face.

"You'd like to be reacquainted with your old friend, wouldn't you, Menrick?"

The vampire spawn dropped the bone he'd been gnawing on and turned to hug Lady Shyressa's legs.

"That's right," she said, enjoying the adoration from her beloved follower. "I thought you'd like that."

CHAPTER 4

Wake up, you pig-slopping bastard!"

A wave of water hit Ryder in the face, and he sat bolt upright.

"Wha ... Where am I?"

"Shut up, you," came the same voice.

Ryder wiped the water out of his eyes with the back of his hand. He was sitting on a soldier's cot in a cold, dank stone cell. A pair of weak torches, one on each side of a single door, lit the room. Four men—all but one wearing the jade green and royal blue uniforms of Lord Purdun's elite guard—surrounded him. The fourth held an empty bucket.

Unlike the others, this one sported a dirty white shirt, the sleeves rolled up, and a worn leather vest over the top. His head, face, and exposed forearms, all completely hairless, shined in the dim torchlight. A handful of scars crisscrossed the man's cheeks and forearms. Ryder recognized him immediately—Captain Phinneous. He was notorious among the Crimson Awl. Ryder had heard some of the older members tell stories about Phinneous around the campfire. Ryder never believed them. No man could be that cruel. Ryder's lips curled up into a grimace. Guess now he'd know for sure if the tales were true.

Ryder looked down at himself. His shirt was torn and bloodied, but the gash in his stomach was no longer there. He grabbed his gut, running his fingers along the fresh scar where the soldier's blade had cut him.

"I'm not dead."

The guardsmen laughed.

"Not yet," said the captain.

Ryder swung his feet around and planted them on the floor. He gripped the edge of the cot with both hands. "What is it you want from me?"

Captain Phinneous spun the bucket upside down, slapped it to the ground, put one foot atop it, and leaned down into Ryder's face. "We want you to tell us all you know about the Crimson Awl."

Ryder looked at the floor and shook his head. "Afraid I can't do that."

A sharp thud filled the small room, and the wooden bucket flew off the floor, hitting Ryder. The lights in the dungeon room flashed brighter as the heavy wood hit him in the face and his head flew backward, slamming against the stone wall. He could feel blood dripping from a new wound on his cheek, and his head began to thump with pain.

"That was uncalled for."

Captain Phinneous's fist connected with Ryder's jaw, and the lights flashed again.

"And that?" inquired the captain. "I suppose that wasn't needed either?"

Ryder gripped his jaw, jiggling it a little. It felt as

though it might come unhinged. "Yeah, that too."

Four hands grabbed Ryder by his torn shirt and lifted him to his feet.

"I want you to know," said the captain, his voice even, "that I don't intend to play these games with you."

Ryder, held like a rag doll between the burly guards, looked up at Phinneous. "Is that what this is? A game? You boys really need to get out and have more fun. Now horseshoes, that's a good game. This, this is . . ."

Phinneous smashed him in the gut with another fist. A dull pain flooded his abdomen and ran up his spine. When it reached the back of his head, it grew sharper and spread out, like a handful of skeletal fingers. The clawing bones scratched at his skull, and Ryder had to close his eyes simply to hold himself together.

"You're right," said Phinneous. "We do need to have more fun."

Ryder pried his eyes open to see the captain cross the tiny dungeon cell and lift one of the torches out of its sconce.

"If you don't like that game, maybe you'll like this one better." Phinneous's face broke into a huge grin as he came back. His upper lip curled, pulled awkwardly to one side by old scar tissue. "I call it 'burn the rebel.'" He lowered the torch next to Ryder's face. "It's one of my favorites."

Liam sat in the same spot he had for the past two days, looking into the fire. The flames grew quickly, then fell back again. Rising and falling, rising and falling. It was as if they were trying to leap off the log and fly up the stone chimney to escape. But there was no escape. They were chained to the source of their life, stuck to the burning log until it was completely consumed and they were extinguished.

A heavy knock came at the door.

"They've come," said Angeline.

Liam jumped to his feet, grabbing his sword from the table.

"Calm down," soothed Samira. "It's probably just the neighbors." She glared at the older woman as she crossed to the door.

Liam lowered his blade but didn't put it down.

Samira slid aside the wooden slat in the door and peered through. "Yes?" she said. "What do you want?"

"Ma'am, my name is Captain Beetlestone," came the voice through the door. "I'm here for Liam of Duhlnarim."

Samira turned to look back at Liam.

Liam shook his head. He'd been so stupid. That door was the only way in or out of this house.

Samira nodded and turned back to the door. "He's not—"

"We know he's in there," said Captain Beetlestone. "Don't make this any harder on yourself than it has to be. Let us in, or we'll be forced to break down the door."

"Now you listen here," said Samira, leaning closer to the slat. "You can't just come to my house, pound on the door, and call me a liar."

Liam could see her body stiffen as she wound up to tell the captain off.

"I pay the overblown taxes the baron levies like every other good citizen, and in return I expect to get some respect from his thugs." She slammed the slat shut. As she backed away, she placed both hands on the heavy crossbeam and gave it a little shove, checking to make sure it was closed tight. The thick wood didn't budge. It was closed as far as it would go.

Samira spun around, a smirk on her face. "Let's see them try to break through that."

As if in response, something heavy crashed against the wood. The door groaned and some dust floated out from between the seams, but it held.

Liam had helped Ryder install the extra-heavy crossbeam not long after the two of them had joined the Crimson Awl. Ryder had wanted it as an extra precaution. "For Samira's sake," he had said.

Back then, Liam never imagined it would be his life the heavy wood would protect.

"Get over here, away from the door." Liam grabbed Samira by the shoulder and pulled her back toward the other side of the house, next to his mother. He put himself between the two women and the door.

Again something smashed the door, but this time it sounded heavier. If the first sound had been a boot heel, this had been a warhammer or a heavy maul. The crashing sounds grew in frequency, landing on the door too fast for them to be made by just one man.

Liam looked back at Samira. "How many of them are out there?"

Samira shrugged. "Through the slat, I only saw three . . . no, four guardsmen."

Three he could maybe take. Four was pushing it, and if there were any others, he'd be far too outnumbered to have any chance. Liam started to look around the house. There were no windows, and the only other access to the outside world was through the chimney. For a heartbeat, Liam thought perhaps he could squeeze himself up and out onto the roof. But the fire had been burning all morning and afternoon. Even if he put it out, the bricks would be far too hot for him to touch.

He didn't have much time.

"Liam," his mother gripped his arm, "We're trapped in here. What are you going to do?"

Liam gritted his teeth. "Thank you, mother, for your insightful observation," he spat. "I'm working on it."

"Well, you'd better hurry."

His mother had a way of getting under his skin at the most inopportune moments.

Just then the pounding on the door stopped. Despite their best efforts, Baron Purdun's elite guardsmen had been unable to break through the heavy crossbeam.

Angeline sighed. "Thank Lathander for his protection, it held."

"It's not over yet," said Liam.

"Liam of Duhlnarim," Captain Beetlestone's shouting was muffled by the stone walls and wooden door. "Surrender yourself into our custody, or we will be forced to smoke you out."

"Liam," said his mother, the sound of worry evident in her voice, "what do they mean?"

Samira put her arms around the older woman. "It means they intend to burn down the house."

Angeline gasped.

Liam could see the fear in their eyes. He felt it too. But more than fear, he felt guilt. Guilt over having caused this. Guilt for having put these two women through so much.

"Liam of Duhlnarim," came the dull, shouting voice again. "This is your last chance. Come out now, or we'll light the roof."

Liam looked at the heavy wooden door. He had no choice. Placing his sword on the table, he turned to his mother and Samira and put his arms around them.

"Take good care of each other," he said. "I'll miss you both very much." Then he turned and headed for the door.

Ryder lay on the floor. His body ached from the beatings. His skin wept from the burnings.

Captain Phinneous stood over him, a spent torch in his hand, and a line of sweat dripping from his shiny, hairless forehead. "This is your last chance, Ryder. Tell me what I want to know, or you die here and now."

Ryder's head lolled back on his shoulders. "Go ahead and kill me."

Captain Phinneous gripped the remnants of the torch tightly in both hands. "Are you so worthless that you don't even respect your own life?"

Ryder let his head slide gently to the stone floor. "If you kill me now, I will be immortalized." He coughed, a thick ball of phlegm dislodging itself. He spat the mucus and the accompanying blood out beside him, then continued. "The Crimson Awl shall chant my name as they knock down the portcullis and ransack Zerith Hold." He smiled as the image of the resistance marching on this fortress, killing the guards and overthrowing Purdun, ran through his head. It was the most beautiful sight. "I'll become a martyr."

Phinneous chuckled. "Get a load of this one, boys. Delusions of grandeur." He dropped the spent torch to the ground. "So tell me this. If your death somehow miraculously provides the motivation for the Crimson Awl to overcome this fortress and all the guards inside of it—something they've been unable to do for over two years now—then why didn't you get yourself killed long ago?"

The other guardsmen laughed.

"Seems you've been holding your boys back," said Phinneous.

Ryder just closed his eyes and tried to focus on the parts of his body that didn't hurt so much. Phinneous wasn't going to kill him. It would be too beneficial to the rebels to have a rallying cry, someone to fight for.

"You're missing another very important detail," continued the captain.

"Yeah?" replied Ryder. "What's that?"

"It was one of your own who tipped us off about the ambush."

Ryder's eyes shot open.

"Seems one of your own boys wants you dead." Phinneous leaned over, filling Ryder's view with his scar-encrusted bald head. "Last chance. Are you going to tell me what I want to know?"

Ryder swallowed hard and shook his head. "Never. I don't believe you."

"That's what I thought." Captain Phinneous kicked Ryder in the ribs, knocking the wind from him.

Ryder was already in so much pain that it hurt more to double over than to just lie there and let his ribs throb.

"Ryder of Duhlnarim," Captain Phinneous's voice became more formal. "I hereby charge you with the crime of conspiracy to kill the baron, Lord Purdun. Furthermore, with the crimes of organizing and leading a criminal organization in the action of attempting to murder Princess Dijara, the king's sister and the wife of Lord Purdun—"

"What?" shouted Ryder. "I did no such—"

Phinneous's boot came down on Ryder's stomach, silencing his objection. "And finally, with the crime of conspiracy to overthrow the country of Erlkazar." He leaned down, a big smile on his scar tissue-covered lips. "How do you plead?"

"This is preposterous—"

Captain Phinneous punched Ryder in the jaw. With his head against the hard stone floor, there was nowhere for it to go. His skull bounced as it absorbed the entire force of the blow.

"Right, then." Phinneous stood up. "You all heard the man," he said, pointing to each of the guardsmen. "A plea of guilty will be reflected in the record."

The guardsmen all nodded.

"This is no court," pleaded Ryder. "I demand to see the barrister."

"As punishment, I, Captain Phinneous, commander of Lord Purdun's elite guard, sentence you to a life of hard labor. You will be assigned to a chain gang and marched to the farthest peninsula of the Dragon Coast, where you will be sold as a slave to the traders and businessmen of

Westgate. The warehouses there are overflowing with merchandise, and they have need of strong backs."

Captain Phinneous turned to the door. "Our work here is done, gentlemen." Placing the key in the lock, he let himself out. "Let's leave our friend here alone, so he can enjoy his last few moments as a free man in peace. His life as a slave begins today."

CHAPTER 5

Liam marched across the drawbridge, stopping just short of the portcullis guarding Zerith Hold, Lord Purdun's stronghold in Duhlnarim. The young revolutionary was accompanied by nearly two-dozen guardsmen.

Apparently the baron considered Liam a very dangerous man.

Without a word from Captain Beetlestone or any of the other guards, someone raised the portcullis before them. The clanking of the heavy chains as they lifted the iron gate reminded Liam of the sound of a ship's anchor. When he and Ryder were young boys, they used to hang out by the docks in Port Duhlnarim—only a stone's throw from where he was now—pretending they were pirates about to sail away on an adventure.

The sound of anchor chains meant a ship was

about to leave port. Liam had loved to watch the tremendous sails being hoisted, snapping taut as they filled with air. He had always dreamed of one day taking a voyage far away from Erlkazar. The clanging of the portcullis raising reminded him of those childhood feelings. Now, more than ever, he wished he were aboard one of those ships, sailing away.

The iron gate reached its full height and stopped. Along its bottom edge, a dozen sharp spikes angled downward like a set of dragon's teeth ready to devour anyone foolish enough to enter. The sharpened metal had corroded some over the years. Its marred, pockmarked surface was reddish brown, either from rust or the coagulated blood of its victims.

Behind the portcullis, a set of huge wooden doors, banded together with iron, swung open. Liam imagined it would take an elephant, or perhaps a pair of them, to knock them down. He could honestly say they were the largest doors in Duhlnarim. Hells, they were the largest doors he'd seen in his whole life.

Captain Beetlestone shoved Liam with the butt of his sword. The pointed metal dug into his back and Liam lurched forward through the opening. He had never been inside Zerith Hold before. This had always been the prize the Crimson Awl had coveted. He could hear Ryder's words echo in his head. "When the time is right, we will storm the gates and kill the oppressive bastards inside."

Liam had always believed those words. But he could see it was going to be a lot harder than they had imagined.

Just inside the front gate, the stone walls were lined with archer's ports—murder slits, Liam had heard them called. As he was marched by, he could see that even now they were manned. Past the entryway, the front courtyard was built exclusively to repel invaders. An open staging ground filled most of the space between the stone walls, but there were raised platforms, perches for more archers, arranged around the edges. From his vantage point, Liam thought you could likely station thirty, maybe forty men on these platforms. Anyone entering this killing field would be surrounded, faced with arrows from all sides.

Across the open courtyard, Beetlestone shoved Liam from behind again, forcing him to follow the other guardsmen up a shallow flight of stone stairs. At the top was another doorway. This one, though not as grand as the portcullis and monolithic wooden doors they'd just passed through, would likely hold out against any invading force the Awl could muster.

The double doors were manned by four fully armed soldiers. As Liam and his escorts approached, the guards separated, two on each side, and pulled the doors open. The huge iron hinges made a grinding noise, not the complaint of a rarely used mechanism suddenly having to work after a long rest, but simply from shouldering the burden of a heavy weight.

Liam was ushered inside through an opulent entry hall and up another flight of stone stairs, these covered with a fine red rug. It was like nothing he'd ever seen. Paintings of regal-looking men and woman lined the walls. Treasures of all kinds filled nooks and decorated tables. Suits of antiquated armor, relics from past wars and from foreign nations, stood motionless along the wide hallways. The spoils of war were arrayed in every possible location—a strong word of warning to visiting dignitaries.

At the top of a final flight of stairs, Liam's entourage came to one last set of doors. Unlike the others they had encountered, these were small and unguarded. The dark wood was polished to a high shine, and the ornate brass doorknobs shone brightly in the late afternoon sun.

Captain Beetlestone pushed the doors open, and Liam was ushered into a large, well-appointed room. There were tables and chairs situated in little clusters all about, as if the primary use for this room were for small groups of people to carry on intimate conversations. On the opposite side of the room was another, single door. It was closed.

In the corners, each partially hidden by a tall wooden bookshelf, stood four well-disciplined soldiers. They wore white capes, closed at the front. Their shoulders were adorned with golden embroidery, and their helmets had what appeared to be silver-etched runes running along their edges. All of them had their heads bowed. From this distance, Liam couldn't tell what sorts of weapons they carried. Their capes covered everything.

Though they were tucked away behind the furniture, they didn't appear to Liam as if they were trying to stay out of view. On the contrary, they seemed to be stationed in easy sight of the front door and the windows along the far wall. Anyone entering the chamber would see—and be seen by—them.

Unlike the guards who had escorted Liam from his home, these ones were oddly different. They stood stock still, each in his place, not seeming to care about the events unfolding before them. They stared, eyes to the floor, as if they were golems waiting patiently for their orders.

Captain Beetlestone produced a pair of manacles and held them out before Liam. "Keep your wrists together," he said, "and this won't even hurt."

Liam glanced again at the guardsmen. Deciding it was a good idea to follow the captain's instructions, he lifted his arms, placing his wrists together. "If I'd known your dungeon was this nice, I would have given myself up long ago."

Beetlestone smirked. "And if I'd known you were such a pansy, I would have come to collect you before now." He finished clasping the irons around Liam's wrists, then he slapped him on the back of the head.

Liam stumbled forward a step. "That was uncalled for."

Beetlestone cuffed him again, forcing Liam to one knee. "So was that," said the veteran soldier. Then he turned toward the door. "Come on, boys," he said, addressing the other guardsmen. "We'll leave him to Lord Purdun." The captain led his men out of the room.

"Stupid bastard," Liam said under his breath. "Some day it'll be my turn."

The door closed and latched as they left.

Liam lifted himself back to his feet and took in the furnishings. The walls were lined with shelves, and the shelves were choked with books. Liam was struck with a sense of awe. He could count the number of books he'd read in his lifetime on one hand. Hells, if the baron wanted to lock him in here for the next few years, it would be all right with Liam. He'd be the best-read farmer in all of Erlkazar.

He took a few steps toward the nearest shelf and fingered a leather-bound tome. He hesitated before lifting it out, watching to see if one of the guards was going to stop him.

Not one of the cloaked figures budged.

Liam shrugged. Guess they don't consider me a threat to their reading material, he thought.

The book he picked up was entitled *The Life and Times of Grooble Stonepate*. Liam opened the cover to find a poorly drawn sketch of a rather goofy-looking dwarf. Liam hadn't had many encounters with dwarves. Though it wasn't uncommon to see them doing business or passing through Duhlnarim, very few of them chose to make it their home. Those who did had a tendency to keep to themselves. But even so, Liam knew enough to tell that whoever drew this picture of Grooble Stonepate was either a very poor artist or had even less knowledge about dwarves than he did.

Closing the cover, he placed it back on the shelf, the

chains on his manacles clinking against the wood as he did. He ran his finger along the row of books. Each had a different feel to it, but none of them had titles on their spines. He wondered how people ever found what they were looking for.

"Guess you just match the color of the cover to the mood you're in."

He picked up another book, this one bound in dyed red hide, and turned it so he could see its title: *The Art of Waging War*, by General Bartholemew G. Blazencrow.

"A wonderful read."

Liam started and almost dropped the book.

"If you find the time, I highly recommend it."

Liam placed the book back on the shelf and turned to face the speaker. The young man was not much older than Liam himself. His bright red hair, combed neatly to one side, made a wavy pattern across the top of his head. It was obviously awash in some sort of scented oil. Liam could smell it from where he stood.

The man wore finely made clothes of what looked like silk and a fencer's belt around his waist. Oddly, though, no sword dangled from his hip. But the man's most distinguishing feature was a series of three long scars across his left cheek. Though they seemed old and long-healed, they stood out, a bright burgundy against his pale, freckled skin.

The scarred man looked Liam up and down, seeming to take his measure. "So, you're an educated man."

Liam nodded.

He offered Liam his hand. "I am Lord Purdun, Baron of Ahlarkham."

Liam was momentarily stunned. He had seen the baron before—his portrait hung in every major service building in Duhlnarim—but he'd never been this close before. Standing right beside him, Purdun didn't seem so imposing. In the paintings, he was the oppressor, the icon responsible for all of Ahlarkham's problems. He was a menace, a force of evil that must be stopped at all costs. But in person, old "Firefist," as he was sometimes called, was just a man.

"I know who you are," said Liam, refusing to take the baron's hand.

Purdun smiled. "And I know who you are, Liam of Duhlnarim."

Liam nodded. "I suppose you do." He shook his shackles without lifting them into view. The chain made a satisfying clink.

The smile drained from Purdun's face, and he snapped his fingers. One of the cloaked guards suddenly came to life, stepping out from behind a bookshelf. As he did, he seemed to grow and grow. The cloak's hem lifted from the floor, and the man's legs extended beneath. What had appeared to Liam upon first inspection as a floor-length robe in fact only came down to the guard's knees.

At his full height, the man (though Liam doubted this was a man, never had he seen anyone so massive) needed to duck his head to avoid hitting it on the ceiling. His bulk had been concealed behind the bookcase, but out here in the open, Liam could see that this was no ordinary bodyguard. Easily nine feet tall, the soldier had arms as big around as Liam's middle. His face was mostly concealed. Only a few glimpses of pale gray skin showed through the golden mask attached to his helm.

This enormous creature crossed the room toward Liam, carrying his massive frame with the lithe grace of a predatory cat. Despite his size, Liam could tell this guard had some speed.

As he approached, Liam took a step back. Stopping beside the two men, the bodyguard produced a small silver key and handed it to the baron.

Purdun took the key from the guard. "I also know about your ambush of my carriage several days ago."

Anger flared inside Liam. He could see the soldiers pouring out of the doors, the guardsmen surrounding him and his brother, and Ryder dropping to his knees after being slashed across the gut.

"Tell me something I don't already know."

"Now, now," said Purdun, trying to smother a self-satisfied smile, "I only did to you what you were planning to do to me. You were outsmarted and beaten in a fair fight. Don't be a sore loser."

Liam lashed out, grabbing for the baron's shirt. "You killed my brother."

Purdun's eyes went wide, and he lunged back. Reaching for his hip, his hand grasped at something Liam couldn't see. One moment, the baron was unarmed. The next, he stood on guard, a rapier materializing in his hand as if out of thin air.

The pain of losing his brother drove Liam forward. In a blink he sidestepped and grabbed hold of the bell of Purdun's blade. Knocking it aside, he lunged for the baron's throat. "I'll get—"

His words were cut off when his feet left the ground. The baron's massive bodyguard grabbed Liam by the back of the vest, wrenched his hands off Purdun's neck, and lifted him in the air. Liam was helpless, dangling a gnome's height above the floor like a baby kitten.

Purdun stood several steps away, his sword pointed at Liam. His carefully coifed hair hung now over one eye. His shirt sat cockeyed on his chest, crumpled at the neck where Liam had grabbed hold.

The baron pushed his hair back out of his face. "I'd rather you didn't do that again."

Liam's arms and legs swung freely. He craned his neck to look back at the gray-skinned creature. The bodyguard held him off the floor with only one arm and apparently little effort.

Liam looked back at the baron. "Or what?"

Purdun took a deep breath, looking a little exacerbated. Then his face broke into a smile, and he laughed.

"I like your spirit." He turned his rapier around and

slipped the tip back toward his belt as if he were placing it into a sheath. The blade disappeared slowly, looking as if it were being swallowed by an invisible snake. When the hilt reached his hip, it too vanished, and the baron's fencing belt once again appeared to be conspicuously empty of weapons.

Purdun straightened his shirt and collar and collected himself, then he nodded to the bodyguard. "Put him down."

The creature released Liam, and he fell to the ground, landing on the wooden floor with a thud. Liam scrambled away from the bodyguard and lifted himself to his feet.

Purdun looked him over from head to toe, spared a glance at his bodyguard, then took a step toward Liam, holding the key out.

"Please," he said pointing to Liam's shackles, "I'd prefer if you weren't wearing those."

A shudder ran down Liam's spine. He'd heard about this sort of thing.

He took a quick glance around the room. The other guards were still motionless in their alcoves. The door he'd come in was closed and presumably locked. The only other way out was the stone archways in the far wall that looked out on the bay and the ships in the harbor. It was a long way down—too far for Liam to jump.

Liam shuffled away from the baron. "Is this some sort of game?"

Purdun stopped, still holding the key out before him. "Game?"

The brutality of Purdun's elite guard was common knowledge. Liam had heard the tales of Captain Phinneous letting prisoners free only to claim they were trying to escape. He'd let them get into the courtyard, then sound the alarm. From what Liam had seen on the way in, a prisoner wouldn't stand a demon's chance in heaven of getting out. Anyone caught in that courtyard would be picked to pieces by the first volley of arrows. After that, there probably wouldn't be much left. It was a sick game, another abuse of power and another way to dehumanize the citizens of Duhlnarim.

Liam held up his hands. "Why drag me in here and shackle me, only to let me go?"

Purdun grimaced. "I apologize, Liam. It was never my intention to chain you up."

"I'm not going to give you an excuse to torture me. I'm not going to try to escape."

One of the freighters in the harbor began to weigh anchor, its chain clanking as it rose out of the water. Liam looked out the window, once again longing to be aboard that ship bound for a new place.

Purdun chuckled. "Is that what you think this is?"

Liam's attention came back inside the room. He never would have imagined his life ending like this. Three days ago, before he'd jumped out to attack the carriage, he knew that his actions could get him killed. Somehow though, he figured his end would be a bit more heroic.

He looked Purdun in the face. "There's no one here except you, me, and your goons. You can do what you want to me and make up whatever story you like. You don't need me to play along."

Purdun waved his hand, and the bodyguard took several steps back. "Liam, I have no intention of harming you."

"Then what did you bring me here for?"

Purdun stepped forward again and grabbed Liam by the wrist. Liam jumped back but not before the baron had unlocked and released his right wrist. The shackle swung free.

"I brought you here, Liam," said Purdun, "to offer you a job."

Liam stopped his retreat. "A job?"

Purdun nodded. "Yes, Liam. I want you to join my elite guard."

Liam wasn't sure he had heard the words right. "You want me to join your guard?"

"That is what I said," confirmed the baron.

Liam laughed. "What makes you think I'd want to join your elite guard?"

Purdun shrugged. "The money."

Liam was confused. Less than a tenday ago he'd attacked one of the baron's carriages, and somehow that had qualified him for entrance into the baron's elite guard. "Are all of your thugs ex-criminals?"

Purdun smiled, ignoring the question. "You'd get the best training and the best equipment. Three square meals a day, and extra provisions for your family. You could improve that run-down house of yours. Get your mother a proper wardrobe. Buy your father a new horse."

"I don't think you get it, Purdun." Liam narrowed his eyes. "I despise you. I hate everything you stand for. It's you who made my family suffer in the first place with your laws and taxes. And now you come to me with an offer to make their life better, bring their lives up to the level they deserve." Liam spat on the floor. "You step on our throats, suffocate us, then act as if you were doing us a favor by letting up, allowing us to simply live. Then you have the audacity to ask me to help you suffocate the rest of Erlkazar." He lifted the open shackle and placed it back on his wrist. "No thank you. I would rather live the rest of my life in chains than be party to such villainy."

Lord Purdun took a deep breath. "Well, Liam, I can certainly understand your position." He placed the key in the shackles and locked them once again. "But it's a standing offer. If you change your mind, you know where to find me." Purdun placed his hand on Liam's shoulder and directed him toward the door. "Come."

Liam didn't budge. "Where are you taking me?"

"I'm escorting you to the front gate, Liam." He smiled. "To make sure you make it out of Zerith Hold safely."

❖ ❖ ❖ ❖ ❖

Ryder sat in the bowels of Lord Purdun's dungeon, his legs chained together, his wrists chained together, and the chains chained together. Beside him on the wooden bench were two similarly chained men—one muscular and bald with the tattoo of a blue triangle on his forehead and the other skinny and sickly.

In fact, the entire dank, dripping room was filled with manacled men. They sat side by side by side, three to a bench, twelve benches in all, each man chained to the next. They all wore the same identical clothing: dirty gray baggy hemp pants and matching sleeveless shirts. Down one side of the floor a huge shirtless man, bulging with muscles, paced the narrow walkway between the prisoners. His chest was crisscrossed in old scars, and he carried a whip in his right hand.

"All right, you vermin," started the man. "There will be no talking, no whispering, and no complaining." He cracked his whip against the stone floor. "If you're here it means your life is no longer worth a piss. So until we manage to find someone stupid enough to pay good money for your wasted, worthless hides, you belong to me." He turned and paced back toward the front of the room. "And I'm none too happy about having to spend the next several months with a bunch of criminal low-lifes, inhaling your fumes and watching you wallow in your own filth. Marching several hundred miles across the open plains ain't exactly a picnic with a fair maiden for me either. So mind that you don't make me angry, and you might just make it to your new home in one piece."

He stopped when he got to the front of the room. Atop a raised platform rested a pair of large drums with blackened leather harness straps—the kind that could be hefted over a drummer's shoulders and carried during a parade or festival. The cow hide that covered their tops was stained a deep brown, and there were several tears and holes along the sides and bottom.

Behind the drums was a pair of wooden doors held closed by a monstrous sliding bolt. As an added measure, a heavy metal lock hung from the latch. It was open and unlocked, but having the lock on the inside seemed odd to Ryder. Was there something they intended to keep out of here? Or was the taskmaster really prepared to sacrifice himself if the prisoners managed to break free?

Beside the doors, as if in answer to Ryder's query, hung a half dozen wicked-looking knives, cleavers, clubs, and other implements of pain. Perhaps there was another reason for the latch being on the inside.

The taskmaster picked up a heavy-looking cleaver in his free hand and shook it as if testing its weight. He nodded, seemingly satisfied.

"Now, about the rest of the rules. You address no one but me, and only if you've been addressed first. Any talking out of turn will get you fifty lashes by my own hand." He slapped the whip against the floor again. It made a sharp cracking sound, and a small stone flew into the air. "If I do speak to you, you will address me as 'sir.' If I even think that you are being disrespectful, you will receive fifty lashes. If you look at me funny, you will receive fifty lashes. If I don't like your tone, you will receive fifty lashes." He paused and looked over the prisoners. "And if I just feel like it, you'll receive fifty lashes."

The taskmaster swung the cleaver through the musky air. Ryder watched as the blade glistened in the lanternlight. This scarred, shirtless creature seemed to be enjoying himself. He had a whip in one hand, a cleaver in the other, and was swinging them both like a child might wave its toys. It made Ryder's stomach turn. What sort of man would revel in such torment? What sort of life could have led a man to stoop to such a place? He was barely more than an animal.

Ryder stared down at the chains on his arms and legs. They were trying to turn him into an animal as well. He looked back at the taskmaster. He was still flailing around with his whip and cleaver. The taskmaster's chest and forehead were beginning to shine from sweat. That would be Ryder's challenge here. He could never let himself become like this man, never let them take from him the only thing he had left: his humanity.

A pounding on the door caused the taskmaster to stop his display.

"Prepare the prisoners," yelled a voice from the other side of the door. "The mounted guard is ready to leave."

The taskmaster was visibly deflated by this. He bowed his head then hung the cleaver back on the wall. "All right scum," he said after a long sigh, "that's your cue." He wound his whip around his right hand, making his fist look like a giant's. With his other hand, he grabbed hold of the length of chain on the floor that connected to the first set of three prisoners.

Giving it a rough tug, he shouted, "Get up."

All thirty-six prisoners stood up.

"To your left." He gave the chain another tug. "Move."

Ryder, being on the farthest left side, sidestepped as far as he could. There was enough chain between the shackles on his ankles for him to take a full stride. But the chain between him and the bald man on his right was not as long, and the two of them got momentarily tangled. Ryder came to an abrupt stop, almost toppling over. The bald man reached out and caught Ryder by the wrist, righting the falling revolutionary.

Ryder looked at the man. He had a gruff, surly countenance. His forehead sported a vivid blue tattoo shaped like a triangle. His left ear had a long tear in it, covered with a fresh scab—likely an ornament recently removed by force. His nose was bright red, a telltale sign of one who's consumed a lifetime's worth of mead in much less than a lifetime, and his face was covered with deep pockmarks. Despite his outward appearance, his eyes had a kindness to them, and the man nodded when they made eye contact.

Ryder nodded back, acknowledging the man's help, and continued to shuffle to his left. With several quick steps and a hop to avoid tripping over the chain again, he managed to move far enough for him, the bald man, and the third prisoner in his row to get out from behind the bench.

Once the entire group of prisoners was ready, the taskmaster gave them a once-over and nodded. Clipping the lead chain onto a hook on his belt, he turned around and hefted the drum harness onto his shoulders.

"All right, you worthless pile of dragon dung, this isn't difficult." He pounded one of the drums with his fist. It made a deep boom. "Listen to the beat and move your feet. If I stop beating the drum, you stop moving your feet. If I turn left, you turn left. If I turn right, you turn right. Got it?"

No one said a word.

The taskmaster looked back over his shoulder, shouting this time. "Got it?"

"Yes, sir," said several of the prisoners.

"First beat," he shouted over the drums, "you step with your left foot. Second beat, you step with your right foot. Anyone who can't keep up or keep the beat will force me to stop beating the drum, and if I'm not beating the drum I'll be beating you." He slammed his fist against the first drum.

Ryder stepped his left foot forward. The tattooed man did as well. The skinny man at the end of their row, however, was caught off-guard. He was yanked forward by his shackles, only catching his balance at the last instant. The prisoners in the next row bumped into the skinny man's back, nearly causing a pileup.

"Second beat," shouted the taskmaster. He brought his other fist down against the drum.

Ryder stepped forward with his right foot. This time the skinny man caught the beat, and he moved in unison with the rest of the group. As the prisoners shuffled forward, the chains rattled, sounding like some sort of angry spirit.

"First beat!"

Ryder stepped again. The bruises from the beating Captain Phinneous had given him burned from the strain.

"Second beat!"

Ryder looked up at the taskmaster. The taskmaster beat the drum again, this time without any verbal instruction. Ryder's lip curled with the distain he now felt toward the man.

As a group, the prisoners, led by the drum-beating taskmaster, marched in a wide circle around the wooden benches in the center of the room. When they reached the same place they had started from, the taskmaster abruptly stopped beating the drum.

"Do it just like that until we get to where we're going, and I won't be forced to hurt you."

Pulling the bolt on the door, the taskmaster let it swing open. Outside was a courtyard enclosed by a high stone wall and two-dozen armed guardsmen on horseback. To one side sat a carriage, not unlike the one Ryder had ambushed with Liam.

"Here we go." The taskmaster beat the drum, and the gang of chained prisoners moved forward.

When they reached the middle of the courtyard, the mounted guard captain shouted, "Halt."

The taskmaster stopped beating the drums, and the prisoners came to a stop. The guardsmen moved their horses into positions beside them. Holding loaded crossbows in one hand and the reigns to their horses in the other, they surrounded the prisoners.

The captain lifted his arm in the air then let it fall. "Forward."

Another set of doors opened up across the courtyard, and the drumbeat began again.

The sun was going down on the horizon, turning the sky a deep orange.

Ryder stepped forward, then stepped forward again. "I will not go down easy," he said under his breath.

The tattooed man turned to look at him. Ryder thought he might say something, but all he did was nod.

The taskmaster picked up the pace, and they marched out of Zerith Hold toward the setting sun. The carriage rolled out behind them, taking up the rear.

Boom, boom, boom, boom....

Captain Beetlestone pulled the knob on the door leading into Lord Purdun's private study and entered the room.

He bowed before the baron. "You sent for me, my lord."

Lord Purdun turned away from the windows looking out over the harbor. The sun had gone down. The only light that could be seen was the reflection of the moon off the lightly rippling water.

"You've been with me a long time," he said. "I trust your judgment."

"Thank you, my lord," replied Beetlestone, standing up straighter.

The baron took deep breath. "Tell me honestly. Do you think this is the right thing?" asked Purdun. "Do you think Liam is the right choice?"

The captain nodded. "I was there when they attacked the carriage, my lord. I saw him with my own eyes. He's definitely the one."

"What about his brother?"

Beetlestone shook his head. "He would never give in. Liam is the one we want. He has the skills and the good sense to keep himself in one piece."

Lord Purdun nodded. "All right," he said. "Then we will proceed." He turned back toward the window.

"Yes, my lord." Captain Beetlestone turned and, closing the door behind him, exited the room.

CHAPTER 6

Liam woke up with a start. He was in his own bed. He was warm and comfortable. He touched the pillow, then his own face.

"Dear Tymora, please let that have been a dream."

Then the images of Ryder came back to him. The aching in his chest, the crushing anguish, and the guilt rolled back in, and Liam was certain that it was no dream. That moment of obscurity, between asleep and awake, was a small taste of bliss. But now the realities of Liam's life had come crashing back into his consciousness, and he would have to deal with it.

Swinging his legs out from under his blanket, he put his feet on the floor and lifted himself out of bed. The sun hadn't come up yet. All the better. Darkness suited his mood.

Slipping his clothes on, he grabbed a hoe from a rack on the wall and headed out the door. Down the path, he turned and headed east. He didn't need the sun's guidance to find his way. He'd walked the path so many times that he sometimes felt he could find his way completely asleep.

All of the farmers in Duhlnarim shared the same set of fields. Nobody owned them, of course. They were all the property of Baron Purdun and his wife, the Princess Dijara, who was also the king's younger sister. Each family was allotted an amount of land to work as they saw fit, but every season, the tax collector came around, collecting for the baron. Every year the taxes got higher. It got so a family could barely make a living anymore.

Liam and his folks would break their backs working the land, tilling the soil, planting the crops, then harvesting them, only to have most of what they reaped taken away.

Despite how early he'd arrived, Liam wasn't the first in the fields of Furrowsrich village. It was better to get an early start so one could finish the hard work before the sun got too high in the sky. Already the sound of sharpened metal tilling the hard-packed dirt had reached a steady rhythm. There were at least a dozen other men working here, including Liam's father, Douglas. But none of them spoke, not in the morning.

Liam wasn't sure why the silence was part of the farmers' morning ritual, but right now he was thankful for it. He just wanted to go straight to work—wanted to push himself, to feel something other than the anguish that had ruled his life for the past two tendays.

Crossing over several planted rows, Liam came to the spot where he'd left off the day before. He raised the hoe and brought it down in a quick chop. His first strike was off beat. Raising it again, he brought it down a little faster. The blood flowed through his veins, and soon he had a good sweat going. His down strokes kept rhythm with the other farmers.

By midday, he'd completed two full rows. As he began work on the third, Douglas grabbed him by the shoulder.

"It is time for a break," said the old man.

Liam looked up but didn't stop his swing. "I'm fine."

His father just nodded. "Well, if you won't take a break for yourself, perhaps you'll come help me fix the cart." He hitched his thumb over his shoulder. "The wheel is stuck, and I need someone to hold it while I pound out the axle."

Liam shrugged and followed his father to the small shed situated beside the field. All the farmers built these structures next to the land they worked. It was a way for them to claim a small amount of ownership in a system that allowed them no control over anything Inside the rickety wooden walls, a farmer could do whatever he wished. The land the building sat upon didn't belong to him, but the space inside did.

Next to the shed, Liam's father's cart was turned over, the wheel in the air.

The old man went into the shed and returned with a heavy stone hammer and a steel awl.

"Grab hold of the wheel there," Douglas instructed, "and I'll knock the axle loose."

Liam did as his father instructed, bending over the cart and grabbing it with both hands.

"All right, hold it still now."

They worked in silence, the hot afternoon sun beating down on them. This was how it had always been between the two of them, father and son. Liam had never really related to his father all that much. They didn't talk, except when Douglas needed help with something. And Liam never felt the need to get more out of the old man. Liam didn't like to think that he hated his father. He preferred to think that they just didn't have anything in common. They had a duty to each other because they were family, and that was the extent of their relationship.

With one final blow, the axle on the cart came loose, and the wheel slipped off.

"Good," said the old man. "Now take it around to the other side of the shed. I'll put the new axle on it."

Liam lifted the wheel and carried it around the building. As he came around the shed, he caught sight of Samira. She carried a heavy-looking bucket over her right arm, and she braced it with her left. Every day she mercifully brought fresh water to the fields to quench the farmers' parched throats. She waved at Liam as she approached.

Samira was tired. Liam could tell by the way she carried herself that the past two tendays had taken their toll. It pained him to know how much she was mourning the loss of his brother. Something so beautiful shouldn't have to feel such an ugly emotion.

The other farmers saw her approaching with the bucket, and they flocked over to the shed to get a dipper full of the clean fresh well water. Liam put the wheel down and turned to be the first in line.

"Hello Samira," he said, taking off his cap.

"Afternoon, Liam." She smiled, worry lines creasing her face. "You look thirsty. Care for a drink?"

"Yes. Thank you."

Samira lifted the dipper out of the bucket and handed it to Liam. Covered in dust, standing out in the hot sun, the cool fresh water tasted better than any water he'd ever had. Though he knew this was the same water from the same well that he'd been drinking from since he was young, somehow, it always tasted better after a long day's work.

He finished the water in one long slurp, then handed the dipper back. As he did, he made eye contact with Samira. There was sadness there. Sadness and pain. Her eyes seemed as if they were carrying a heavy weight all by themselves, holding back the emotions Samira was too brave to show off here among the other farmers. It was as if all of her anguish over losing Ryder had been packed away behind those two beautiful blue eyes. They struggled to hold it all back. But somehow, while Liam looked on, they softened. For a moment, the burden they carried was lifted, and a wave of happy relief swept over them.

"Come on, son, don't hold up the line." The farmer behind him gave a light shove, and Liam looked away from Samira as he stepped aside and out of line.

Liam went back and lifted the wheel he and his father had been working on. Standing up, he found himself face to face with Captain Beetlestone. The veteran was backed by four other soldiers.

"Well, well," said Beetlestone as he doffed his helm. "Back hard at work, are we?"

Liam shifted his grip on the wheel. "What do you want?"

"Don't you know?"

Farmers in Furrowsrich village were a notoriously nosey bunch, and a crowd began to form behind Liam, watching the interchange.

"No, Beetlestone, I don't."

The guard captain smirked. "It's been two tendays. Lord Purdun wants to know if you've thought about his offer to join his elite guard."

Liam looked back at the group of farmers. Everyone was silent, pretending to mind their own business, but he could tell they were hanging on every word.

"No, I haven't."

"Well—" the captain said, taking a step closer to Liam— "let me give you a piece of advice. If I were you, I'd take him up on it." He stepped back, examining in the entire crowd in one long, slow glance. "Someone like you doesn't get too many opportunities. Could change your life."

Liam blinked.

The farmers began to murmur. Beetlestone wasn't lying. Many of these people would give all they had to see their son or daughter taken into the baron's elite guard.

Life in Furrowsrich was hard. No money, long days in the fields, barely enough to get by. Taking this position would mean an easier life for him and his family. But that was exactly why he couldn't take it. It was Purdun who created this situation, and if Liam let himself be bought, then who would look after the interests of these other folks? If every revolutionary in the Crimson Awl could be bought, then Purdun would win. At least if Liam held out, there was a chance, albeit a small chance, of the Awl overthrowing the baron and changing everyone's lives at the same time.

Beetlestone put his helm back on his head. "Well, think about it. Think real hard about it." He turned to the rest of his men. "Let's go." The guard captain walked away, his men falling into step behind him.

Liam took the wheel into the shed. Though it was hot, the shade was a merciful relief from the sun beating down on his head and the farmers' staring eyes on his back.

His father followed him in. "What was that about?"

Liam shook his head. "Nothing."

"Nothing? Sounded like something to me," said Douglas, raising his voice and moving closer to his son.

Liam flinched. Ever since he was a little boy, his father would use his superior size to gain the advantage in an argument. Despite the fact that Liam was no longer five years old, and he was now taller than his father, Douglas was still well-muscled from his time in the fields, and his father's commanding tone intimidated him.

"I told you already, Lord Purdun asked me some questions."

"Captain Beetlestone said something about an offer." Douglas moved in even closer, his chin nearly touching Liam's cheek. "What offer is he talking about, Liam?"

Liam squirmed. "All right," he said as he took a step away from the older man. "Purdun offered me a spot on his elite guard."

"And you didn't take it? What kind of fool are you?"

Liam's anger rose at his father's goading. It replaced his sorrow and gave him strength. He squared his shoulders and glared down at Douglas. "Not the kind of old fool who waits around, toiling his whole life just so that fat pig Purdun can get rich off my hard work." He shoved his father.

Douglas lost his balance and had to take a step back. It wasn't that the shove was so hard that it actually overpowered the old man, but the action surprised both father and son.

Liam's heart pounded. He was tired of being muscled around, and now he'd done what he'd never before had the courage to do. The feeling thrilled him. But there would be consequences, and that also terrified him.

Douglas came back with both fists balled up, ready for a fight. "You prepared to back that up, boy?"

Liam instinctively reached for his belt, but he hadn't brought a sword. Glancing around the room, he looked for something to defend himself with. It was too late to talk his way out of this; he'd seen that look in his father's eyes too many times. Their arguments had often ended this way over the years. But this one was different. This time, Liam had made contact, and the old man wasn't going to let that go unpunished.

Liam remembered back to a time when he was only ten years old. They had been out in these very fields, and he and Ryder had been practicing their sword fighting with a couple of hoes. Douglas had stepped between their little game, and Liam had feigned a blow to the old man's head. His father had grabbed him by the arm and lifted him clean off the ground.

Looking Liam in the eyes, Douglas had said, "If you hit me, you'd better make sure I don't get back up. Because if I do, you'll be sorry."

Liam had never forgotten those words. They had been burned into his permanent memory, and since that day, he'd never laid a finger on the old man.

Until now.

Liam caught sight of a broken pickaxe leaning against the wall of the shed, and he made a lunge for it. Douglas saw him move, and swung down with his powerful fist. But Liam was too fast, and he spun away, grabbing the pick and avoiding the blow as he sidestepped the slower, burly old man.

The move had saved Liam from a painful sock in the gut, but it had humiliated his father, adding insult to injury.

Douglas's face was now red, and he sneered at his son, his tremendous frame heaving with exertion as it blocked the path to the open door. "You're gonna get it, boy."

Liam lifted the broken tool.

"What's going on in here?" Samira appeared in the doorway. Her face was obscured by the sunlight behind her. Liam could only see the silhouette of her hand placed firmly on her slim hip. Her hair was tied on top of her head, exposing the long smooth curve of her neck, backlit by the sun's rays.

"Oof." Liam staggered back, slamming into the wall as his father's fist collided with his chin. He slid down the wall to the ground.

"Stop it!" shouted Samira. "Stop it right now." She pushed past Douglas to get to Liam's side.

"This doesn't concern you," said the old man, rubbing his knuckles.

Samira bent down and touched Liam's cheek. "You're bleeding."

Liam put his hand to his face. His father's punch had split his parched lip.

Douglas shuffled his feet. "Leave the little sissy be. He got what he deserves."

Samira spun on the old man. "Don't you have work to do?" she said. "You've done enough here already."

"Bah." Douglas sneered at Liam then turned and walked out the door. The opening no longer blocked, the sun beamed in from outside.

Liam pushed himself up on one arm and started to get up off the ground.

Samira grabbed him by the shoulder and helped him up. "Oh, be careful."

"I'm fine. I'm fine." He waved her off as he got to his feet. "I had it coming."

"What happened?" She tore off a piece of her skirt and dabbed at the blood on his face. "And what was all that with Captain Beetlestone?"

Liam touched his chin. It was sore and probably would be for a while. "That discussion is what got me this fat lip."

"Ah," Samira nodded. "A little fatherly advice."

Liam smirked. Ryder had started courting Samira when they were still just teenagers, but she had known their family for much longer. Though she had been kind and friendly toward Douglas, Liam had always thought she disapproved of the way he related to the rest of the family.

The doorway went dark again. "Liam of Duhlnarim," came a voice. Three men shuffled into the shed. All of them wore hardened leather armor, and each of them carried a long sword. "You have some explaining to do."

The speaker stepped forward, out of the backlit doorway and into the shadows where Liam could see him. He was tall with long black hair tied back in a ponytail. There were dark circles under his eyes and his skin was pale, making his face look sickly in the strange light of the shack.

"Montauk!" said Liam, recognizing immediately one of his fellow Crimson Awl. "You've heard about Ryder, then?"

Montauk nodded. "Yes, I did. And I also heard about your little visit with Lord Purdun. Seems you've gone over to the other side."

Liam raised his hands. "No. You don't understand. I turned him down. I told him to go to hell."

Montauk shrugged. "Tell it to the Council."

The two men flanking Montauk stepped forward and grabbed Liam by the arms.

Liam shook them off, shoving both away. "Let go."

Montauk pulled his sword.

Liam froze at the sound of the grinding metal. Samira's hand tightened around his arm.

"Don't make this any harder than it needs to be," said Montauk. "Come with us peacefully, and you'll get to tell your story."

Liam looked at the two men, then at Montauk. Until just a few moments ago, he had thought they were on his side. "Do I have a choice?"

Montauk shook his head.

"Then lead the way." Liam touched Samira's hand, then let himself be taken from the shack out into the afternoon sun.

CHAPTER 7

I'll kill you—" Ryder woke up with a start. The nightmare of his failed ambush played over in his head, a persistent dream for nearly a month.

"Shh," said the bald man to his right. "You'll wake the taskmaster."

The realities of Ryder's situation came rushing back to him. It was very early morning. The sky had just begun to lighten, but the sun had yet to come up over the rise. He sat up straight and peered over the men in front of him. A few yards ahead of the chain gang, the taskmaster was hunched over his drums, still dead asleep.

They had stopped for the night, now over two tendays outside of Duhlnarim. The guards had made camp in a shallow valley, chaining the prisoners to a large oak tree. Ryder could see their fire about a hundred paces away. At least two of the guards were awake. He could hear their voices intermingling with the crackling of the fire.

Ryder lifted his hand to cradle his sore neck, but the chains connecting him to the bald man didn't reach that far. He was stiff, and his whole body hurt from sleeping on the hard-packed dirt.

"What'd they get you for?" whispered the bald man.

Ryder stopped moving. "Sorry, I didn't mean to wake you."

The bald man shook his head. "I wasn't asleep." He lifted his arm, putting some slack in the chain.

Ryder smiled. "Thanks." Then he reached back to rub the sore muscles in his neck.

"So," repeated the bald man, "what'd they get you for?"

Ryder shrugged. "I'm not sure. Conspiracy, I guess."

"Conspiracy? What, the baron caught you thinking impure thoughts?"

"That and ambushing one of his carriages."

The bald man smirked. "Sounds more like thievery to me."

"I guess you could look at it that way. But we weren't just stealing, we were trying to intercept a message from Lord Purdun."

The bald man raised an eyebrow. "A message? You don't approve of the baron's correspondences?"

Ryder nodded. "Well, to some extent, yes. This message was a letter of treaty bound for another barony. If it had gotten there, it would have meant more hardship for the folks of Duhlnarim and more trouble for the Crimson Awl."

The bald man's eyes narrowed. "A revolutionary, huh? Not much of a criminal then, are you?"

"Not really," admitted Ryder. "Does that lower your opinion of me?"

The man smiled, exposing a pair of golden front teeth.

"Anyone who puts a thorn in Purdun's ass is all right by me." The man offered Ryder his hand. "The name's Nazeem."

"Ryder." He shook the offered hand. "And what's your story?"

"Smuggling," said Nazeem. "Seems Purdun doesn't like the idea of anything coming into his barony without him getting his fair share of tax."

"Sounds about right—" Ryder froze, his comments cut short at the sound of the taskmaster snorting and rolling onto his side.

The large greasy man sat up and wiped a meaty palm across his face. Then, with a huge yawn and a stretch he got to his feet and began counting the prisoners. Ryder glanced once more at Nazeem, as if to say "we'll continue this later." He avoided eye contact with the taskmaster as the man's sausage-sized finger pointed to him, counting Ryder as number twenty-five.

The sky had gotten much lighter, and many of the other guards were moving around the camp. One of them poured a pail of water over the campfire. Ryder could hear the ashes sizzle as he watched a cloud of smoke rise into the air.

The taskmaster unlocked the chain that held the prisoners to the oak tree and gave it a healthy yank.

"Wake up, you scum," he shouted.

The rest of the prisoners stirred to life, sluggishly waking up from their less-than-restful sleep.

"On your feet."

Though it was difficult to lift his body and the heavy chains with his sore, stiff muscles, Ryder managed to get himself to his feet. Nazeem sat cross-legged on the ground next to Ryder. Without using his hands, the tattooed man attempted to lift himself to standing. The skinny man on the end of their row, however, did not get up, and Nazeem was forced to crouch, unable to hold up both his weight and that of the other man.

"Get up," Nazeem hissed under his breath.

But the skinny man didn't move. Instead, he let out a shallow snore.

All of the other men had gotten to their feet, and the taskmaster was making a slow circle around them, inspecting each of the prisoners.

"Get up, you fool," said Nazeem, this time a little louder.

The skinny man didn't hear his plea, but the taskmaster did. One moment he was at the front of the chain gang; the next he was right beside Nazeem.

"I told you never to talk." The taskmaster's whip cut the air, snapping as it slashed Nazeem's bare shoulder.

The bald man sucked in air through his clenched teeth, but he did not scream. Ryder hadn't noticed it before, but Nazeem's shoulders were covered with long, thin scars. He was no stranger to this sort of beating.

The taskmaster pulled his whip back over his head and cracked it again, catching Nazeem along the side of the face. Ryder cringed. Though he couldn't see exactly where the whip had hit the man, he knew it had to hurt. Nazeem handled it the same way he had the first lash, cringing from the obvious pain but refusing to give the taskmaster any satisfaction.

"We got ourselves a tough one here," said the taskmaster, pulling his whip up again. "Good. Good. You should fetch a high price in Westgate. Might even find interest for you with the Quivering Thumb." He leaned in closer. "You could actually live long enough to earn your freedom in the arena." Standing up straight, he snapped the whip again. This time though, he targeted the skinny man.

Awakened rudely from his sleep, the skinny man yelped when the tip of the whip slapped against his back.

"Get up," shouted the taskmaster. He kicked the skinny man in the gut.

The little man's entire body lifted off the ground from the impact, and he let out an "oof," then doubled over.

The taskmaster kicked the man again. "I said 'get up.'"

"Mr. Cobblepot," shouted the guard captain. "Quit messing around and get ready to march."

The taskmaster looked up at the mounted captain, being careful not to make eye contact. "Yes, Captain Tully."

"Be quick about it," said the captain, then he turned his horse around and rode off.

The skinny man convulsed, spitting up a glob of blood. Mr. Cobblepot reached down and with one arm lifted the beaten prisoner to his feet.

"I'll deal with you later," he said, shoving the man. Scuttling around to the front of the gang, the taskmaster wrapped his whip around his hand and lifted his drums to his shoulders.

"All right, scum," he yelled, "it's double-time all morning. Compliments of sleeping beauty there."

Ryder looked over at the skinny man. He could barely hold himself up. Beyond having just been beaten, he seemed sick, depleted. Ryder didn't think the poor man would make it through the morning. He wished there were something he could do, some way to help the poor bastard lift his burden.

"We march," shouted the taskmaster. He slammed his drum. *BOOM ... BOOM. ...*

The chain gang lurched forward. Ryder stepped in time with the drum.

The sun finally crested the rise, spilling light over the valley. It was going to be a hot one. The skinny man coughed and gagged, stumbling forward with the marching group and spitting out another long stringy strand of mucus and blood.

Ryder shuddered as he thought about what would happen when the skinny man finally collapsed. Stopping without orders would get a prisoner severely beaten. If the taskmaster didn't notice when the man fell, he might be dragged by the rest of the gang.

The skinny man coughed again, this time so violently that he doubled over. The chains on his feet—bound to the man in front of him—pulled taut.

Nazeem reached out and grabbed the skinny man by the back of his vest, dragging him forward on the next drum beat. Ryder moved closer to Nazeem, giving him as much slack in the chains as he could manage without falling over himself. If one of them fell, the others likely would as well.

The skinny man finally recovered from his coughing fit, and he regained his balance. He looked up gratefully at Nazeem, tottered a bit, then pasted his gaze to the ground, concentrating on each and every step.

This time the carriage took the lead. The mounted guardsmen fell into place alongside the chain gang, and they continued their march out of the valley. The taskmaster beat the drums at double the usual speed, and the prisoners followed the dirt road up the western slope, running from the rising sun.

❧ ❧ ❧ ❧ ❧

"All right, you vermin," shouted the taskmaster as he lowered his drums from his shoulders, "we stop here for the night."

The entire gang collapsed to the ground in a cacophony of moans and groans. They had stopped in open lowlands on a big, flat, damp piece of ground surrounded by several small groupings of trees on the east and a large pile of boulders on the west. Thick swarms of bugs moved around like tiny rain clouds, shifting and circling overhead. The air reeked of rotten vegetation and stagnant water.

Ryder felt a wave of relief flush through his aching body as he crashed to the ground. They had marched from sunup to sundown, stopping once and only briefly for water. His feet throbbed, feeling as though all the blood in his body had somehow found its way down there and now threatened to burst through his skin, spilling out over the open plain.

To his right, Nazeem sat cross-legged, his arms resting on his knees. The tattooed man sat like this every time they stopped. He would close his eyes, sit up straight, and breathe through his nose. Nazeem looked so calm, so peaceful. Ryder wished that he could feel the way Nazeem looked. But right now, there was no peace or tranquility to be had on the hard, rocky ground.

Beside Nazeem, the skinny man had slumped over into a heap. Ryder was surprised he had made it. He'd had a rough start at the beginning of the day, but after that he'd more or less kept pace with the rest of the group. Only a few times did Nazeem have to help him along or keep him from falling. Making it to the end of the day without being trampled or beaten seemed like a tremendous success.

Someone shoved Ryder.

"Water."

Ryder looked up at a young guardsman holding a wooden bucket and dipper.

Ryder nodded and took the offered water gratefully. He swallowed the entire dipperful in one giant gulp—and immediately gagged. His mouth was covered with a gritty film, and his stomach felt nauseated. He looked down into the dipper. The inside of it was covered with mud and slime.

"You scum should be right at home drinking swamp water," said the guard, laughing.

Ryder tried to keep the contents of his stomach from coming back up. It was a struggle. He coughed and burped, swallowing hard with each breath.

The guard grabbed the dipper back, filled it again from the bucket, and passed it over Ryder to Nazeem.

The tattooed man took it, looked into the bowl, sniffed the water, then drank it down. Unlike Ryder, the tattooed man didn't seem to have the same reaction, simply swallowing and handing the dipper back to the guard.

Ryder tried to scrape the film off his tongue by rubbing it back and forth against his teeth. Some of it came off, but the taste of rotten vegetation still lingered in his mouth. He would be burping up stinkweed juice for at least another day.

"Hey you," said the guard, looking at the skinny man. "Time for water."

The skinny man didn't move.

"Hey. I'm talking to you." The guard flung the sludge from the bottom of the dipper at him.

Still, he didn't move.

The guard shrugged. "Suit yourself. But there won't be any more until tomorrow." He started to move on to the next row of prisoners.

"Just a moment."

The taskmaster appeared, hovering over the skinny man, a huge grin on his face.

"This man is very thirsty." Cobblepot took the bucket from the guard. "I'm sure he wants to drink every last drop." Squatting down, he grabbed the skinny man by the hair and lifted his head from the ground. Then he put the edge of the bucket up to the skinny man's mouth.

Even being jerked back like that didn't elicit a response. His eyes opened, and he moaned, but otherwise he let the taskmaster move his body around like a rag doll.

"Open wide," said Cobblepot, forcing the scummy water down the prone prisoner's throat.

The skinny man's mouth filled quickly and the murky water spilled out the sides, flooding over his face, nose, and cheeks, then down his chest. For a moment, the skinny man didn't move, letting the swampy fluid just flow over him. Then Ryder could see his mouth move, and the skinny man's chest heaved. The skinny man kicked pathetically against the taskmaster's hold, trying to fight the bucket away. He managed to get his lips away from the edge long enough to take in one huge gasp of air. Fighting to breathe, he made a sound like a strangled chicken and coughed up sludge.

"Taste good?" taunted the taskmaster. He continued pouring the muddy water into the prisoner's mouth.

The skinny man raised his hand. The chains on his arms rattled as they pulled tight. Though the bucket was up against his face, he couldn't get any leverage, and he pushed feebly against its edge.

Ryder leaned on Nazeem's shoulders, reached over and shoved the bucket. "You're going to kill him."

Mr. Cobblepot released his grip on the skinny man, letting him fall back to the ground, coughing and puking. He eyed Ryder, a look of hatred and frustration plain on his face. Then he smirked.

"Guard, fill this up," he said, handing the now-empty bucket to the soldier, "I think we have another thirsty prisoner."

The guard took the bucket and headed off toward the swamp.

Cobblepot stepped over the skinny man and stood on the chains between Ryder and Nazeem. He loomed over the two of them.

Ryder settled back into his place, trying to separate himself from Nazeem. He didn't want whatever was about to happen to him to flow over to any of the other prisoners.

"It's been a while since I've given a proper lashing," said the taskmaster as he unwrapped the whip from his massive fist. "I'm going to enjoy this." He let the whip dangle on the dusty ground, dragging its tip around in a small circle.

Ryder looked down at the whip. There was no way he could escape, no way he could fight back, shackled to the other thirty-five men in the chain gang.

This was going to hurt.

Cobblepot brought the whip over his shoulder and snapped it once against the ground, sending dirt and dust into Ryder's eyes. Sitting on the ground, helpless, Ryder was reminded of the beatings his father used to give him as a child. The man used to take his belt off in preparation for delivering his punishment. Then he would slap the hardened leather against the sturdy oak table a handful of times. Ryder wondered what it was about the torturer that made him revel in the torment, why the first few blows seemed intended not to inflict physical pain but to increase the mental torment. Ryder already knew what was going to happen to him. He didn't need reminding. This was just a way to extend the pain. Make it not only last longer but also seep in further, so that it hurt deep inside as well as against the skin.

Straightening his back, Ryder crossed his legs underneath him as he had seen Nazeem do. He took a deep breath and closed his eyes. He did not know if he could find solace the way the tattooed man seemed to, but he had no better option.

The whip cracked again, then the familiar sting of leather crossed his chest. Ryder hissed at the pain. The tip of the whip was much narrower than his father's belt had been. The blow was so sharp; it felt like a razor carving into his skin. He tightened all the muscles in his body, trying to steel himself against the sensation.

Again the whip cracked, slapping his shoulder. The pain was so poignant that even with his eyes closed he could sense the mark it left on him. It was as if the backs of his eyelids held a map of his body, and he watched as the taskmaster drew lines upon it. Ryder got lost in this image, escaping into himself, away from the beating. He would take the best the taskmaster had to offer, and he would be stronger for it.

The taskmaster continued his beating, the blows landing one after another in a regular rhythm. He was trying to beat the humanity out of Ryder, trying to turn him into a version of the taskmaster—an animal with no respect for human life or dignity.

Ryder fought against this transformation. But the whip burned him, and with each new attack, he lost more ground. Though he battled against the pain, his grip on his humanity was slipping. The whip's sting was all-consuming, and he lost track of all other sensation. He was adrift in a world of pain, and it was all he could do to hold on and not break down.

The whip struck the side of his face. Ryder breathed then braced himself for the next blow.

It never came.

"Bandits!"

Ryder opened his eyes.

The taskmaster was several paces away, looking out to the west. In front of him, a few of the guardsmen were scrambling to get to their horses. The rest however, were in a fight for their lives.

A band of mounted bandits had come out from behind the boulders and encircled the guards as they began preparing the camp for the night. They wore baggy pantaloons and loose-fitting tunics that fluttered behind them as they rode. Every one of them had wrapped their heads and faces with scarves, leaving only their eyes exposed. They carried a hodgepodge of mismatched weapons—the spoils of other raids—and they howled as they descended upon Lord Purdun's guardsmen.

Taskmaster Cobblepot was rushing now to the guardsmen's aid, swinging his whip over his head, Ryder and the other prisoners seemingly forgotten.

Ryder's body throbbed from the lashing he'd received, but somehow the pain felt diminished by the sight of the bandits. Under different circumstances, he might have been terrified. But right then, anyone who would fight Purdun's men was all right with him.

Nazeem leaned over. "Are you all right?"

Ryder shook his head. "I've been better."

This made Nazeem laugh. "I've never seen a man take such a beating without even making so much as a whimper. You are very brave."

A second wave of billowing riders rode out of the trees behind the prisoners. The prisoners in the rows behind Ryder and Nazeem gasped and stood up, forcing both men to get to their feet. The skinny man was lifted into the air, his full weight carried by the chains.

The entire chain gang got up off the ground and began to move, but the riders were much faster and overtook them. Ryder craned his head to see what was happening. As they approached, two of the bandits dropped down off their horses, leaped to the ground without slowing, and landed on their feet at a full run.

"Hold still," shouted the first one. "We're the Broken Spear. We're not going to hurt you." His voice was high, like that of a boy not quite fully a man.

Nazeem looked to Ryder. "Do you know of these men?"

Ryder nodded. "I've heard of them. My father used to tell us stories about them when we were little. I thought they were a myth, something he had made up to scare us into being good."

"Perhaps your father is not as much of a liar as you thought," replied the tattooed man.

The two dismounted bandits reached the last row of prisoners. Both of them were relatively short, and Ryder lost sight of them behind taller men.

"Please don't hurt me," screamed someone in the back, followed by the sound of metal crashing against metal.

A chill ran up Ryder's spine. This was not the way he wanted to die. Trapped like a hunter's quarry, unable to fight back.

"Be quiet, you coward," yelled the young bandit. "Now go fight your oppressors."

There was more pounding, and the sound of metal bending then giving in. Out of the corner of his eye, Ryder watched several prisoners, their sleeveless gray tunics stained with sweat, running toward the taskmaster, large rocks in their hands.

There was a lot of commotion. The men behind Ryder were shoving. The men in front were craning their necks to see what was going on. The sounds of men fighting and dying floated on the wind, surpassed only by the crack of the taskmaster's whip.

There was another loud metallic snap behind Ryder, then the bandits were standing beside him.

"Hold out your hands," ordered the young one.

Ryder did as he was told.

The man produced a pickaxe and a glass vial. He poured a thin, clear liquid on the two chains that connected Ryder to Nazeem and the skinny man. It seemed to smoke, and the metal touching Ryder's skin grew terribly cold.

The other bandit stepped up and grabbed hold of the chains. This one was much larger than the young one. Ryder could feel the man's strength through the shackles as he pulled them taut.

"Hold your hands as far apart as you can," ordered the muscular bandit.

Ryder nodded.

The younger one reeled back and slammed the pickaxe against the chains on Ryder's wrists—right where he'd poured the liquid. The pointed weapon sparked as it struck, but the chain remained intact.

"Damn," shouted the young one. He hit it again, and again the chain didn't budge.

The muscular bandit let go of the chains. "Try the lock."

The young one nodded and held out the vial of liquid. "Don't move," he said, "or you might lose your hand."

Ryder looked into the man's brown eyes. He had the purposeful look of someone with an agenda—an inner demon that drove him to do great things, perhaps despite himself. Ryder had seen that look before in the eyes of the men of the Crimson Awl. They had a reason to live for, something so dear that they would risk everything to protect it.

Just looking into his eyes, Ryder knew this man was the same.

"You understand?" The bandit poured the liquid directly on the cuff holding Ryder's left hand. The locking mechanism smoked just as the chains had.

Ryder nodded.

"Speak up, man," shouted the bandit. "Do you understand?"

"Yes." It felt strange to speak. The only words he'd spoken in the past several days had nearly gotten him killed.

"Good." The bandit raised the pickaxe.

Ryder held his arms as still as he could and braced himself.

The head of the weapon came down. *Clank.*

A buzzing pain ran up his arm, and Ryder looked down at his wrist. The shackle hung open, the lock broken, and with a quick shake it dropped away. The chain dragged on the ground, about five feet of it still attached to the cuff on Ryder's right arm.

"That did it," said the muscular bandit.

The younger grunted his acknowledgment and went to work on the other chains. They came away with much less effort, leaving only single links attached to the cuffs on each ankle.

"You are not truly free," said the young one, "until we all escape these oppressors." He slapped Ryder on the shoulder. "Now go. Fight back against the men who would make you into a beast."

CHAPTER 8

Liam followed Montauk and his men to the woods just outside Duhlnarim.

"Stop right here," said Montauk. He pulled from a pouch a long thin strip of fabric. Holding it up, he pushed it toward Liam's face.

Liam pulled away. "What do you think you're doing?"

"What does it look like I'm doing?" replied Montauk. "I'm blindfolding you."

"Montauk, what's with you? I've been a loyal member of the Awl since its inception. You know this. You were there."

Montauk nodded to the other men. Each grabbed one of Liam's arms.

"Yes, Liam, I know how long you've been around. Frankly, that's what surprises me so much about your betrayal."

Liam struggled only slightly as the other men held him in place. "Betrayal? What betrayal?"

"That's what we're going to find out," replied Montauk. "Now play along, or I'll be forced to hurt you." He held up the blindfold again.

His arms pinned to his sides, Liam let Montauk place the fabric against his skin. He felt the knot press against the back of his head, grabbing at his hair as it cinched tight. The two men pulled his arms behind his back. Liam heard the heavy clanging of a chain, then he felt the familiar sensation of manacle cuffs closing over his wrists.

"Am I a prisoner?" Liam tested the shackles. There wasn't much play in the chain.

"Of a sort," replied Montauk. "You never can be too careful."

A hand on Liam's back urged him forward.

They walked on in silence for a long while, the regular crunch of dried pine needles underfoot keeping time as they went. Liam counted his steps, trying to distract himself from the uncertainty of what was to become of him. Ever since the morning Ryder died, his life seemed to be spinning out of control. The world moved by in front of him. He tried to reach out, to grab hold of something. But it was no use. He was powerless to affect the sights and sounds running before his own eyes. It was as if he were watching a play. The story would work its way to its final conclusion, regardless of whether he was in the audience or not.

Eventually, Liam's mind wandered. He lost track of the number of steps. He lost track of the forest and the men. He thought back on the days not so long ago when he and Ryder would come out into the woods to play hide-and-seek. Ryder would blindfold him like this and spin him in circles. When he fell down from dizziness, Ryder would run off to hide.

Liam had always hated the sensation of being dizzy. It

made him sick to his stomach, and the feeling wouldn't go away for some time afterward. Still, Liam had enjoyed these games with his older brother. By this time, both of them had different sets of friends. Liam was still in school, and Ryder had taken to helping their father in the fields full time. The brothers didn't get to spend much time together anymore. So when they did, Liam did whatever his brother wanted. It didn't matter. Somehow, just playing games like they had when they were both younger felt right. Ryder had been the one person Liam could count on to understand him. He had been the one person who would always be there to back him up when things got tough. Liam couldn't say that about his father, or even his mother for that matter. Ryder had been the anchor for Liam.

"I wish you were here right now," whispered Liam.

"What?" said Montauk. "Speak up."

Liam shook his head. "It was nothing."

"Well, you'd better have *something* to say. You have plenty of explaining to do."

Someone jerked Liam to a stop. Without unlocking his shackles, Montauk pulled down the blindfold and left it dangling from Liam's neck.

They had brought Liam to a clearing. It looked to be the old, abandoned druid's circle—Dowmore Glen. Liam had never met any of the mythical druids who were reputed to live in the forests outside Duhlnarim. No one had seen them. Still, the stories of their existence and of the rituals they carried out deep in the woods were generally taken for truth by the farmers of Duhlnarim. Everyone had heard the hunters' stories of this place.

Liam himself had always believed they were there. At the very least it was an easy way of explaining the strange behavior of the animals during the full moon, and the odd crop growth during times of drought. But if ever he needed any proof, the scene before him would be plenty.

A low rock wall encircled the entire clearing. Years of

the elements had worn the edges of the stone down into a series of softly sloping curves. Vines grew up over large sections of the wall, but unlike the roots and brambles Liam had seen tearing apart the buildings in Duhlnarim, these formed patterns and shapes, decorating the wall rather than fighting its unnatural presence.

The vines climbed over the wall and up the sides of four crumbling stone monoliths. Carved into each monolith was a depiction of the same nude female drow, her long flowing hair strategically twisting and turning to cover her more private parts. Liam was no divine scholar, but judging from the carving, he supposed this was the goddess Eilistraee.

In each monolith the goddess struck a slightly different pose than in the last. But the theme was the same in all of them. The goddess stood on one leg, holding a large sword over her head with the full moon large and glorious behind her. The carvings all faced the center of the circle, presumably looking down on the proceedings.

At the far end, opposite where Liam was standing, three large oak trees reached up over the wall. They leaned over the middle of the circle, and their branches grew into each other, woven together like crisscrossed fingers. As a farmer, Liam had spent much of his life attending to the needs of growing plants, but never had he seen anything like this. It was as if the trees had at some point come to life, twisting their trunks toward each other to engage their branches and leaves in one giant embrace, creating a natural canopy over the circle.

Underneath the trees' outstretched arms stood six of the seven members of the Council—the official decision making body of the Crimson Awl. Though most of the decisions were made in the Awl through a vote of all the attending members, when there were disputes, the Council was the final authority.

The members now stood in a line, three on each side—an obvious absence in the center. Up until the ambush,

Ryder had been the seventh and most senior member of the group. The open space between the other Council members was there for him. Despite the circumstances, it made Liam feel a small amount of warmth for these men that they would honor his brother in such a way. He began to relax. Surely they would realize that he was no traitor. They would show to him the same honor they showed now to Ryder.

Arrayed around the wall, standing two and sometimes three deep, were many of the other members of the Crimson Awl. Liam recognized all of them. He'd seen them at meetings, even fought with them side by side against Purdun and his men. He had come to think of them as his extended family. They looked out for him, and he did the same for them.

Behind the Awl, standing in the shadows several steps off but still within earshot, was a group of odd-looking people. All but one wore heavy cloaks of dark gray wool that were hard to see in the shadow-laden forest. At first, Liam couldn't tell how many of them there were. They seemed to fade in and out, blending in with the darkness. Two in the group stood out. One because he was the sole person among them with his hood pulled down and his face exposed. The other, like those behind, wore a hood over its face, but unlike its companions, the fabric was a deep red, like the color of blood.

Liam looked at them for a long moment and decided that there were six of them in all. He didn't recognize the man without a hood, and the others showed no distinguishing features. They were intently focused on the proceedings, looking on with obvious interest.

The cuffs of his shackles bit into Liam's wrists, and he twisted them to see if he could make himself more comfortable. If the Council wanted to talk about betrayal, he'd talk about betrayal—namely the way they were treating him after he'd lost his brother in the raid.

Montauk left Liam's side, stepping over the low stone wall and into the circle. He passed by the other members and took the empty place among the line of Council members.

Liam's heart sank. "You've given Montauk Ryder's seat on the Council?" He glared at them.

All of the Council members except Montauk averted their eyes.

"How long did you wait in respect for his passing?" said Liam, sadness slowly filling his chest. "A day? Perhaps a full tenday?"

"It's not like that, Liam," said a portly man standing beside Montauk.

"Then what is it like, Meirdan?"

The portly man grabbed his long, graying beard, seeming to use it to steady himself and collect his thoughts. "We mean . . . Well, it's . . ." Meirdan took a deep breath. "Your brother would have wanted it this way."

"How do you know what Ryder would have—" started Liam.

"Enough," interrupted Montauk. "It is not the Council that has to justify its actions. It is you."

"Yes, yes," said Meirdan, obviously glad to have the spotlight moved onto Liam. "You have some explaining to do."

"And what would you like me to explain?" spat Liam. "How we got ambushed? How Ryder was killed when the elite guard—?"

"Why don't you start with your visit to Zerith Hold and your little chat with Lord Purdun?" interrupted Montauk.

The collected members of the Crimson Awl stirred angrily.

"He took me prisoner," defended Liam. "I had no choice."

"You didn't resist?" probed Meirdan.

Liam nodded. "I did," he replied. "But they threatened

to burn down my home. Samira and my mother were inside. Surely any of you would have given yourselves up to save your family."

"Then why didn't you do the same for Ryder?" jabbed Montauk.

Suddenly, Liam hated this man. "Why don't you unlock my hands and ask me that question again?"

"Now, now, Liam. I am only trying to get to the bottom of what happened and what was said."

"We were ambushed, Montauk," shouted Liam. "Somehow they knew we were coming, and they were ready. They had us outnumbered. When things got tough, Ryder pushed me out of the way of a guardsman's blade." Liam bit his lip. He could see Ryder in his mind. He watched again as the soldier's blade pierced his gut. "He saved my life, then begged me to run." Liam looked out into the crowd of Awl. He spotted Kharl. He shoved his chin toward the young man. "Ask Kharl, he'll tell you. He was there."

The Awl mumbled to themselves. Behind them, the newcomers stood stock still, unmoved by Liam's words.

Montauk took a step forward and put his arms up. Instantly the circle fell silent. "You are avoiding the issue. Get to the point. What did you tell Lord Purdun? What does he know about the Awl?"

Liam held his chin up defiantly in the face of this thinly veiled accusation. "I told him nothing."

"Surely the baron wanted something from you," goaded Montauk.

Liam took a breath, looking out at the other Awl. He didn't know how this next part was going to sound. He looked to the ground. "Yes, he did."

"And? Out with it, man. What did he want?" demanded Montauk.

"He offered me a job."

"A job?" Montauk's voice rose to an incredulous pitch.

Liam nodded. "He wanted me to join his elite guard."

This brought another burst of mumbles from the rank and file.

Montauk laughed. "You expect us to believe that you were taken by force to see the Baron of Ahlarkham after you ambushed one of his carriages so that he could offer you work?"

Liam nodded again. "That's what happened."

"And what was your answer?"

Liam stood up straight, puffing out his chest. "I told him I'd rather die than do his dirty work."

This brought a few hoots from the crowd, and a "That a boy!"

Montauk glared at the Awl, and they fell silent again. "And after you told him this, he just let you go, no punishment, no exchange of information, no nothing?" He spun a slow circle, making a big deal out of making eye contact with everyone present. When he had completed his turn, he faced Liam again. "Well, I don't know about your other brothers and sisters of the Awl, but I for one do not believe you."

Liam looked around at the men and women he had thought were his friends. They stared at him with accusation in their eyes. Even Kharl, who would have been lying dead next to Ryder if it hadn't been for Liam, seemed to condemn him.

There was a loud noise behind Liam, and a whole lot of rustling.

Then someone shouted, "It's Purdun's men. Run!"

There were a few choice swear words, then commotion broke out. Dowmore Glen became a frenzy of activity. The veterans in the group organized quickly, forming a line, trying to give the others time to flee. They grabbed the younger ones, forcing them behind the line. The Council members and those on the fringes of the circle ran for cover.

As Liam spun around, he caught one last glimpse of the strange robed group on the fringe of the Glen. Only two of them remained. The hoodless man and the red-cloaked person looked on with the same stoic gaze they had worn while watching Liam fight accusations of treason. Then they turned and walked calmly from the clearing. As they left, four gray wolves padded out from behind the trees, following them deeper into the forest.

Liam wondered about them for a quick moment, then the hum of bowstrings brought him back to the soldiers raiding the clearing. He turned around to see a host of well-armed elite guardsmen charging through the woods toward the druid's circle.

"Damn," he said under his breath, and he took off running. He made for the defensive line, following the rest of the Awl as they ran from the clearing.

The crossbowmen were only a few large strides away. They had crouched behind the low stone wall for cover, and Liam wanted to get behind them. Reaching the wall, he lifted his foot to leap over, but Montauk moved in front of him. The man who had usurped Ryder's place as head of the Crimson Awl gave Liam a shove. Off balance from preparing to jump over the stones, Liam couldn't catch himself in time and fell backward. With his hands cinched behind him, he tumbled, landing on his tailbone with all his weight. It hurt, and he gritted his teeth. His eyes watered from the pain, and he looked up at a blurry image of Montauk leering down at him.

"This is your fault." He pulled a dagger from his belt, turned the point toward Liam, and lifted it over his shoulder. "You're a traitor to the Awl and a disgrace to the memory of your own brother."

Liam's heart raced. He scrambled sideways, bending his knees and lifting his weight with his bound hands as he slid one foot under his rump. But as he shifted his weight the pine needles moved, and he slipped, falling again on his tailbone.

"Good-bye and good riddance," said Montauk.

"Incoming," shouted one of the Awl.

A volley of arrows came raining down near the crossbowmen. Most of them shattered harmlessly against the stone wall, but a few hit home.

Montauk let out a cry and stumbled backward, holding his right arm. "Damn."

One of Purdun's men had grazed Montauk with his shot. Two of the crossbowmen stood up to help him, pulling the usurper back and away from the stone wall. Most of the other Awl had already fled the clearing, leaving only the veterans and Montauk.

"Fall back," shouted another of the crossbowmen.

The crouching revolutionaries stood slowly and backed away from the druid's circle, keeping their crossbows pointed at the oncoming soldiers. One at a time, they fired off their bolts, turned, and ran, leaving Dowmore Glen and those who had fallen behind.

Liam struggled again to get to his feet. This time the sharpened tip of an arrow blocked his path, and he lay back down.

"Well, well, if it isn't our old friend Liam."

Liam looked up into the face of Captain Beetlestone.

"So," said the captain, a huge grin on his face, "have you reconsidered our offer? By the look of things, I'd say you haven't much choice."

CHAPTER 9

Ryder stretched his back. It was the first time in a month that he'd been able to move without the help of the man chained beside him. The feeling was euphoric, completely erasing the bruises and aching muscles, the marching and the beatings. He was free again, and nothing in the world could take away from that.

He examined the shackle attached to his wrist. He moved his arm back and forth, making the heavy chain swing. Without a sword, it would have to do.

Ryder looked up to the swirling melee before him. A couple of Purdun's guardsmen had managed to get on their horses, but most of them—those who hadn't already been killed— were still on foot. Small pockets had formed, the guards standing back to back, lashing out at the bandits encircling them.

Closer, standing a full head taller than anyone else, was the taskmaster. His whip in one hand, a meat cleaver in the other, he swatted at a freed prisoner. The smaller man threw a rock at Mr. Cobblepot, which the taskmaster batted away. Then the huge man stepped forward and brought his cleaver down, slamming it into the prisoner's head. The man's skull split in two, drenching the taskmaster's bare chest with blood.

The dead man stayed on his feet for a moment longer, swaying, then he toppled to the ground, chunks of red and gray spilling from the massive wound in his head.

Ryder closed in on the taskmaster. His tormentor stood in the middle of the battle, reveling in his last kill. Fresh blood dripped from his chest, arms, and neck as he looked for his next victim. He didn't see Ryder right away, and the revolutionary turned freed prisoner took advantage of the opening.

Charging forward, Ryder swung the chain on his wrist up over his head in a quick circle. The heavy end lagged behind his arm, picking up speed as it came around. Cobblepot turned to see Ryder just as the chain hit him square in the face. The shackle cuff made a resounding clank as it collided with the huge man's skull, slapping closed then open again as it hit.

The taskmaster blinked his eyes and shook his head, obviously stunned by the attack. Ryder took four large steps back, pulling the unwieldy chain with him. It shook and rattled as he prepared to swing it again.

Cobblepot regained his composure, and he turned to face off with Ryder, a red welt forming on his forehead where the chain had hit him.

"You should've stayed put, filth," bellowed the huge, bloody man. He cracked his whip toward Ryder, slapping at the dusty ground. "But I'm glad you didn't." The whip cracked again. "Because now I can take you apart."

The big man lunged, eating up two of Ryder's backward

paces with one of his own. He came on with his heavy cleaver, swinging it as effortlessly as though it were nothing more than an extension of his own hand.

Ryder jumped back and brought his arm around reflexively. The chain swung slowly through the air, and the taskmaster bashed it aside with a quick blow. The chain clanked back, jerking Ryder's arm with it, and he stumbled sideways.

The taskmaster retaliated with his whip, catching Ryder on the chest and shoulder. The strike burned his skin and tore his gray tunic. But more than anything, it infuriated Ryder. The last time the taskmaster hit him with his whip, Ryder had been bound, unable to fight back. This time, things were different. Ryder was free to take control of his own destiny, and he intended to do just that. Gritting his teeth and forcing the pain from his mind, Ryder spun around, accelerating as he went. The chain rose into the air, carried by his body's momentum. At the end of the spin, a bit disoriented, he raised his arm and lunged toward Cobblepot's head. The heavy cuff slammed against the taskmaster's ear, dropping the big man to one knee.

Cobblepot let out a yell, dropped his cleaver, and lifted his hand to the side of his head. When he pulled it away, it too, just like the rest of his body, was covered with blood. This time, however, it was his own.

Ryder fell back, trying to catch his balance, keeping the bare-chested man in front of him.

Cobblepot looked up from his place on one knee. "I'll get you for that."

Standing up, he cracked his whip, snapping it forward and back. Pop, pop, pop, pop. The whip sang through the air. The taskmaster began to advance.

Ryder swung the chain, the whistling sound of air rushing through the links growing with each circle it made over his head. He held his ground as the big man charged.

The whip snapped as it came for his face. Ryder dodged to the left and ducked. The whip caught him on the top of his head, making a painful crack as it connected. But it didn't stop Ryder's advance. He lunged forward, sending the chain out at Cobblepot's ankles. The cuff wrapped around the big man's leg and the chain made a full loop, flopping over and tangling itself on its own links—just as Ryder had hoped it would.

Dropping to his knees, Ryder leaned back with all his weight, pulling the chain toward him with every last ounce of strength he had left.

The move caught the taskmaster off guard, and Ryder managed to pull the man's legs out from under him. Cobblepot swung his arms in wide circles, trying to stay upright, but all that did was prolong his fall. The taskmaster landed on his back, sending up a huge plume of dust from the dry plain. Ryder immediately jumped to his feet, the chain on his arm still entangled around the taskmaster's leg. Turning a quick circle to give himself as much slack as he could, Ryder lifted his foot in the air and came down on Cobblepot's head with the heel of his boot.

The big man let out a howl, his whole body convulsing from the blow, and he pulled his hands to his face. The chain around his leg pulled taut, yanking Ryder back. He stumbled to his knees, but the sight of his torturer lying there on the ground drove him on. He leaped to his feet and came at the man again.

Ryder brought his foot up, this time stomping harder. His heel landed against Cobblepot's hands, smashing them into his face. Blood poured out from behind his fingers, and the taskmaster shook, his body twitching. Ryder repeated his attack, nearly losing his balance with the momentum of his foot.

His boot connected with a loud snap, and the front of Cobblepot's face collapsed. Ryder's boot heel sank deeper than he had expected it to, and a jolt of fear and exhilaration ran up his spine. The taskmaster screamed and started to thrash. Ryder was thrown to the ground.

The chain, still tangled around Cobblepot's leg, pulled at Ryder's arm, yanking him around like a dog on a leash. He tried to get closer, to loosen the slack, but the big man was thrashing so hard, there just weren't enough links in the chain. Struggling to his feet, Ryder changed his approach. Risking being pummeled to death by Cobblepot's flailing boots, he looped his arm forward and around, trying to shake the chain free.

Cobblepot sat up and lunged forward, pulling both hands away from his face to grab at Ryder. The piggish man had been ugly before, but now he was downright hideous. His nose had been completely caved in. Instead of a protruding ridge, there was a deep recess. Blood flowed from the wound, spraying out in speckled drops with each labored breath.

The rest of the taskmaster's face had shifted, filling in the gap where his nose had been. Where before the cartilage had held the skin taut, it had now gone slack. Large wrinkles of flesh gathered across his cheeks and forehead. It looked to Ryder as if the man's face was now longer, thinner. His eye sockets were closer together, and his gaze seemed to wander, his eyeballs shaking as they tried to focus.

Ryder easily pulled away from Cobblepot's grasping hands. The man reached, then reached again, as if trying to catch an elusive butterfly. His clumsiness was only accentuated by the agility of his prey. For a moment, Ryder felt pity for the man. Sitting there, bathed in his own blood, the one-time tormentor of men looked like a newborn baby, unable to defend himself against the dangers of the world.

With his arms in the air, the taskmaster's legs had momentarily stilled, and Ryder took advantage of it. Untangling the shackles from the big man's leg, he took several steps back and breathed. He was tired, perhaps more so than he'd ever been in his entire life. Turning around, he looked out to see the rest of the battle.

Huge dust clouds rose off the plain. The bandits' horses kicked the dirt into the air as they rode circles around the surrounded guardsmen. There were screams and the other telltale sounds of battle, and Ryder couldn't get a good sense of what was happening.

Out of the corner of his eye, he caught sight of something moving in on him. Leaping back without knowing for certain what was coming, Ryder threw himself to the dirt.

He didn't see much more.

"Now it's my turn." The taskmaster grabbed him by the throat, lifting Ryder from the ground.

Ryder was shocked at how fast the big man had gotten to his feet. He clawed at Cobblepot's hands and kicked at the ground with the tips of his toes as he dangled from the big man's grasp.

"I'm going to break your neck." The taskmaster began to squeeze Ryder's throat.

Ryder struggled as best he could, but there was little he could do. Cobblepot was much stronger, and even beating on the big man's hands had little effect. Ryder's vision blurred and blood filled his head. The pressure built until it felt as though the whole thing would pop off.

Into his field of view came the form of a man. His arms were bare and his chest was covered with gray cloth. Over his head he carried what appeared to be a large rock. The man closed on the taskmaster, and Ryder caught sight of his face—and the tattoo on his forehead.

Nazeem's feet came off the ground as he hit the taskmaster in the head. Ryder could feel the shock of the blow course through Cobblepot's grip around his neck. The big man jerked, then seemed to relax.

Ryder pulled free of Cobblepot's chokehold and fell gasping to the ground.

The taskmaster staggered a step, his upper body swaying. He put his hand on the back of his head and turned around to look at Nazeem. As he did, Ryder could see the oozing wound the rock had made. Both the front and the back of his skull were caved in. Blood ran freely down his chest and back. He took one more step toward Nazeem, then collapsed to the ground in a puff of dust.

"Are you all right?" Nazeem came to Ryder's side, grabbed hold of his arm, and helped him to his feet.

Ryder shook his head to clear it. "I'll be fine." He looked the tattooed man in the eye. "Thank you."

Nazeem smiled, bowing his head. "I am sure you would do the same for me."

A loud hoot came from behind both men, and they spun toward the sound. Ryder grabbed hold of the chain on his wrist and dropped into a crouch, prepared to start swinging.

As the dust settled, Ryder could see men strewn all over the ground. Some of them wore gray tunics. Others wore the dusky robes of the sand bandits. But most of them Ryder recognized as Purdun's men.

The fight was over. The bandits had won. They stood on top of the carriage, holding up handfuls of gold and bolts of silk cloth. Others sat on their horses shaking their clubs, swords, and crossbows in the air. Many of the freed prisoners joined them in the revelry.

Nazeem put his hand on Ryder's shoulder. "I think you can relax."

Ryder straightened, still gripping the chain. "Can I?"

The young man who had freed Ryder from his bonds stood on the back of a horse, shaking his fist in the air. He put his fingers to his lips and let out a shrill, rolling whistle. All of the bandits immediately stopped their celebrating.

"This has been a fine victory for the Broken Spear," he said in his high, adolescent voice.

The bandits let out a joyous cheer.

"And we have liberated many from their oppressive bonds!"

This got a cheer out of many of the freed prisoners.

Ryder, however, kept his mouth shut.

"Gather all you can carry; we make for Fairhaven."

The bandits went to work immediately, packing up the riches from the looted carriage and picking through the belongings of the fallen guardsmen.

"I have a bad feeling about this," said Ryder.

"You feel bad about being freed?"

Ryder shook his head. "No, it is good to be free." He looked at the tattooed man. "I just don't know if we should trust these men. Perhaps we should just slip away and head back to Duhlnarim."

Nazeem shrugged. "They did not want us in Duhlnarim."

Ryder shrugged. "I have family there. We would be safe among people we could trust. We'd have time to take some rest." He leaned in close to Nazeem's ear. "Come back with me. You could become one of the Crimson Awl. Help us overthrow Purdun."

"The revolutionary spirit lives strong in you." Nazeem smiled. "But we are thirty days' march from your home. We have no food or water. And you are covered from head to toe in bruises." He looked out at the bandits as they prepared to leave. "As much as I would like to get my revenge on the dog Purdun for placing me in chains, I think we need time to recover our strength."

Ryder looked around. None of the bandits were paying any attention to him. He could easily just turn and walk toward home.

"There will be plenty of time to achieve your revolution after you have healed. Purdun will still be there when you return. And if he is not, then so much the better."

The bandits were nearly ready to leave. They had packed their horses and were gathering up the freed prisoners. The young man who apparently led the bandits looked right at Nazeem and Ryder.

He raised his hands to his mouth and shouted, "Come, it is time to leave. We have food and shelter for you in our camp, just east of here. You will be safe with us in the Giant's Run Mountains."

Ryder looked again at the road that led back to Duhlnarim. He felt Nazeem's hand on his shoulder.

"My friend, you will never make it," said the tattooed man. "A wise revolutionary is one who lives to fight another day. Better to delay your return than to never return at all. I do not think it would be wise for you to go back to Duhlnarim just yet. But if you are going to go, you must do so now."

Samira was down that road, waiting for him. It pained Ryder to think about what she must be going through. Every moment he delayed his return would only extend that agony.

"Only a few more days," he said softly. Then he turned around and headed with Nazeem toward the waiting bandits.

CHAPTER 10

I know you might think me cruel, but I do the things I do for the safety of the barony," explained Lord Purdun. "Sometimes they might seem harsh, but there are things at stake here greater than personal freedom."

Liam was seated on one of the many couches in the baron's sitting room. He laughed. "Spoken like a true dictator."

"I apologize for having you followed like that," said the baron, standing up from one of the plush upholstered chairs. "But I'm sure you would agree, all is fair in these sorts of situations."

Liam spat in Purdun's face.

Purdun slowly wiped the gob off his cheek.

Liam smirked. "All's fair, right?"

Baron Purdun lifted a handkerchief out of his breast pocket and wiped the mucus off his hand. "You don't have any idea what sort of forces you are dealing with."

"I know enough of how you've treated my family and the villagers of Duhlnarim," said Liam. "I know enough to want you out of power. And, yes, I have a real good idea of what you and your men are capable of. I've witnessed it firsthand."

Purdun shook his head. "I'm not talking about my elite guard, and I'm not talking about the Crimson Awl."

Liam wrinkled his forehead. "What are you babbling about, Purdun? I'm getting tired of your games."

The baron clenched his teeth, visibly trying to maintain his patience. "Listen, Liam. The members of the Crimson Awl aren't what they seem."

"Why should I believe you? Why should I believe anything you say to me? You used me. You picked me up and brought me here to try to discredit me. You used me as bait to get at the Awl. You put my family in jeopardy, and you destroyed my life."

"I understand you're angry," said Purdun, "But you should be thankful I didn't throw you in the dungeon for ambushing my carriage."

This didn't make Liam feel any better about the situation.

The baron continued. "Think about the meeting at Dowmore Glen. Were there any new people there? Anyone who wasn't already part of the Awl?"

Liam thought back on the group of hooded strangers he'd seen watching the proceedings. "No," he lied.

Purdun shook his head. "Come now. Think hard. Did no one seem out of place?"

Liam narrowed his eyes. "What are you getting at?"

"The Awl is being manipulated by an outside power." Purdun said, slightly exasperated. "Someone who has reason to see me removed from power."

Liam shrugged. "Then perhaps I should meet them. Sounds like my kind of person."

Purdun turned around, pacing between the chairs, holding his chin in contemplation. "If you met this one, you'd think differently."

"Anyone who wants to see you out of power is a friend of mine."

Purdun stopped his pacing and turned to face Liam. "This person is a very powerful, ancient undead spellcaster. A vampire by the name of Shyressa."

A chill ran down Liam's spine, just hearing her name.

"And I can assure you, she doesn't have your best interest at heart," explained the baron.

A vampire? Liam thought back on the clearing, on the strange group of robed figures followed by a group of wolves. He'd heard legends of vampires and their spawn having the ability to turn into wolves. Maybe what Purdun was saying was true. How could he have known about the strangers at the meeting? None of this made any sense.

Liam shook his head. "You're making this up."

"I wish I were." Purdun rubbed the back of his neck, looking as if he were quite stressed. "But I'm not. Shyressa has it out for me, and she's using the Awl as a way to destabilize Ahlarkham."

"Why are you telling me this?"

Purdun walked across the room to stand in front of Liam. "Because I want you to understand why I did what I did. I want you to see that I had to have you followed so that I could try to get to Shyressa before she gets to me. It was nothing personal. I ordered my men to do everything in their power to ensure your safety."

Liam was confused. "You ordered them to protect me?"

Purdun nodded.

"Why would you do that? I'm not on your side."

Purdun took a deep breath. "Because, despite what you think of me, I am not an evil man. I don't want to see you or any of the citizens of Duhlnarim harmed." The baron sat back down in the chair he had started in.

"And I know you're not on my side, but I want you to be. I want you to join my elite guard."

"Again with the elite guard." Liam didn't understand any of this. "Why are you doing this to me? What is so special about me?"

"You have passion. You genuinely believe in what you are doing, and you care about the well-being of the citizens of Ahlarkham. I could use a man like that."

"How?"

"Well, for one thing, if you were to join us it would add a lot of legitimacy to the guard that is currently lacking. You and the Awl have done a pretty good job convincing the people of Duhlnarim that we're a no-good bunch of despots."

Liam couldn't help but feel a small amount of pride swelling in his chest. To hear from the baron's own mouth that his work had made some impact was a heartwarming thing.

"And you want me to switch sides and tell my friends and family that I was wrong all this time. Is that it?"

Purdun nodded. "The people listen to you. If they see you—a man they look to for leadership, a man they trust—put his own faith in me and the elite guard, then I believe they will follow suit."

"Well," responded Liam, "thanks to you, they no longer believe I'm on their side."

"Your reputation has been called into question with the compromised leadership of the Crimson Awl, not with the people at large."

"You stand here and tell me incredible stories about a vampire who wants you out of power, saying that I don't understand the forces at work. But it is you who don't understand." Liam shook his head. "The Crimson Awl *is* the people at large. This isn't some bought-and-paid-for group of thugs or mercenaries. The members of the Awl are the people who suffer daily under your heavy-handed taxation and your brutal guardsmen.

They are one and the same."

"Fine, say what you will. There are other reasons I want you to join the elite guard."

"Like?"

"Of all the members of the Awl I could approach, you are the only one I am completely convinced is not in cahoots with Shyressa."

"What makes you so sure?" Liam shot back. "Your story is starting to come apart. If the Awl really are being manipulated, why would you think you could trust me?"

"Simply put, it's because no man fights as hard as you do unless he truly believes he's right. If you were in the vampire's employ, you wouldn't carry so much conviction."

Liam stood up. "I fight you as hard as I do because I find you despicable."

"Calm down." The baron made a gesture with his hands like he was pushing a cloud toward the floor. "Don't you see a compliment when it's given to you?"

"Your words are poison. No matter what you say, you will never convince me that you are a good man."

Purdun threw his hands in the air. "Why won't you listen to reason?"

"Because I refuse to believe that the man who killed my brother can be reasonable."

Purdun's face turned very serious. "It was not my blade that killed your brother."

"It might as well have been," Liam raised his voice. "It was your fault we were out there that morning. It was your order that put those men inside the carriage. And it was your money that paid for the steel that cut him through the gut. You are as guilty as any one of your murderous guards."

Purdun stood up. His fair skin was flushed red. His fists were clenched so tight they shook, and the skin on his knuckles had turned white.

"Your brother attacked one of my carriages. He killed five of my men. Men who had families. Men whose lives were at least as precious as his own." Purdun glared at Liam. "In my opinion, your brother got what he deserved."

Liam lunged at Purdun. This was the second time he'd tried to attack the feudal lord inside his own private chambers. It was also the second time he found himself dangling from his tunic, held off the ground by one of the baron's half-giant bodyguards.

Purdun shook his head as he looked up at Liam. Then he turned toward the door and shouted, "Captain Beetlestone."

The doors flew open, and the guard captain came into the room. "Yes, my lord."

"Take this man to the dungeon." He glared one last time at Liam, then turned and walked toward the door on the other side of the room. "Maybe the rats can talk some sense into him."

Ryder marched up the steep, walled canyon that lead into the Giant's Run Mountains, limping the entire way. Every step seemed another lesson in agony. They were escorted by the bandits on horseback, none of whom talked during the trip. The carriage that Purdun's guard had been protecting was packed full of the wounded and the freed prisoners who simply couldn't walk any farther.

Beside Ryder, just as when they had marched from Duhlnarim, walked the tattooed Nazeem. There were no chains binding them together, but they traveled side by side nonetheless.

As they walked, Ryder tried to think about things other than the pain that sank through his flesh and seeped into his bones. If he focused too much on the bruises and wounds, they became unbearable, so he thought about his home and his family. He longed to be back there with his lovely wife. He could see her long dark hair and those beautiful blue eyes. It pained him to think of her alone. He knew that Liam would look after her, and there was a small consolation in that. He vowed as he traveled that as soon as he was able, he would find a way to get home.

"Ryder." Nazeem's voice brought him out of his daydreaming and back to the painful reality of climbing up the mountain pass.

"Yes."

"Why do you think the guards were carrying so much treasure?"

Ryder hadn't thought about it until the tattooed man pointed it out. "I'm not sure. Perhaps they intended to trade for something in Westgate."

Nazeem nodded. "Yes, but they had all of us to trade. Had we made it there, they could have easily auctioned us for several thousand gold apiece."

"So, they could have gotten a lot of money for us," said Ryder, tugging at his torn pants, trying to make his journey just a little more comfortable. "Maybe they wanted something even more valuable than slaves."

Nazeem shook his head. "In the Pirate Isles, few things are more valuable. The merchants in Westgate know this. It's just a short trip out to the islands from their port. No, with that kind of money, Purdun could have purchased the fastest warship in the Shining Sea." Nazeem chuckled. "In some places, he could have bought himself a small castle—or an army of mercenaries."

Ryder looked at his companion. "How do you know all this?"

Nazeem smiled. "I am a criminal," he said pointing at the tattoo on his forehead. "I know this sort of thing."

Ryder pointed to his own forehead. "What does this mean?"

Nazeem rubbed the blue triangle with his index finger. "This is the mark they give you in Mezro when you break the law."

"Mezro? You are Chultan then?"

Nazeem nodded. "Born and bred."

"What were you doing all the way out in Erlkazar?"

Nazeem smiled. "I have told you this already. I was a smuggler."

Ryder chuckled. "Yes, I know. But why did you leave Chult? Why go so far from home?"

"Mezro is a peaceful city. No one there even carries a weapon. If the undying Chosen of Ubtao catch you breaking the law, they brand you with this tattoo and throw you out of the city." Nazeem's smile faded. "I had to leave the Chultan peninsula in order to survive. No one will deal with you if you have been shamed by this mark. So I decided to go someplace where nobody knew or cared what it meant."

The two men walked on for a while in silence. Then Ryder spoke up. "Nazeem?"

"Yes?"

"What was your crime?"

Nazeem seemed to think about the question for a moment. Then, "I killed a man."

Ryder thought back on all of Lord Purdun's guards he'd faced in hand to hand combat. Many of them had died by his hand. "Did he deserve it?"

Nazeem only nodded.

More or less, Nazeem's story was the same as Ryder's. He'd been thrown out of his home for committing what the baron considered to be a crime. Ryder didn't see his actions as criminal. They were necessary. They were the means of a revolutionary. If his oppressor was going to slowly kill the citizens by taking their food and taxing their wages, then he would respond by killing them back.

The caravan came to a U-shaped bend in the road. The path led up north, farther into the mountains. The south side of the curve was defined by a forest of tall, prickly trees, each standing thirty or more feet tall. A pair of Broken Spear warriors stood in front of the trees, holding back the branches and ushering people single file through to the other side.

Nazeem went first. Ryder ducked his head and followed him through the foliage. There were several rows of these trees, and their branches were covered with long, needle-sharp thorns. At each new row of trees, another pair of Broken Spear warriors stood holding back the branches. The treacherous tunnel was difficult to navigate, made doubly so by Ryder's limp, beaten body. More than once he felt his flesh tear as it caught on the thorns.

As Ryder finally came out of the trees to stand next to Nazeem, he straightened his back and found himself looking up at a huge multitiered stone palace, seemingly carved right into the side of the mountain.

"Gods," said Ryder under his breath.

"Giants," corrected a voice.

Ryder turned to see the young robed bandit leader standing beside him and Nazeem.

"Welcome to Fairhaven." The robed leader pulled down the mask that covered his head, revealing long dark hair, mocha skin, and a smooth, hairless face. The leader of the bandits wasn't a boy. "I'm Giselle."

She extended her hand in greeting.

Ryder looked at Nazeem, then back at the lithe woman standing before him. There were women in the Crimson Awl. He'd fought beside them on many occasions. But none of them looked like Giselle. She was beautiful, and her eyes had a keen sharpness to them. It made Ryder feel as if she could anticipate his thoughts. The combination of these two things was so powerful that Ryder was at a loss for words.

She cocked her head to one side, looking from one man to the other. "Are you unfamiliar with this custom?" She reached out and took Ryder's hand in hers, shaking it up

and down. "Taking a proffered hand is a show of greet-
ings and friendship."

"Uh, yes, of course," said Ryder, stuttering a bit. "I'm
Ryder."

Giselle smiled. "Nice to meet you, Ryder." She let go
of his hand and offered hers to Nazeem.

The Chultan took it and bowed his head. "They call
me Nazeem."

"A pleasure," said Giselle. She turned to face the huge
spiraling stone stairs that led up into the palace in front
of them. "This used to be the home of a powerful stone
giant clan. But it's abandoned now, so the Broken Spear
call it home." She turned and headed for the huge, four-
foot-tall steps.

Giselle put her fingers to her lips and let out a rolling whistle, as Ryder had seen her do after the battle on
the plain. From high above came a response—a similar
whistle but much lower pitched. A rope appeared from the
second level of the palace, with something dangling from
it. As it came closer to the ground, Ryder realized that
the something was actually a pair of small ladders.

Giselle stepped forward and took them off the rope,
then gave it a quick tug. The rope shot back up into the
sky.

"Come," she said, waving for them to follow. "It's not
much farther." Placing the first ladder against the stone,
she climbed to the next step.

CHAPTER 11

Liam drifted in and out of consciousness. The only hint that time was passing in the dark, foul-smelling dungeon was the slow drip of water, the occasional exploratory scratching of the rodents, and the rumbling of his empty stomach. He'd been down in the dungeon for what must have been several days. To Liam, it felt like more than a month. His arms and legs were chained to the wall, and though he had enough slack to move around, there was nowhere for him to go. Even if there were, the room was in complete darkness.

So Liam had taken to sitting on the floor against the wall, trying to sleep just to pass the time. With no light and consumed by absolute boredom, it wasn't hard to drift off into blissful nothingness. But it was difficult to stay there.

The hard stone was cold and it dug into his flesh. He would wake up what seemed like every few moments with a new pain in his neck or side or back. And he would shiver.

From time to time, one of the rodents would become emboldened and try to take a nibble out of him. They didn't bite hard at first, just testing to see if he tasted good. But a couple of times he was brought kicking out of his disoriented slumber by a sharp pain and the sound of squealing as the creature who had tasted his flesh was booted and went flying across the cell.

During the times when sleep did not come to him, Liam thought about Ryder. He missed his brother. More than anything, he just wished he could see him one last time, spend one more evening at the Broken Flagon Inn drinking mead and reminiscing over their childhood. He had never contemplated a life without Ryder, and now that it was here he didn't know what to do. He felt as though in the two months since his brother's death, he'd been simply drifting. Life had *happened* to him. He had no control, and he didn't want any. To have control meant that he knew where he wanted to go. But he didn't.

It hurt to think about his brother and the fact that he was gone. But it hurt more to think about the day when that pain would drift away. He didn't ever want to stop grieving for Ryder. That aching was all that he had left, and if he couldn't have Ryder back, then he would hang on to that pain forever if he could.

After a time sitting in the darkness, his thoughts wandered, and he must have dozed off again. The sound of the bolt sliding startled him awake. The next thing he knew the door to his cell was opening, and a blinding light filled his vision. He held up his arm to block it. His eyes burned and watered as he peered around the back of his hand to see Captain Beetlestone and a pair of guardsmen, each holding a torch, step through the threshold.

"You have visitors," said Beetlestone. The captain leaned down and unlocked the chains that held Liam to the stone wall. "Get up."

Liam rolled to one side and lifted himself off the ground. It was harder than he imagined it would be. His legs were sluggish, and his joints complained at the effort.

"How long have I been down here?" asked Liam, struggling.

"More than a tenday," said Beetlestone. The captain grabbed Liam under the arms and helped him get to his feet.

Liam wobbled a bit, his legs tingling and numb.

"Here," said Beetlestone, handing Liam a small package wrapped in a handkerchief.

Liam, transferring his weight back and forth between his legs in an attempt to get feeling back in them, grabbed hold of the package and unwrapped it. Inside, he found a whole loaf of country bread. He didn't waste any time in tearing into the crusty loaf and shoving large bites into his mouth. The hunger pangs were just another constant reminder of how messed up Liam's life had become. He filed them next to his sorrow and his aching body. But now that he had food, his empty stomach became all he could think about. He devoured the bread in great bites.

"Slow down," warned Beetlestone. "If you keep eating at that rate, it'll come right back up."

His mouth full, Liam stopped chewing and took in a big breath through his nose. He finished the bite and swallowed. "So, who wants to see me?"

"You'll find out soon enough," said Beetlestone. "Come on."

A cold chill ran down Liam's spine. This couldn't be good.

His loaf in one hand, Liam followed Beetlestone out of the cell and down the hall. The guard captain led him into a large room at the far end.

Obviously Purdun didn't want whoever it was to see

how they had been keeping Liam. Though this new room was still a cell, it was much larger and cleaner than the one Liam had just been in, and there were barred windows high up in the walls that let in fresh air. Liam took in a lungful of the stuff. It felt so good.

In the middle of the room, hanging from the ceiling, were at least a dozen sets of shackles. Unlike the chains in his last cell, these didn't allow the prisoners to sit on the ground. Beetlestone gently nudged Liam toward the hanging shackles.

"Left," he said, grabbing at Liam's wrist.

Liam complied, too tired to fight back.

"So, what do you think of our dungeon now?" quipped the captain.

Though the remark was meant to sting, Liam could tell Beetlestone didn't really put his heart in it. His voice was somehow sad, almost apologetic.

When Liam was securely fastened to the ceiling, the captain and his two guards exited the room, leaving the wooden door wide open. Once they were gone, Liam gave the chains a hard tug. They rattled against each other, swaying back and forth, but they held him fast. Letting the chains hold his weight, he leaned forward, holding his arms out to his sides. Up on his tiptoes, he twisted to one side then the other, feeling a little bit like a child on a playground. His mind had wandered for days on end, and now he finally had some light and something to play with. If he was going to be held against his will, at least he could entertain himself.

Standing up straight, he broke another piece off the loaf of bread and stuffed it in his mouth. Though it wasn't very pleasing, it did satisfy his grumbling stomach.

From down the hall Liam heard footsteps. Then two people appeared in the door.

"Gods. Look at you, Liam."

Liam lowered his head. He had expected some sort of interrogator, someone who would try to coax information out of him now that he'd had some time to suffer in the dungeon. He didn't expect this.

"Hello, Mother."

Angeline came running into the room only to stop several steps before her son. "Are you all right?"

Liam looked at himself. His clothes were filthy. He smelled, and he was slouched from having spent the last few days sleeping on a stone floor. "What do you think?"

Angeline put her hand to her mouth, and tears welled up in her eyes.

Liam instantly regretted his gruff response. "I'm fine. A little worse for the wear, but I'll live."

"That's what you get for being involved with those Awl," said Douglas.

Liam looked up at his father. "Now that I'm chained up you've come to finish that fight, pop?"

"Stop it," interjected Angeline. "Both of you." She looked at Douglas then turned and put her hands on Liam's shoulders, trying to calm the situation.

Liam glared over her at his father. He hated the man. He'd never had the courage to even think that before. In his exhaustion, he'd lost his inhibitions, his fears over the consequences of having such thoughts. He had been afraid of what the other farmers in Duhlnarim would think about him if they knew his secret feelings for the man who had brought him into the world. But sitting for more than a tenday in a stone-walled dungeon had given him plenty of time to fear much larger things. He had very little left to lose, and this man no longer scared him.

"Then why did you come?" he asked, not lowering his eyes.

"One of Purdun's guardsmen came and asked us to," replied the old man, staring back at Liam, a look of disgust on his face.

"We came because we were worried about you," interjected his mother. "You just disappeared. We didn't know where you were. We thought maybe you'd been killed on one of those stupid raids, like Ryder."

The sound of his brother's name made Liam break his staring contest with his father. He took a step back from his mother.

"Ryder died fighting for what he believed in," he said, not raising his voice. It hurt him to hear her belittle Ryder's sacrifice. "You both are just too stupid or thoughtless to recognize that."

"Oh, Liam." Angeline began to cry.

Douglas put his arm around her. "See what you did?" he shouted.

Liam looked at them both. He was tired of feeling sorry for them. "What do you want from me? Why did you come here?"

"We just came," said Angeline, trying to hold back a sob, "to try to talk some sense into you."

"Well," said Liam, holding his arms out to make the chains shake, "I'm a captive audience. Talk all you like." He leaned back, falling backward until the chains caught him, holding him off the ground by his wrists.

Liam hung there, his head resting back, his eyes closed, smiling to himself. He'd never been able to tell his folks off like that. There was no guilt, no fear of reprisal, none of the feelings he'd had when getting in a fight with his parents as a child. His captivity had changed him. The chains of the dungeon had set him free. Despite the aches in his bones, and the weakness from lack of sleep, Liam was stronger now, and it felt great.

He leaned farther back, stretching the tired muscles in his neck. Then he lifted his head. He wanted to see the look on Douglas's face. Opening his eyes, he looked up at Samira. Both Douglas and Angeline were gone.

"Hi," said Samira, a reserved smile on her face.

Liam stood up, suddenly feeling ashamed of his appearance. "What are you doing here?" He blushed, his sense of triumph transformed into flustered insecurity.

"I mean, hi."

"Oh, look at you," she said, stepping up and taking hold of his face.

Where she touched him, it stung, and he pulled back. Putting his own hand to his face, he felt a long fresh scratch, complete with dried blood, running across his right cheek.

"Where did that come from?" he asked.

"I was hoping you'd know that."

Liam shrugged. "Must have been the rats."

The smile on Samira's face dissolved into a look of disgust. "Rats?"

Liam nodded. "In my cell."

Samira scanned the floor.

Liam shook his head. "Not here. They had me in another cell before you came." He looked around. "One about a third of this size. No windows. Kind of damp."

Samira put her hands on his cheeks and turned his face to hers. "What are you doing this for?"

"Doing what?"

"Putting yourself through this," she said.

"What choice do I have?" replied Liam. "I didn't ask for this."

"If I ask you a question," she said, letting go of his face, "will you answer me honestly?"

"Of course."

"Did you try to attack Lord Purdun in his own chambers?"

Liam smiled. "You heard that, did you?"

Samira nodded. "Is it true?"

"Yes," he said. "Twice."

"Twice?" Samira's voice rose as she said the word. She put her hand over her mouth, as if embarrassed of her outburst. In a more hushed tone, she said, "Really?"

He nodded, still smiling. The thought of how bold and truly stupid that was made him warm inside. Oddly, he was proud of himself for being so foolish.

Samira covered the smile on her mouth, but Liam could see in her eyes that she too was amused by his brash behavior.

"Ryder would have been proud of you," she said.

Liam nodded his agreement. "Yes, I think he probably would have been."

"But he also wouldn't want to see you like this." She grabbed hold of his filthy, tattered shirt and gave it a tug.

"*I* don't want to see me like this."

"Then be done with it," came a voice from behind Samira.

Liam looked around his brother's wife. Lord Purdun stood in the doorway.

"Well, if it isn't my old friend," said Liam. He grabbed Samira by the arm and turned her around. "Samira," he said, his voice thick with sarcasm, "may I present to you the Baron of Ahlarkham, Lord Purdun."

Purdun obviously didn't get the slight, because he smiled and bowed as he entered the room. "Thank you, Liam. And you must be Samira." Purdun crossed the stone floor and took Samira's hand.

Samira dropped into a curtsy. "Yes, my lord," she said.

"So, Liam, are you ready to accept my offer?" asked Purdun.

There were no guardsmen here, and Purdun's personal bodyguard likely wouldn't fit inside the tiny room. Liam noticed that though he was chained up, Purdun kept a good distance from him.

"What offer?" asked Samira.

"Liam hasn't told you? I've asked him to join my elite guard."

"And my answer is still no," spat Liam.

"Has none of this—" Purdun spread his arms to indicate the stone walls and hanging chains of the dungeon— "had any impact on you?"

Liam's eyes narrowed. "Yes it has," he said, his voice rising. "It's strengthened my—"

"Liam," interrupted Samira, squeezing his arm. "Don't be foolish. Do what the baron asks, and get yourself out of this place."

"Stay out of this," said Liam. He gave her a stern look, which she returned.

"Liam, be reasonable," said Purdun. "Listen to Samira. If you stay here in the dungeon, you will live a short, miserable life."

"Then let me go," said Liam, holding his arms out so the locks could be removed.

Purdun didn't budge. "If I did, then what? Where would you go? Home? The Crimson Awl thinks you're a traitor. Your life wouldn't be worth a single shaft of wheat. Would you leave Duhlnarim? Leave Ahlarkham all together? I'd be willing to bet a man like you has never been farther north than Llorbauth, maybe Shalane at best. Do you think you'd be safe only a hundred miles away? You know the Awl better than I, but in my estimation, even they could track you down if you stay in Erlkazar. Are you willing to abandon everything? Give up your family and everything you know and start over again with nothing?"

Liam glared at the baron.

Purdun continued, "Or you could join the elite guard. You'll be out of your chains." Purdun put his hand in his coat pocket and produced a key. "You'll be able to stay here and keep your family." He nodded toward Samira. "You will be safe. You will be well trained, well equipped, and well paid."

"He's right, Liam," coaxed Samira. She squeezed more tightly. Despite the soreness in his muscles, her touch somehow soothed him. "You really don't have another choice."

"No, you don't." Purdun shook his head, a smug smile on his lips.

Just the look on his face was enough to make Liam's innards burn. That self-righteous bastard! It was easy for him. He held all of the cards, and he knew it. It infuriated Liam. Purdun had the money and the army, and in his eyes, that made him right. It gave him whatever he wanted. Liam wondered if the spoiled little brat had ever had to go without anything in his entire life. He'd probably never had to work a single day in the fields, or go to bed with his stomach still grumbling. No one ever said "no" to him.

Well, thought Liam, let me be the first then. He lifted his chin and stared at Purdun, defiance in his chest. "I do have a choice. I can choose to say no. I can choose death over betrayal."

The smug smile on Purdun's lips disappeared, replaced by the mixed, tight-jawed look of frustration and anger.

Samira's hands slipped from Liam's arm. The sudden absence of her touch was saddening. With her there, standing beside him, he had strength, the power to fight back.

"Please don't do that," she said, her lip quivering. "I don't think I could stand to lose both of you."

In his mind, Liam conjured his image of Ryder—the last moment they had spent together. His older brother lay dying on the ground. His last words played in his head: "Look after Samira. Tell her I love her."

Liam looked down at Samira. There were times when he'd seen her be as tough as bulette hide. Then there were other times. This was one of those.

He closed his eyes. He could clearly see Ryder, looking at him expectantly. He gritted his teeth and shook his head. "Fine," he said. "I'll do it."

CHAPTER 12

Ryder reached the top of the enormous stairs and turned around to look out over the plain. The sun was already beginning to set, but from here he could still see far to the west, deep into the Giant's Plain. He thought he could see the point at which the caravan had been ambushed, but he couldn't be sure. From this height, one copse of trees was indistinguishable from every other, and the rolling plain looked as flat as a blacksmith's anvil.

Behind him, a long stretch of pathway led up to the huge broken stone archway of Fairhaven. Battered pillars carved to look like gaunt, muscular humans carrying huge rocks or spears lined the path on both sides. They were nearly twice Ryder's height, and their deep, inset eyes stared straight ahead, unconcerned and uninterested in anything happening below their knees. Nearly half of them were smashed beyond recognition. Of those still standing, many looked as if they might topple over at any moment. By the dour looks on the faces of those remaining, Ryder assumed this wasn't a very happy place when it was originally occupied.

At the end of the path, carved right out of the dark gray stone of the mountain itself, stood a grand palace. By Ryder's estimation, its walls rose straight up over eight times the height of a man. Behind that, the top of a spiral tower jutted up even higher. From the plain below, the tower probably looked like one of the jagged, natural peaks of the mountain. Up close though, Ryder could see that some artisan had spent much time carving ornate designs all along its surface.

The walls themselves were covered with paintings. They were hard to see at first. Large bits of rock had been chipped away by what Ryder guessed had been a siege some time ago. On what remained, the brighter colors had faded from time and exposure to the elements, so the images blended in with the speckled mountain rock. As Ryder got closer, he could make out shapes and scenes. They appeared to be paintings of giants. The paintings depicted giants hurling rocks at one another or sitting in drum circles around the nighttime fire. In one particularly ruined image, Ryder even thought he could make out the image of a giant painting upon the wall—a self-portrait of the artist.

Ryder and Nazeem followed Giselle and the rest of the caravan under the archway at the end of the path and through what must have at one time been a huge wooden door guarding the entrance to the palace. All that remained were a few smashed wooden planks and two sets of huge rusty metal hinges.

Ryder leaned over to Nazeem. "What sort of creatures do you think could have caved in the walls of such a place?"

Nazeem shrugged. "Demons? Dragons?"

"Dwarves," corrected Giselle.

"Dwarves?" Ryder could hardly believe it. "But they are so small."

Giselle looked at Ryder, a sly look on her face. "You are bigger than me," she said. "Do you think that makes me less mighty?"

Ryder thought about it for a moment. "Well, yes," he said nodding.

Giselle cocked her head to the side. "Really?"

Ryder realized his faux pas. "Though," he stammered, trying to cover for himself, "I suppose there are exceptions."

"Exceptions?" Giselle put her hands on her hips and looked him up and down.

Ryder shrugged. "Well, all I mean is, were I not so beaten up, I would have an advantage over you in a fight."

"If you think so," said Giselle, smiling, "then perhaps you should prove it."

Nazeem chuckled. "I believe you have just been challenged, my friend."

Ryder blushed. "I . . . I didn't—"

"Don't worry." Giselle nodded and touched his arm. "I'll wait until you are fully healed before I beat you again." She added her laughter to Nazeem's.

Ryder just shrugged, not knowing any other way to pull his foot out of his mouth.

"The dwarves have always had a particular hatred for the giants. But despite your lack of tact, your point does have relevance here," continued Giselle as they walked into the bustling open courtyard behind the wall. The brown-robed Broken Spear busied themselves with many different tasks. Fires were being lit. Wounded were being tended to. And on the walls above, sentries climbed atop huge stone blocks that gave them a view of the path and the plains beyond.

"You see," continued Giselle, "the giants were involved in another battle when the dwarves arrived at Fairhaven. They had already taken many casualties, and were not prepared to take on two foes at once. They fought until they realized all was lost, then they fled to the Underdark."

"The Underdark? I thought only the drow dwelt there," said Ryder.

Giselle shook her head. "There are many creatures who make their home below the surface of the world. The giants founded a new village there. It's called Cairnheim. It is said that there are passages to it scattered all over the Giant's Run Mountains." Giselle stopped walking when they reached the base of the tower.

There was a long pause, then Giselle clapped her hands. "And that concludes our history lesson for today. Please forgive me if I prattle on. I get excited about the past. Anyway," she stepped past the two men, "I'm sure you are both very tired." She looked up into the sky. "It will be getting dark soon. Find yourself a place to rest. There will be a feast tonight, to celebrate the great haul we made." She looked at them both. "And to welcome our new friends. Until then, be at ease. I have much work to do, but I will make sure to have a healer come take a look at your wounds."

With that, Giselle turned and walked away into the busy center of the courtyard. Ryder watched her go.

"I think she likes you, my friend," said Nazeem.

Ryder felt his heart race. "What?" He shook his head. "I didn't get that impression at all." The thought of this powerful woman being attracted to him did sort of excite him. He might have let himself enjoy it a bit more if it weren't for the guilt he felt over Samira.

"You know," replied Nazeem, "for a man with two good eyes, you see very little."

Ryder shook his head at the smiling Chultan. "I see what I choose to see."

"My point exactly."

As Giselle disappeared into the crowd, Ryder turned away and headed for a pile of straw under a canvas lean-to. He lay down on it, letting his aching body rest for the first time in what seemed like his entire life.

"Doesn't matter what she thinks anyway," he said as he settled in. "We'll be leaving soon."

That night there was a terrific feast and celebration. The tales of the battle grew longer. The foes they fought grew larger, and the heroic deeds grew more frequent. Ryder sat near the fire speaking with Nazeem, eating fresh meat off the bone.

A portly man wearing a leather apron with several huge stone mugs hanging from his belt approached them. He staggered when he walked, and his cheeks were a bright red. Under his left arm he carried a sloshing bucket full of a greenish liquid.

"Krogynth, gentlemen?" asked the overly jolly man.

Nazeem was on his feet in a flash, taking a giant-sized mug of whatever it was the man was peddling.

"Krogynth?" asked Ryder.

Nazeem's eyes were wide as he looked down into the grog. "It's a type of moonshine," explained the Chultan.

"Made from a fermented green mold," expanded the jolly man.

"And you drink this?" asked Ryder.

Nazeem took a large quaff then smacked his lips, wiping off any leftover drips with the back of his hand. "Don't knock it until you try it. Krogynth is hard to make and even harder to come by if you don't know the recipe." He held his mug out to Ryder. "You may never again get the opportunity to try it."

"Well," said Ryder, reaching out to take the mug from his friend. He sniffed it. The green liquid smelled vaguely like licorice root. "Since you put it that way." He lifted the stone mug with both hands and took a sip.

Despite its mild scent, Krogynth had a rather abrasive flavor. "It tastes like currants mixed with earwax."

The jolly man let out a belly laugh. "Don't it though?" He dipped another mug into the bucket and offered it to Ryder.

He pointed to the Chultan. "Let him have it." He looked down into the huge mug in his hands. It was more than half full. "I'll just finish this one."

"Suit yourself," said the jolly man, giving the fresh vessel of Krogynth to Nazeem.

The Chultan lifted his mug. "To freedom," he said.

Ryder lifted his own. "To going home," he replied.

Then both men drank.

As Ryder lowered his mug from his face, he looked up at Giselle standing over him.

"Having a good time, I see." She knelt beside him.

Ryder swallowed his mouthful of the foul-tasting liquid. The first sip he'd taken was starting to hit his head. His muscles relaxed, and the aches in his bones seemed to ease some.

"Yes," he said. "I do believe we are."

Giselle smiled. She had the most beautiful brown eyes.

"Good." She grabbed hold of his arm. "Now let me take a look at those wounds of yours."

Ryder let her have his arm. He enjoyed the touch of her skin. "I thought you were going to have a healer come look at me."

She pushed back the edge of his tattered gray tunic. "That's what I'm doing."

"You're a cleric?"

Giselle ran her fingers along his arm, poking at the bruises. She hit one that hurt like the nine hells, and Ryder bit down on his lip to keep from shouting.

"Does this surprise you?" she asked.

As the pain subsided, Ryder lifted his mug, struggling

a bit with only one hand, and took a big gulp of the green stuff. "No," he said after swallowing. "I guess nothing about you should surprise me anymore."

Finishing her examination, Giselle fished around inside of her pouch and pulled out a stoppered bottle with a waxy substance covering the top. "Well, I'm not," she said, laughing as Ryder's jaw dropped open. She shoved the bottle into his free hand. "Unless you count handing out healing potions."

Ryder put down his mug of Krogynth and opened the bottle. "You're full of surprises." Then he downed the contents. Immediately he could feel the magical warmth spread out through his body, reaching from his stomach and touching everything out to the tips of his fingers. He exhaled as he lowered the bottle from his lips. He felt whole again, the most exquisite sensation he'd experienced in recent memory.

"Thank you," he said, letting the bottle slip to the ground.

"I'm glad you enjoyed it."

Ryder tested his joints, relishing the feeling of his body working the way it was supposed to without experiencing any pain. "I'll be ready to make the journey home tomorrow."

"Journey home?" asked Giselle.

Ryder turned to her. "I appreciate everything you have done for me," he said. "I owe you my freedom, and if I can ever repay that to you, I will do it gladly." He touched her hand. "But I must return to Duhlnarim." He looked away. "To my family."

Giselle pulled away from him. "I'm sorry, but you can't. You can't leave."

Ryder got to his feet. "What do you mean? Of course I can. Look." He did a little jig in front of the fire to prove that he was healthy. "See. I'm fine."

Giselle shook her head. "No, I mean I can't just let you leave."

Ryder looked down on her, sadness filling his heart. "I know it's hard to let go, but I have responsibilities in Duhlnarim, Giselle, and there could never be anything between—"

Giselle stood up. "No. I mean that once you've seen Fairhaven and the route that leads you here, you have to stay." She looked at Nazeem. "That goes for you too. And all the other freed men. Now that you know how to get to us, we can't let you go. None of you can leave."

Ryder shook his head. It was clouded with Krogynth. "So, what are you saying?"

"That you can join the Broken Spear and become one of us," said Giselle, "or you can stay here, in Fairhaven, as our prisoner."

Ryder dived for the broken chain that had been his shackles. His fingers wrapped around the rusted links as he tumbled back to his feet. Swinging the chain over his shoulder, he looked out at a half-dozen naked blades, their tips pointed at his chest.

"I would think twice if I were you," said Giselle.

Ryder took in the scene before him. Six Broken Spear warriors had him backed in a corner. Giselle stood behind them. Her sword was still in its sheath, and she made no move to pull it out. She was fast, though, and Ryder had no doubt she could have it out and on him in a single heartbeat. Nazeem was outside of the ring of warriors. He stood on guard, his gaze darting from the Broken Spear to Ryder and back again, watching to see what was going to happen next.

"What do you intend to do, Ryder?" asked Giselle.

Ryder released the chain, letting it clatter to the ground. Then he lifted his hands in the air, putting them up so everyone could see he was unarmed.

"Please," he said, looking at Giselle. "How would you feel if our roles were reversed? What if you were in Duhlnarim needing to get back here to the Broken Spear?"

Giselle took a deep breath. "Then I would try to get

accustomed to life in Duhlnarim."

Ryder grit his teeth. "You wouldn't even try to come back here, to return to the people who mattered to you most? I find it hard to believe that you would so easily give up all that you had worked for."

"I understand what you are trying to do, and perhaps you are right." Giselle grimaced. "But I can't risk the safety of everyone in Fairhaven just because you are homesick. And no matter how persuasive your arguments, I don't intend to change my mind."

"You know," replied Ryder, "it doesn't matter what reason you give yourself for putting me in chains. Call it whatever you want. You'll still be an oppressor, just like the men you rescued me from."

Giselle took a deep breath and sighed. "So," she said, a look of disappointment on her face, "what's it going to be? You can keep your freedom if you promise to stay."

Ryder shook his head. "I can't do that."

"That's what I thought." Giselle shook her head. "All right." She turned and started walking away. "Take them to the cage."

"Not Nazeem," shouted Ryder. "He has nothing to do with this."

"Your actions have condemned you both," said Giselle over her shoulder, then she disappeared into the shadows.

"Let's go," said one of the armed warriors, shaking his bare blade.

Ryder and Nazeem were guided across the courtyard at the tips of the Broken Spear's swords. On the far side, opposite the broken gate, a huge cage was recessed into the stone wall. It looked as if it hadn't seen much use. The bars were rusted and the ground was covered with rocks and silt. In the corners, large mountain brush plants had grown up through the hard-packed dirt and in some places out of the cracks in the stone itself.

The armed warrior produced a key and unlocked the bars. Ryder and Nazeem were ushered inside.

"Welcome to Fairhaven," the warrior said, closing the gate.

Huge flakes of rust rained down on the ground as the bars clanged and locked.

CHAPTER 13

Liam woke with a start, feeling rats nibble at his legs. His arms flew to his sides. He thrashed, and panic filled his chest. Liam opened his eyes, and he didn't recognize the room. He was in a soft bed with fine linen sheets. There was a nightstand with a candle and a washbasin on one side, and a wooden door with a lock on the inside on the other. In the corner was a set of fine scale mail armor neatly arranged on a rack.

There was a pounding at the door.

"Liam."

Liam shook himself further awake. This was the third day in a row he'd woken to that dream, but he remembered where he was now. This was his new room. He remembered having a hot bath and having been fitted for armor. He had agreed to join Lord Purdun's elite guard. His entire life, for good or for bad, had changed.

Another knock on the door. "Guardsman Liam, it's time for roll call."

Liam rolled out of bed, got to his feet, and crossed the stone floor. Opening the door, he looked out at Captain Beetlestone. "You sound different," said Liam.

The captain nodded. "We're on the same side now. Get yourself together. The bugle for roll call will sound soon. We will be assembled in the parade grounds." He turned and pointed down the hall. "Just go to the end of this corridor and head out the double doors to the left."

Liam nodded and ran his hand over his face. He was trembling.

Beetlestone must have seen it, because he said, "It's all right. You'll be fine. It'll be rough at first, but you'll do all right." Then he turned and walked down the long stone hallway.

Liam watched him go. This was all very strange. This day was going to be telling. To be honest, he wasn't sure he could even do what it was they asked of him. Could he cut it as a soldier? He took a deep breath, trying to steady his hands, then he shrugged. Guess he was going to find out.

Shutting the door, he turned and proceeded to put on his new armor. Behind the rack were a helm and a pair of new swords, one long and one short. He pulled the longer out of its sheath and examined it. The handle was wrapped in fine leather, and the hilt was inscribed with several ornate runes. He ran his finger over them and they flashed a light blue under his touch.

"Enchanted," he said. He'd never handled such fine weapons. Then he smiled to himself. "The elite guards have some help."

Liam had just finished strapping on the last piece of his armor when he heard the bugle blow.

"This is it." Dropping the two new swords into the belt on his hip and placing his helm on his head, Liam took one last deep breath then headed out the door to the parade grounds.

Outside in the cool morning air, the rest of the elite guard had already assembled. Several units were lined up in military-style rows, all facing a set of steps at the far end of the courtyard. The soldiers stood at attention before a collection of armored men, none of whom Liam recognized.

Beetlestone had conveniently forgotten to tell Liam where he was supposed to report. He didn't have any idea who most of these people were or where he was supposed to go, so he just sort of stood there, taking it all in. There were a lot of guardsmen, but fewer than Liam would have guessed. He had always imagined them as an inexhaustible supply of faceless warriors. They were the insurmountable force that the Awl was to somehow find a way to beat despite impossible odds. The odds were still in the favor of the elite guard, but not by as much. Maybe that's why Purdun wanted him to join so badly. His inexhaustible supply was starting to dry up.

"Liam of Duhlnarim." A big bald guardsman with scars crisscrossing his face came marching right at him. "You're late."

Liam looked up at the man as he came to a stop. He was pretty good sized, and up close, Liam could see that not only was the man's head bald but so too were his forearms and face. It looked as if the man had no hair at all.

"Who are you?" asked Liam.

The man's face wrinkled. "I'm Captain Phinneous," snarled the bald man. "I'm the commander of your unit."

Liam's heart sank. He'd heard of Captain Phinneous. Everyone in the Awl had heard of him.

Phinneous looked Liam over from head to toe. "I'm not particularly happy about having one of you revolutionary types in my command."

Liam waited, expecting the captain to say more, but Phinneous just stood there silently, glaring down at him. As time passed, it became increasingly more uncomfortable for Liam. He felt as if all eyes were on him, expecting him to do something.

Finally, when he couldn't take it anymore, he said, "Well, I'm not particularly thrilled about this arrangement either."

Captain Phinneous sneered at Liam, the corner of his lip curling up like a growling wolf. He snapped his fingers and three of his guardsmen were at his side.

"So it's like this, huh?" said Liam, sizing up the four men.

Captain Phinneous smiled. "Well, we need to see what kind of man you are, Liam of Duhlnarim. If we're going to be fighting by your side, we'd like to know if you can handle yourself." The bald man pulled his long sword out of its sheath. The enchanted metal made a slow grinding ring as it came free.

The other guards followed their captain's lead.

Liam gripped the hilt of his new long sword. He'd never taken more than three guardsmen at a time by himself. He'd always had Ryder to watch his back.

"Draw your weapon," commanded Phinneous.

Liam didn't budge.

Captain Phinneous took a step forward. "Draw your weapon," he repeated. "That's an order."

Liam still didn't move, holding the hilt of his sword and watching the other soldiers instead.

Phinneous snapped his fingers again and all three guardsmen advanced on Liam. He barely had time to pull his blade from its sheath and step back before they were on him. With a wide swing, he slapped aside their first attack. He could already feel the effects of the enchanted blade. Though it didn't make him faster, it did feel as if the blade followed his intentions more readily than his previous sword.

The three men separated and spread out, forcing Liam back another step. They were trying to surround him. He didn't have much room, and unless he intended on taking this fight into the stone hallways of Zerith Hold, then very soon he was going to have to take a stand.

Lifting his short sword from its sheath, he felt its weight in his hand. He'd never fought with two weapons before, but there wasn't a better time than the present to learn.

All three guards moved in at the same time. Liam stepped to his right and lunged with his long sword, running the length of the blade along his opponent's. The hand guards on both blades connected with a deep clank, and Liam twisted his wrist with a quick snap. He managed to lodge the ornate bell of his sword on the other guardsman's. Then he yanked the swords toward himself. The other guard wasn't expecting such a bold maneuver. He teetered forward and before toppling over, he let go of his weapon to avoid losing his balance and falling onto Liam's short blade.

With another quick twist and a flip of his wrist, Liam tossed the extra sword away. Then he turned to defend himself from the other two soldiers. The nearest guardsman was coming down on him, both hands on his weapon. Liam barely had time to raise his short sword to parry the blow. The guard pressed his advantage, overpowering Liam's off hand and forcing him down to one knee. Liam pushed back, but he wasn't strong enough to hold back the guard's two-handed attack. Bringing his long sword around, he went on the offensive, swinging at the other man's feet.

The guardsman pulled back just in time, leaping in the air and lifting himself over Liam's flying blade. Pushing off with all of his might, Liam threw himself away from his attackers. He tumbled once and came back to his feet, both blades out before him. He didn't have long to reassess the situation. The tip of another sword came right for his face. He twisted his torso, dodging to his right to avoid losing his left eye.

Though his new, enchanted sword was a boon, the new armor was somewhat of a hindrance. Though it was lighter than he had expected it to be, it was more restrictive than his typical studded leather, and it slowed his movements just a touch. His attacker's sword slipped past his cheek, but he wasn't fast enough to avoid it all together. The sharp tip connected with his pauldron, and he felt the blow jolt through his shoulder.

Liam was thrown back, and he stumbled as he caught his balance. His shoulder hurt, and he looked down at it, expecting to see blood. There was none. The scale mail had done its job. It had caused him to miss the dodge, but it had also saved him from serious injury. It was a trade-off, but perhaps one that he could use to his advantage.

By now the disarmed guardsman had retrieved his weapon. He joined his comrades as they closed in on their prey. They had Liam backed up against the wall. Though his back was protected, they outnumbered him, and they could use the wall as a way to force that advantage. He wanted to avoid that.

Liam lifted his elbows away from his sides a few extra inches and watched them come in, waiting for the right moment. The three soldiers took a different strategy this time. The first man came in alone, staggered shortly thereafter by the second, while the third circled, looking for the right moment to move in.

As the first guard lunged for him, Liam sidestepped the blade, taking it under his left arm. Dropping his elbow, he clamped down on the sword, letting his armor protect him from the blade's sharp edge. He couldn't completely hold the guard's sword in place, but the extra pressure slowed the man's retreat, and Liam came around with a right hook, catching the man in the jaw and sending him sprawling to the ground.

There was an audible gasp from several of the assembled guardsmen, and Liam allowed himself a smile. Didn't expect him to last this long, did they?

Liam stepped to his right, putting the downed guardsman between him and the next opponent. The charging guard had to slow down to avoid stepping on his companion, and this gave Liam the opportunity to circle around and get away from the wall.

The two remaining guards stopped, exchanged a glance, then moved around to try to flank Liam. Liam matched their steps, keeping them at the same distance. They were backing him into a unit of guardsmen still in formation.

Not knowing what the other soldiers would do when he came crashing into them and also not wanting to be caught between two attackers, Liam changed his strategy. Turning his shoulders, he charged the nearest of the two attacking guardsmen, leading with his short sword and coming around right behind it with his long sword. His opponent was fast, though, parrying both attacks with one blade then countering. Liam simply dodged the attack and countered himself with the tip of his long sword.

The two men traded blows, neither able to gain the advantage. Liam feinted right then came back left, turning his head as he did so to check behind him. He didn't intend to trick the guard with this obvious move, merely to buy himself some time to check on his other opponents.

Glancing back, he found what he was looking for—or it found him. The metal-reinforced fingers of Captain Phinneous's heavy gauntlet appeared in his sight only a moment before they smashed into his face, sending sparks flying across his vision. His eyes watered. The world pulsed in and out of view, and his head exploded with pain.

Liam shouted, staggered back, and swung both blades in a wide arc, defending the area around him while he recovered. He shook his head, trying to clear his vision. The point right between his eyes felt as if it might crack wide open. The insides of his head throbbed, and they screamed to be let out. He knew every moment it took him to regain his vision was an opportunity for Captain Phinneous and his henchmen to attack him unprepared.

As if they had heard his thoughts, Liam felt the tip of a blade catch him in the rib, and he was forced back again. The armored plates had stopped the blade from puncturing his skin and skewering his lung, but the impact hurt like the nine hells.

Squinting back the pain, Liam spun, taking in what was before him. He found himself once again surrounded, and Captain Phinneous had joined the fight. The four elite guardsmen walked a slow circle around Liam, their blades out before them as if they were closing in on a tiger.

This was going to require drastic measures.

Liam shoved his short sword back into its sheath and tossed the whole thing to the ground. Better to stick with the things he knew best. He'd keep the armor, because that seemed prudent. But trying to learn to fight with two weapons and still stay alive seemed like competing goals.

Placing his now-free hand on the end of his sword's hilt, he looked right at Captain Phinneous.

"That hurt," he said.

The captain laughed. "I hope so."

Liam took two quick strides and charged at Phinneous. The guard captain shifted his weight, adjusting his feet and taking a defensive stance.

Liam's feet kicked up dust as he propelled himself forward. When he was within a single step, Phinneous swung down on him, but Liam managed to slip to one side, just missing being cleaved in two by the bigger, slower man.

Inside the captain's reach, Liam dropped his shoulder

and plowed right into the man's chest. As he connected, Liam realized how stupid the move was. Running full force into the huge captain had felt much like he imagined running straight into a barn wall would feel. The man was solid and armored, and Liam immediately regretted his decision.

Liam drove forward with his legs, but he could feel his momentum slowly being drained as he tried to push the bigger man backward. Phinneous seemed to simply absorb the blow. Liam came to an almost complete stop.

In the next moment, it felt as if the world had tipped sideways, toppling the entire parade ground and Captain Phinneous with it. Liam found himself charging forward again, moving his legs as fast as he could to try to catch up with the rest of his body. Phinneous had started to fall backward. The man was so muscular it had taken Liam an extra heartbeat to get his massive frame moving, but once it started going, it really started going.

The captain backpedaled, but his feet got caught on each other, and he tripped. Liam pulled up, slowing and catching his balance. The captain continued on, stumbling into a row of soldiers standing at attention and knocking three of them to the ground. There was a crash, and the four men fell into a jumble of armor and meaty limbs.

Liam stood up, breathing hard, and checked behind him for the other three soldiers. But none of them moved, each standing stunned, looking at their captain in a heap on the ground.

Phinneous struggled to free himself from the other men. Several still-standing soldiers bent down and helped lift him up.

Shaking them off as he regained his feet, Captain Phinneous glared at Liam. "You're going to pay for that." His bald forehead wrinkled, and he took a step toward Liam.

"That'll be enough, Captain." Captain Beetlestone stepped in front of Phinneous.

The two men locked eyes, and they stared at each other. There was complete silence in the parade yard. Every guardsman watched the conflict between the two captains. Liam watched right along with them.

After a long moment, Phinneous made a sound like an angry kobold then stepped around the blocking captain, leveling his gaze on Liam.

Beetlestone again cut him off. "I said that's enough. Take your beating like a man."

The mood in the parade grounds shifted. There had been a sort of animalistic excitement while Liam had been the subject of attention. He had felt like a gladiator in an arena. The guardsmen were the crowd, and he was the show. It had been entertainment to these men.

Now things had changed. The look in the guardsmen's eyes told the whole story. They were afraid. There was dissension among the commanders, and that shook these soldiers. The men who led them into battle disagreed on something.

The air grew thick with tension. The outcome of this conflict had become more than just the fate of Liam of Duhlnarim.

Phinneous took another step to the side, moving around Beetlestone as he did, not taking his eyes off Liam. For his part, Beetlestone didn't move, letting Phinneous simply step around.

The blood in Liam's veins had begun to slow as he caught his breath, but the sight of Captain Phinneous coming for him again filled him with a new burst of adrenaline. Would this man ever stop trying to kill him? Liam hadn't been an elite guardsman for even a whole day, and he was already regretting his decision.

The bald man advanced. The scars on his face had grown red, and they stood out against his otherwise pale skin. Liam stretched his neck to one side then the other. The anticipation sent a tingling across his skin as the guard captain grew closer and closer.

Behind Phinneous, Captain Beetlestone turned around and drew his sword. "It stops here."

Phinneous, hearing the sound of steel being drawn, stopped, though he didn't turn around. "What do you intend to do, Beetlestone? You gonna stab me in the back?" His words dripped with doubt and ridicule. Yet the man didn't move.

"If it comes to that," replied Beetlestone.

Captain Phinneous's jaw grew taut, and his eyes narrowed.

Liam watched the bald man, waiting. The entire parade yard sat silent and still. No one breathed; no one blinked. The only movement was a bead of sweat that slowly made its way between Liam's shoulders.

Then Phinneous pointed his blade at Liam. "This isn't over." He turned around and headed back toward his unit, knocking aside two of his guardsmen as he disappeared into the sea of soldiers.

Liam lowered his guard. He was breathing hard, and his arms were shaking from the exertion. Sheathing his blade, he bent over to retrieve his castaway short sword. As he stood back up, Captain Beetlestone filled his view.

"You'll be reporting to me from now on," said the captain. "Fall in."

CHAPTER 14

Ryder tried to ignore the current state of his life—
namely, that if it weren't for the cage, he'd be on
his way back home. His captivity for the past few
months afforded him no luxury except time, which
made him long for it all the more. His wounds were
now completely healed. He could easily make the
trek, but there was little he could do to realize his
desires. In the meantime, he focused his attention
on getting accustomed to Fairhaven.

Once a day a young man by the name of Jase—
a night watchman for the Broken Spear—would
come and get Ryder out of his cage and escort him
around the grounds so he could stretch his legs
and get some exercise. There wasn't much to the
place. There were a few artifacts left over from
the giants, but other than that, the abandoned
palace was sparse.

The Broken Spear was composed of warriors. They had no families, no attachments, and no need to make aesthetic improvements. They didn't even keep livestock or pets. Ryder assumed this was because it would be too difficult to get them up the ladders.

When he wasn't out on a chaperoned walk, Ryder thought often of his home and of Samira. He wondered how Liam was doing. Probably already leading the Awl against Baron Purdun. He smiled to himself. Liam would keep everything in order while he was gone. The thought of Liam planning a raid against Zerith Hold made him swell with pride.

Nazeem spent his imprisonment tinkering with things. He had scavenged the entire cage, broken the thin branches off the brush growing in the dirt, and woven them together into mats, which he placed on the ground for the two of them to sleep on. With a small pile of dead leaves underneath them, they weren't bad.

The Chultan had taken his imprisonment with the same even-tempered acceptance as he had the long, forced march from Zerith Hold. He had an amazing ability to accept the inevitable. Nazeem never seemed to get angry or sad. He just took everything as if it were all part of the plan. It made Ryder feel rather childish for being so homesick.

Over the past day the Chultan had also managed to fashion himself a sling out of a strap of discarded leather. There was plenty of ammunition, and Nazeem was sorting through every pebble and stone he could reach, looking for the pointy ones.

As day turned into night, Nazeem sat cross-legged in the corner of their cell. He dropped a double handful of stones on the ground and began sorting them.

"You better be careful with that," said Ryder, looking at the sling his friend had built. "You could give a man a nasty headache with one of those stones." Ryder laughed at his own joke.

Nazeem only smiled, then stood up and placed one of the rocks in his sling. He spun it around once quickly, then let the stone fly. The projectile whizzed through the air and slammed into the stone wall behind Ryder with tremendous force. It shattered into countless tiny shards and rained down on Ryder's head.

"Be careful," reiterated Ryder. "If Giselle catches you with that thing, there is no telling what she'll do to you."

The Chultan lifted the leather to his forehead and tied the ends behind his head, turning the sling into a headband. He held his hands out, presenting his new fashion. "Surely it is of no threat to anyone."

Ryder lay back on the woven mat Nazeem had made for him. "I stand corrected."

It was quiet up in the Giant's Run Mountains, especially tonight. The air was calm, so the little whistle of the wind through the broken gates and over the ramparts was noticeably missing. All Ryder could hear was the crackling of the small cook fire on the other side of the courtyard and the tumbling of Nazeem's stones across the ground as he sorted them.

"I see the warriors of the Broken Spear are leaving on another raid," said Nazeem, changing the subject.

Ryder lifted his head. In the dimming light, through the bars of the cage, he could see a group of the robed warriors walking out the open doorway. "All of them?"

"No." Nazeem smiled as he looked down on his pile of rocks. He pointed to the top of the wall. "The lovely little one you watch so closely is staying here."

Ryder followed the Chultan's hand up to see Giselle standing atop a stone near the crenellations. "Nazeem, I am a married man," he protested.

"Yes, but married or not, you are still a man."

Ryder thought about it for a moment as he watched Giselle lean out on the wall, cupping a hand to her mouth to yell something down to the departing warriors.

She was certainly beautiful. And that beauty was only enhanced by her rugged surroundings and seemingly inexhaustible ability to cope with changing situations.

"It's hard to argue with your logic." Ryder rested his head back down on the mat. He closed his eyes and thought about Samira. She was strong too, though in a different way than Giselle. Samira had put up with a lot more from him than any person should have to. She held her ground, even when she didn't know the odds. She waited patiently, not having any idea when her waiting might come to an end. While he had gone out to fight, raising his sword to satisfy his own feelings of frustration and powerlessness, Samira was strong without having to take action. That, thought Ryder, might be the more powerful type of strength, and the more difficult to master as well.

With thoughts of his beautiful wife on his mind, Ryder drifted off to sleep.

A nearly full moon was high in the night sky when he was awakened by the sound of the cage door opening. It was Jase. He looked a little panicked.

"What? What is it?" said Ryder as he came out of his sleep.

"Shh," said Jase. "Be quiet and follow me."

Ryder got to his feet. Peering out through the bars, he could see Giselle and several other Broken Spear warriors up on the wall.

"Jase, if you're trying to help me—"

"There is something coming this way," interrupted the young night watchman. "Giselle asked me to wake you and your Chultan friend."

Ryder was puzzled. "She asked you to come get us?"

Jase nodded. "Please, it's urgent."

Ryder turned to shake Nazeem, but the tattooed man was already standing.

"All right," said Ryder to the young man, "lead on."

Jase tossed Ryder the ruined shackles that had bound him on his way out here.

"You'll need these," said Jase. Then he turned and headed across the courtyard, past a line of dead trees beside the wall, and over to the ladders that lead up.

Ryder and Nazeem followed.

When they got to the top, they found Giselle standing on a stone block, peering over the edge with a captain's glass, a length of rope slung over her shoulder. There were several Broke Spear guards beside her.

"Is it them again?" asked one of the sentries.

Jase climbed up on the stone and motioned for Ryder and Nazeem to do the same.

Without looking away from the view, Giselle started speaking. "Sorry to wake you, but many of our warriors are out on another raid, and we are shorthanded for a fight."

"A fight?" asked Ryder, trying to look over the wall. The stone was irregularly shaped, sloped up at one end, so only Giselle and the one Broken Spear guard standing beside her had enough height to look out. "With whom?"

"See for yourself," Giselle stepped aside and let Ryder climb up to her vantage point.

Looking out over the wall, the mountain pass beyond was very dark. The bright moonlight penetrated only the very center of the canyons and pathways that led up to Fairhaven. The plain beyond was well lit, but Ryder was certain whatever it was they were looking at wasn't that far off.

"What am I looking for?"

"Find the stairs," directed Giselle.

Though Ryder wasn't all that familiar with Fairhaven or the view from this height, he followed the statue-lined path to the end of the stairs he had come up when he'd first arrived. He could see where they wound down the mountainside and disappeared into the darkness beyond.

He scanned back and forth, but he could make out only rock and more rock. Nothing out of the ordinary.

"I don't see—" Ryder stopped in the middle of his sentence. Just there, where the stairs came out of the shadow into the moonlight, he saw something move. Then it disappeared again in the darkness.

Ryder blinked and ran his hand over his face, clearing the last of the sleep. Then he opened his eyes as wide as he could and looked again. Out of the shadows stepped a tall, gaunt man carrying something heavy in one hand. The intruder walked upright, and though it was a long way away Ryder could have sworn that whoever it was took one of the four-foot-tall stairs in a single step.

Then it dawned on him. "Giants."

"Yes," replied Giselle. "We've seen them in the surrounding hills from time to time. They mostly come out at night."

"Mostly?" asked Ryder.

Giselle nodded. "There was something I didn't tell you when you first arrived in Fairhaven."

"You mean other than the fact that you were going to imprison me against my will?"

Giselle turned from looking over the wall to glare at Ryder. "The other foe the giants faced when the shield dwarves attacked was one of their own kind," explained the Broken Spear leader, ignoring Ryder's obvious slight. "A giant called the Dodkong."

"The Dodkong?" Ryder had never heard of such a creature. "Should this name mean something to me?"

Giselle shrugged. "Depends. How much do you know about giants?"

Ryder shook his head. "Not much. There aren't any in rural Duhlnarim. I don't know that there are many in all of Erlkazar."

"Don't be so sure," said Giselle. "For many hundreds of years, the dwarves traded enslaved giants to the human royalty of the various baronies around the continent as a way to build political capital. Though many of the old alliances are broken now, the ruling families still keep giants or their offspring as servants. Erlkazar is not an exception."

Giselle smirked, obviously enjoying instructing Ryder on the subject of giants.

Though her attitude was irksome, it was also strangely sexy, and Ryder had to look away from her. "So, who is this Dodkong?" he said, trying to stay on track.

Nazeem answered. "He is an undead stone giant."

"You've heard of him, then," said Giselle. She pointed to her forehead and traced the symbol of a triangle. "All the way over in Chult."

Nazeem nodded.

"The Dodkong is the chief and ruler of the giant clans in the Underdark," explained Giselle. "He wages war against the other giants, slowly killing off the chiefs and reanimating them into his undead minions."

"And how do you know all of this?" asked Ryder.

Giselle pointed down into the courtyard. "When the Broken Spear found this place, we discovered that the giants had left behind most of their belongings. The dwarves must have not cared much for the giants' possessions. There were piles and piles of scrolls, paintings, and stone etchings." She shrugged. "I read them."

Ryder turned to her in amazement. "You speak Giant as well?"

Giselle shook her head. "I can read it, but I've not the vocal chords to pronounce the words."

"There will be plenty of time for you two to get to know each other after the giants are gone," said Nazeem.

Ryder got the hint. "How many of them are out there?" he asked.

"We've counted at least three, but there could be more," replied Jase.

"And how many warriors do you have left in camp?"

Giselle spread her arms. "You're looking at them."

Ryder looked down at the group of Broken Spear warriors. Including Giselle and Jase, he counted only a dozen. He and Nazeem brought the total up to fourteen, but considering their foe, those weren't the best odds.

"If we help you, will you grant us our freedom?" asked Ryder.

"Will you try to leave?" replied Giselle.

"Yes," said Ryder.

"Then the answer is still no."

Ryder headed down the stone toward the steps.

Giselle grabbed him by the arm. "I could have left you locked in that cage."

Ryder pulled away from her and continued toward the stairs.

"Ryder, please," said Giselle.

He stopped, not turning around.

"People's lives are at stake here," said Giselle.

Ryder looked down into the courtyard. There was only one way out. If the giants breached the walls of Fairhaven, they would be trapped.

"I'll need a sword," said Ryder, turning around.

Giselle shrugged. "I don't even have enough for all of my warriors."

"What about the weapons the guards in the caravan were carrying?" he asked. "Surely you took them with you."

"And now more of my warriors are equipped with good steel," replied the bandit leader. "All that is left is the gold in their chests. But if you think throwing handfuls of coins at the giants will help, I am more than happy to show you where you can get all you need."

Ryder looked down at the shackles he carried. He swung the chain side to side, feeling the weight of the cuff. They worked well enough while he fought Cobblepot. They would have to do the same here.

Nazeem's sling seemed even punier than it had earlier. The little rocks would be little more than mere annoyances to a trio of undead giants.

"So," asked Ryder, looking to Giselle, "what's the plan?"

"We wait in the shadows just inside the door," said Giselle, lifting the rope off her shoulder. "When the first one enters, we pull this taut from both sides. We can take out one before they even know what hit them."

"That's it?" asked Ryder. "That's the whole plan?"

Giselle started down the stone block toward the stairs. "That's the whole plan." She stared at him. "Unless you've got something to add?"

The Broken Spear warriors all began to file off the stone, following their leader. Nazeem looked to Ryder.

"Yes," said Ryder. "Yes, I do."

Everyone stopped.

"Well, spit it out then," said Giselle. "We haven't much time."

Ryder nodded. "Nazeem and I will sneak out the front door and hide behind the statues," he explained. "The rest of you stay here with the rope. As soon as the first giant passes, the two of us will attack from behind, taking him by surprise." Ryder looked into each person's eyes in turn as he spoke. "Once we have the giants' attention, we'll try to draw them away from the gate. At the very least, this will buy you some time. At best it will distract them, and you'll be able to attack when they turn around. If we play our cards right, we might be able to confuse them enough to constantly attack their backs."

The Broken Spear warriors seemed to roll the idea around in their heads. Giselle's glare turned to dubious optimism.

"What if they don't come after you?" asked Jase.

Ryder scratched his chin. "Then you go through with the original plan, and we'll follow up from behind."

"Well," said Giselle, "it's not much better than my plan, but it's not any worse either."

Ryder would take that. He turned to Nazeem. "Good?"

The Chultan nodded. "Good."

"All right, then, if no one else has any objections," said Giselle, sarcasm dripping from her words, "then I suggest we get on with it."

At the bottom of the ladders, Ryder and Nazeem crossed the courtyard. The only person still in camp was an injured and badly beaten prisoner who had been marched out of Duhlnarim in chains. The rest of them, having been criminals—or at the very least unwanted in Erlkazar—were more than happy to join the Broken Spear. They had marched out with the raiding party who had left earlier in the day.

The last man was curled up in a ball and appeared to be sleeping. He was likely in no shape to fight, but considering the circumstances, he didn't have much choice.

"Quickly," Ryder said, placing his finger to his lips. "You must wake and defend. . . ." As he rolled him over, Ryder recognized him as the skinny man who had been chained to Nazeem.

The man's eyes were open, and he stared up at Ryder with a look of utter terror. "Please. Don't hurt me."

Ryder took a step back, stunned. "I . . . I'm not going to hurt you."

"You're not?"

Ryder shook his head. "No." He grimaced. "But there are things outside this wall that will if you don't get up."

The skinny man nodded and scrambled to his feet. He was quick—quicker by far than Ryder had anticipated. And he was tall, almost two inches taller than Ryder. As skinny as he was, he looked like a cornstalk. Though his skin was pale and he was shaking, the rest of him looked to be in fine shape.

"Are you all right?" asked Ryder.

"No," replied the skinny man.

Ryder looked the man over once again. No blood, no bruises. He could see nothing to indicate that the man was in poor shape.

"What's wrong with you?"

"I don't want to be killed," replied the skinny man.

Ryder laughed. "Neither do I." He extended his hand. "My name's Ryder."

The skinny man shied away, startled by Ryder's gesture. After a moment, he tentatively reached out and shook his hand. "My name's Curtis."

Ryder smiled. "So, Curtis, I'm guessing you aren't the type who carries a sword."

Curtis wiped his forearm across his face. "No."

"Well," said Ryder, starting to get a little frustrated with the man's lack of explanation, "do you have any other skills that might be useful in a fight?"

"In a fight?" said Curtis, shifting his feet. "No." He shook his head, puckering his lips as if the mere thought of a fight put a bad taste in his mouth.

"Well, maybe it's best if you stay out of sight, then," said Ryder, ushering Curtis toward a pile of rubble in a shadowy corner of the courtyard.

Curtis nodded, again shying away from Ryder's hands, but moving where he was directed.

Then he stopped and lifted his hand, pointing his index finger in the air. "I know a little magic."

"Magic? I think that qualifies as useful." Ryder turned to gauge Nazeem's reaction.

The Chultan shook his head, looking skeptical.

"What sort of magic?" prodded Ryder.

"Illusions," said Curtis. "Illusions, mostly."

Ryder shrugged. He didn't know what good parlor tricks were going to be in a fight, but it certainly couldn't hurt to have a magic-user on their side. Better than having one cowering in the corner.

"Come on then," he said, shepherding Curtis toward

the ladders. "You should be up above, where you can get a good view of everything unfolding."

Curtis nodded nervously. "Will I be safe up there?"

Ryder tried to put a smile on his face. "As safe as anywhere."

❦ ❦ ❦ ❦ ❦

With Curtis on the wall above and the Broken Spear in their places, Ryder and Nazeem headed out of the front gate, running through the shadows cast by the towering wall. Skirting around the first of the statues on the northern side of the pathway, the two men sneaked closer to the stairs.

Ryder pulled up about halfway between the gate and the first of the stairs behind a half-broken statue of a giant holding a tremendous spear. The entire upper body had been toppled, so the head and shoulders lay on the ground beside the plinth that supported the rest of the statue. The rubble provided a larger area to hide behind, and if the undead giants came to investigate, the two men could climb under the fallen statue's arm, further hiding themselves.

Ryder could hear the giants talking to one another. They sounded a little like an old man suffering from a nasty head cold and a little like the noise of two large rocks being rubbed together.

"Do you speak Giant?" he asked Nazeem.

The Chultan shook his head. "Why would you think that I might know how to speak their jibber jabber of a language?"

Ryder shrugged. "I don't know. You seem to know everything else and I figured it couldn't hurt to ask."

The first of the undead giants climbed up over the last step. The creature was tall and lean, resembling very much the giants depicted by the statues lining the pathway. In the pale moonlight, the creature's flesh was dull gray. Its tattered skin hung from its bones, flapping as the giant shifted its weight forward and back with each step. Its ribs were exposed on its left side, and a stream of dark, viscous fluid leaked from the opening.

The creature lumbered toward the gate, dragging a huge club in one hand and a boulder in the other. A second, then a third undead giant climbed over the rise of the last step. They were a little smaller than the first, but they were still massive in comparison to Ryder and Nazeem.

The trio continued to talk to each other until the largest spotted the first of the statues. It went still, raising its club to alert the others. As a group, they approached, being careful to circle around behind the statue as they came. When they got close enough, the big one swung its club, smashing the stone with a mighty blow.

The giant's club knocked the head loose, and it fell to the ground, spinning toward the gate of Fairhaven. It took an irregular path as it rolled down the walkway. Each time it turned over, the protruding nose and ears would cause the whole thing to jump into the air and change directions. It came to a grinding rest just in front of Ryder and Nazeem's hiding place.

"They think the statues are real giants lying in wait," said Nazeem.

Ryder looked down the pathway. Many of the statues were battered beyond recognition. But there were several that could be whole giants.

"If we just wait here, they'll find us." Ryder watched the giants pummel the statue.

"Then we must change our plans," said Nazeem. "There is no value in an ambush that does not come as a surprise."

Ryder nodded. "Very true. But I have an idea." He shuffled toward the shadows closer to the gate. "Follow me."

Nazeem nodded and crouched beside Ryder, sling in hand.

Ryder watched the undead giants as they moved to the next intact statue, circling around behind and preparing to attack.

Just as the big one raised it club, Ryder whispered, "Now."

He dashed out into the bright moonlight and across the open pathway. The giants beat on the statue, not paying any attention to the two men as they sneaked across and into the darkness on the south side of the path.

Safely on the other side, Ryder ducked behind a fully intact statue and examined the stone creature's feet.

"What are you doing?" asked Nazeem.

"This statue is loose," replied Ryder.

"Ah," said Nazeem, understanding. "And you want to bring it to life."

Ryder nodded. "Precisely." He looked to the top. "We'll need something to leverage it with—a piece of wood or something to shove into the cracks here at the base."

Nazeem began scavenging the ground around the plinth.

Down the path, the undead giants had finished dismantling their latest stone victim and were moving on to the next—the last intact statue between the giants and the two men.

"There is nothing here," said Nazeem, turning away from the search. "Only small rocks and dirt."

"Then we'll have to do this the hard way," said Ryder.

Taking a step back, he set his chain in motion. He let the heavy end make two revolutions then hurled it toward the statue. The cuff of the onetime shackles landed on the giant's outstretched arm, wrapping around once and catching. Ryder gave the chain a hard pull using the statue's height to get leverage, and the carved stone shifted on its unsteady base.

The undead giants went silent, turning away from the now-ruined statue they had just pummeled.

Nazeem ducked into the shadows, crouching down and loading a stone into his sling. Ryder pulled himself up close to the carved giant, trying to stay out of sight.

The giants came up to the loose statue, circling around as they had with each of the others. The largest of the group came around to the front, dragging its club. The other two swung around, moving behind the statue, right in front of Nazeem.

This close, Ryder could smell the creatures' rotting flesh. It turned his stomach, and a quick wave of nausea flushed through him. Steeling himself, Ryder fought back the impulse to toss up whatever was in his stomach.

Eying the statue, the big giant lifted its club into the air.

Ryder dashed out of his hiding place and behind the biggest giant. When he ran out of chain, he yanked as hard as he could. The statue shifted and teetered.

Confused, the undead giant shifted his gaze between Ryder and the statue, ready to smash one or the other with his club.

That's what Ryder had been hoping for, and he leaned back, putting his legs into his pull. The stone made a terrific grinding sound as its cracked base gave way. It slipped, and the statue toppled toward the undead giant. The creature let out a roar and swung its club at the falling carving. The heavy maul collided with the stone, smashing the statue's head as it fell. Despite the accurate blow of his club, the lumbering undead monster wasn't fast enough to get out of the way.

The statue smashed into the giant's chest and left shoulder, the head of the stone spear sinking into its rubbery flesh and shattering as it tore through. The undead giant's left arm was torn from its body and the flesh made a soft splashing sound as it hit the paving stones and splattered into a viscous puddle. The rock it had been holding in its left hand bounced once, sending up a puff of dry dust, then lay motionless on the ground.

The giant's torn shoulder wept a runny black fluid. The undead creature stared down at the stump. Then it growled and turned its gaze down on Ryder, standing at its feet.

The statue rolled a bit as it settled into its new place on the ground, making a sound not unlike that of the giants talking. Ryder tried to unhitch his chain as the statue came to a rest, but it was wrapped firmly under the statue's heavy arm. The undead giant in front of him reeked of rotten flesh, and Ryder breathed through his mouth to avoid gagging on the smell. The stench was so foul, he swore he could taste it.

On the opposite side of the plinth, the other two giants let out grinding growls, then shuffled toward Ryder.

The one-armed leader swung its club. The swing was slow but mighty. Ryder ducked, dodging a blow that would have caved in his skull. He could feel the wind behind it ruffle his hair as the head of the weapon slipped past. The giant's heavy club slammed into the fallen statue, and the stone giant exploded into dozens of sharp fragments—releasing Ryder's chain.

Ryder stood up and darted to his right, coming at the giant from its armless side. Then he swung his chain at the undead giant. The cuff slapped against the creature's calf, tearing a large chunk out and sending the rotting flesh flying off into the night. The giant growled and swung its club again. Ryder stumbled, just barely able to get out of the way before the club smashed into the ground right where he had been standing.

Dropping to one knee, Ryder used the ground to steady himself, and he hurled the end of his shackles at the giant. The cuff wrapped around one leg, hitching itself on the links of the chain—not what he had been trying to do.

With the chain wrapped around the giant's leg, he had little choice but to try to pull the brute off its feet. He leaned back and put his back into it. The leg didn't budge. The giant was just too strong.

The giant brought his club down toward the kneeling human. Not letting go of his chain, Ryder dropped to his belly and rolled to his right. Dust flew as the creature's weapon slammed into the dirt.

Getting to his feet, Ryder pulled the chain again. It still didn't move, and he cursed, wishing he had a sword instead of his rusting, ruined set of shackles.

The other two giants finally made their way over to their leader. They encircled Ryder, surrounding him with their bulk, their clubs raised and ready.

"I could use a little help here," said Ryder through gritted teeth. He gave the chain one last hard yank. It drew taut, but the giant attached to the other end held firm.

The two new giants swung down on him at the same time. Ryder had nowhere to go, and he didn't even have time to get out of the way. He flinched back, reacting on instinct.

The two clubs crossed in midair, just missing their target and slamming into the chain instead. Alone, Ryder had not been strong enough to pull the undead giant leader from his feet, but with the help of the other two. . . .

The chain slammed to the ground under the tremendous blow. Ryder was thrown forward, his chest flying into the crossed clubs, knocking the wind from his lungs and his chain from his hand. On the other end of the chain, the giant's leg was yanked out from under it, and the creature toppled backward. With a great roar, the beast fell back onto the jagged stone fragments of the shattered statue, and the giant was impaled a dozen times on the pointy shards.

The creature tried to regain its feet, but the heavy stones through its back held it pinned down, and it thrashed against its gruesome imprisonment. The violent movement shifted the broken boulder-sized stones back and forth inside its body, tearing the rancid flesh from the creature's bones.

The monster struggled for a moment more and let out one last grinding noise. Then its body went limp, and it slipped into death once again.

One moment, Ryder lay atop a pair of clubs, looking up at the two remaining undead giants. The next, he was flying through the air, hurled toward the broken gate of Fairhaven. His arms and legs flailed as he fell through empty space. Then he came crashing down, tumbling as he landed. The back of his skull slammed into the base of another statue just a few steps from the painted wall of the palace.

Ryder saw stars, and his head exploded in pain. His eyes teared up, and he could hardly open them. It hurt too much to focus on anything, and when he tried to stand up, his stomach would pitch and yaw.

Ryder managed to get to his knees, and he placed his forehead in the cool dirt. "Dear Ilmater, make it stop."

The sound of lumbering footsteps forced Ryder to open his eyes again. Though his head felt as if it might split open, his vision had cleared enough for him to see the giants closing in. Through sheer force of will, he managed to get to his feet.

Unarmed, wounded, nearly blind, and with a pair of undead giants charging down on him, Ryder teetered on uneasy legs. To his left was the entrance to Fairhaven. Giselle and the Broken Spear waited there for the first giant to pass through. If he could only make it to that gate, he'd have a chance.

Ryder turned and started to run toward the opening, but the ground seemed to shift, and his legs felt as if they were made of warm candle wax. His knees buckled, and he had to put his hand down to keep from falling again. Though he was no longer nauseous, he was still in bad shape.

The undead giants reached him in just a few steps, and Ryder made one last attempt to dart away. His feet crossed, and he got tangled. With tremendous effort, he remained upright, but he was once again standing under the glowering glares of two undead giants.

There was a flash of light and suddenly a figure appeared next to Ryder. He shied back, not sure what he was seeing. The fighter from Duhlnarim blinked and did a double take. There, standing beside Ryder was . . . another Ryder? He rubbed his eyes. Was he really seeing this?

The second Ryder saluted the first then drew a sword from a scabbard on his belt. He ran right up to the two remaining undead giants, waving his sword, and shouted, "Over here, you big louts!"

The giants swung their clubs at him, but the sword-wielding Ryder managed to dodge out of the way.

"That the best you can do?" he taunted. Then he ran around behind the two lumbering monstrosities.

The undead giants turned to face the new Ryder.

"Psst. Ryder," came a voice from above.

Ryder looked up. He could just make out Curtis's head sticking out over the edge of the palace wall.

"Ryder," he called. "Hurry through the gate. The illusion won't last forever."

Ryder looked back at the giants and the illusionary version of himself. Guess the skinny man knew more than a few parlor tricks.

Ryder turned and ran unsteadily through the broken gate to Fairhaven. He was attacked the moment his foot crossed the threshold, and he landed on the ground, chest first.

"Hold," whispered Giselle. "It's only Ryder."

A pair of Broken Spear warriors got up off the downed fighter.

"Thanks," said Ryder as he got back to his feet, "you really go the extra step to make a person feel welcome."

Giselle stepped right into his face. "So much for the plan."

Ryder dusted himself off. "We had no choice. They were going to find us, so we improvised."

"And where's Nazeem?"

Ryder spun around to look out on to the path leading away from the gate. "Hells. He's still out there."

CHAPTER 15

We'll be riding out a communiqué for Baron Purdun to King Korox of Erlkazar," explained Captain Beetlestone. "The road will be treacherous, and we expect resistance either from the Awl—"

Liam squirmed a little when he said this.

"—or from another source."

"Sir?" One of the other soldiers stood up from his chair.

"Yes, Buckwald?" acknowledged Beetlestone.

"Another source?"

The captain took a deep breath, looking at each of the soldiers around the table. All of them belonged to the unit that reported directly to Beetlestone. He was going to be leading this mission, and none of the other troops in the baron's army would accompany them.

He nodded. "There have been an alarming number of scouting reports recently about an incursion of the walking dead in the region surrounding Duhlnarim, particularly in the areas near Dajaan and along Shalane Lake."

Though no one spoke, Liam could feel the room tense. They would no doubt be headed to Klarsamryn, the king's stronghold in Llorbauth. The road to the capital ran parallel to Shalane Lake almost the entire way.

"If there are no other questions," said Beetlestone, "then we will mount up and head out immediately." The captain placed his hands behind his back, waiting.

The room remained silent.

"Very well, then," he said. "To the stables."

The soldiers all stood and filed out of the briefing room. Outside, the sun was just coming up.

The stables had been a late addition to the north end of Zerith Hold. It was attached to a special holding cell used to deal with large groups of prisoners. The dungeon in the Hold wasn't very large, so long-term criminals were moved to other facilities. Or so Liam was told.

The stable boy brought the soldiers' horses into the courtyard. The young man approached Liam and handed him the reins of a beautiful brown mare.

"This one's yours," said the youth.

Liam took the reins. "Thank you." He'd never had a horse of his own. And this one was magnificent. Tall and lean, it was a young horse in its prime. It had been well cared for, and its eyes were bright and clear.

"Hello, there," he said, running his hand along the horse's mane.

The horse let out a whiny.

"Liam," shouted Captain Beetlestone.

Liam looked up from the horse to see that all the other soldiers were already mounted and ready to ride.

"Do you know how to ride, son?" asked the captain.

Liam placed his left foot in the stirrup and swung

himself up onto the horse's back in a single fluid motion. Once he was situated, he turned and saluted the captain. "Yes, Captain."

Beetlestone smirked. "Very good." He turned his horse and headed toward the gate out of Zerith Hold. "Let's ride."

The gate opened, and the soldiers filed out of the courtyard. They fell into line, two abreast, and headed down the cobbled path, the horses' hooves clanking on the stone.

Liam rode beside a gray-haired man. Though he didn't appear to be too old, his skin was beginning to wrinkle on his forehead and below his eyes. He had an easy confidence about him that put Liam at ease. The man smiled when he saw Liam looking at him.

"The name's Knoblauch." The veteran soldier touched his helm in a familiar greeting, one Liam had seen other soldiers use with each other.

"Liam," he replied, repeating the gesture.

The older man nodded. "I know who you are."

Liam shrugged. He didn't know how the old man was going to react to him. Judging from the way Captain Phinneous had responded, he didn't want to make any assumptions. So he kept his mouth shut.

Knoblauch must have sensed Liam's reservations. "Don't worry," he said. "I hold no grudges."

"That's good to know," replied Liam.

"In fact," the veteran leaned in his saddle closer to Liam, lowering his voice, "Captain paired me with you as a precaution. Asked me to look after you, make sure none of the other men got any wrong ideas."

"Oh," said Liam, "aren't you the martyr."

"Well," said Knoblauch, sitting up as he rode, "if you're going to be like that about it."

Liam sighed. "I apologize. It's just that things have been pretty rough for me the past few months."

Knoblauch gave Liam a knowing nod. "I'll bet."

The two men rode on quietly into late morning. In the silence, Liam mulled over all the thoughts Knoblauch could be having about him. What if their roles were reversed?

"Hey, Knoblauch," Liam said after some time, "can I ask you a question?"

The veteran nodded. "Yeah."

"Did you ever fight the Crimson Awl?"

Knoblauch squirmed a bit in his saddle. Then he nodded. "Yes."

Liam felt a chill run down his spine and a knot formed in his stomach. He steeled himself then asked his next question. "Did you ever kill any?"

Knoblauch took a deep breath. "I already told you I don't hold grudges."

Liam shrugged. "Yeah, but maybe I do."

Knoblauch laughed. "All right. The answer is no. I never killed any of your 'Brothers' or 'Sisters.' " The veteran continued to chuckle to himself.

Liam nodded. He wasn't sure he believed the man, but he guessed it didn't matter. Would it make a difference in his situation if the guard next to him had killed members of the Awl? Probably not. And knowing for sure which of the soldiers around him had killed his friends and which hadn't would only serve to torture him more.

The same was likely true for many of these men. They surely had friends and comrades killed by the Awl. None of them would know if it had been by Liam's hand or some other. Liam looked around at the soldiers in his unit. If they got into a fight, would one of them turn on him?

Then he looked at Knoblauch. Guess the captain already thought of that.

Liam settled into his saddle. He wished Ryder were here.

Up ahead, the road took a turn to the east, and Shalane Lake came into view. It was a beautiful deep blue.

"There she is," said Knoblauch. "Big Blue."

"Big Blue?" asked Liam.

"You've never heard of Big Blue?"

Liam shrugged. "Should I have?"

The veteran looked at Liam with astonishment. "Then you don't know the tale of Ellhimar's Tower?"

Liam shook his head. "No."

A smile bloomed on Knoblauch's face, and he rubbed his hands together. "Well," he started, "lakes this far inland usually look green and less pristine than Shalane Lake. This one, however, is the sapphire blue of the tropical ocean."

Liam looked at the water. It was remarkably blue. He'd never seen the tropical ocean before, so he'd just take the veteran's word for it.

"As the story goes," continued Knoblauch, "there is a wizard who lives at the bottom of the lake."

"At the bottom?"

Knoblauch nodded, a knowing smile on his face. "At the bottom. Ellhimar's Tower is said to be surrounded by a protective magical bubble that keeps the water out and the air in."

"Sounds reasonable," said Liam, trying his best to keep a straight face.

"The brilliant blue of the water is a result of the magic that powers the wizard's enchantment." Knoblauch looked at Liam, who obviously wasn't buying the story. "You can ask Lord Purdun if you like. He studied with old Ellhimar before becoming baron."

"What?"

Knoblauch nodded. "That's right. Purdun is a mage."

"But..." Liam stumbled for words. "He pulled a sword on me."

"I heard about that." The veteran chuckled.

"You and everyone else in Ahlarkham," said Liam, sulking.

"Well," said Knoblauch still laughing, "I'll give you

this—you certainly have courage."

Liam tried to hide his smile by turning his head and covering his face with his hand. Finally he couldn't hold it back, and the two men had a good laugh.

"Purdun only dabbles in the martial arts," explained the veteran, his laughter subsiding. "At heart, he's an evoker."

"An evoker. Really?" Liam didn't know what an evoker was, but he didn't want to reveal his ignorance.

Knoblauch smiled. "You don't know what that is, do you?"

"Uh," Liam started. "Of course. An evoker, sure I know what one is."

"All right." Knoblauch shook his head. "I'll let you off the hook. Evokers manipulate arcane energies to create things out of thin air."

The regiment rode around the bend. The road turned west again, away from the lake and into the surrounding forest. The clopping of the horses' hooves grew quieter as the ground turned soft and damp under the canopy of trees.

Liam shrugged. "Yeah."

"You know the battle mages who patrol the top of the wall at Zerith Hold?"

Liam nodded.

"They're all evokers."

Liam understood. "You mean the ones that shoot the big balls of flame?" He blurted.

"Have you heard Lord Purdun ever referred to as the Firefist?"

"Yes." Liam had heard him called that more than a few times. Ryder had even used that nickname the day they had ambushed the carriage.

"Do you know how he got this nickname?"

Liam relaxed, glad to get to a different topic. "No, I don't." Making up stuff to sound like he knew what he was talking about was hard work.

"Well, you might not guess it now, but as a younger man, Purdun was a brash, foolish, hothead with a quick temper." Knoblauch leaned away in his saddle, taking a long look at Liam. "Not unlike someone else I recently met."

"Is this part of the story?" asked Liam.

Knoblauch ignored him and continued. "Just after he married Princess Dijara and became baron, Purdun had a meeting with one of the princess's previous lovers, a minor noble by the name of Stanley Smorthby."

"Stanley Smorthby? What a name," replied Liam.

"I know. Anyway, Stanley had been in line to marry the beautiful young princess and become the Baron of Ahlarkham. So naturally, he was a bit uppity when meeting the man who had taken away not only his woman but also his political power."

"Yeah." Liam scratched his chin. "Must be rough."

"As the story goes, old Stanley Smorthby rubbed Purdun the wrong way. Nobody knows exactly what he said or what he did, but all those present could see that Purdun was mad." Knoblauch shifted in his saddle once again, settling in. "When their conversation finally ended, Purdun offered Stanley his hand—presumably to shake and part on peaceful terms. But when Stanley grabbed hold a huge jet of fire launched out of the baron's fingertips, filling up a quarter of the room and looking like a giant piece of molten cherry pie."

"He burned him? He torched his wife's old lover?"

Knoblauch nodded, a mischievous grin on his face. "Scorched all the clothes and hair right off the corpulent, uppity little snob." The veteran laughed. "It was the funniest thing I ever saw."

"You were there?"

Knoblauch smiled. "I was one of Purdun's personal bodyguards."

"Really?" asked Liam. "So what are you doing back here in the guard?"

Knoblauch paused. "I failed in my duty," said the veteran.

Liam laughed. "What do you mean you failed? Purdun's still alive, isn't he?"

Knoblauch nodded. "Yes, but only by the grace of the High Priest of Gond and an expensive resurrection spell."

Liam cocked his head, a huge smile spreading across his face. "Dear Tymora. It's amazing he even keeps you in the elite guard."

The veteran got a sour look on his face, his smile fading quickly into a powerful scowl. Liam felt like a scolded child. His comment was flippant, yes, but he hadn't intended to make the man angry.

"Hey, Knoblauch, I—"

The veteran held his hand up to silence Liam. Then he pointed to the ground beside them. "See that."

A chill ran down Liam's spine, and he looked to where Knoblauch was pointing. While they were talking, they had ridden deep into the Argent Forest, which bordered Shalane Lake. The trees had grown thick along the side of the road and overhead, blocking out the sun's rays and making it very dark. The road was soft and damp, and though it was midday, it felt like an early summer evening.

On the ground, near the horses' hooves, a wispy, translucent mist was seeping out of the dense bushes that defined the edge of the road. It seemed to move with a purpose, growing as it pulled into view. The sight of it gave Liam a very bad feeling.

"What is it?"

"We have company," said the veteran. He pulled up on the reins of his horse and shouted. "Captain, it's the undead."

The entire regiment came to a halt. The horses whinnied and brayed as their riders turned them to face the bushes and trees. The mists grew, taking shapes—ones that looked vaguely human.

"Vampires," said Knoblauch.

The undead creatures materialized, surrounding Liam, Knoblauch, and the rest of Captain Beetlestone's unit. They hissed at the mounted soldiers, their mouths sharp with teeth, and their skin pale and taut against their bones. As they became fully corporeal, several of them leaped into the trees, climbing with both hands and feet up the trunks and into the canopy above. They moved with a preternatural swiftness that caused the hair on the back of Liam's neck to stand on end.

"Stay close," said Knoblauch. "Your blade has been enchanted to hurt them, but vampires and their spawn are very difficult to kill. Take their heads from their bodies, and if we live through this, we'll deal with the remnants so they don't ever come back." Knoblauch pulled his long sword from its sheath.

Liam nodded and also pulled his blade.

Knoblauch looked into Liam's eyes, his countenance serious and dire. "Watch my back. This may be the toughest fight of our lives, and we're gonna need to be a team if we want to make it out of this."

A pair of vampire spawn—both appearing to have at one time been human men—pounced on the two soldiers. Knoblauch kneed his horse.

"Yah," Knoblauch shouted.

The horse jumped forward and smashed its chest into one of the oncoming undead with force enough to knock a normal man to the ground. But the vampire spawn just latched onto the horse's front quarters with its clawed hands and bit down on the mount's flesh.

Knoblauch's horse let out a tremendous wail—a sound that shook Liam to his bones. Then his mount stumbled and fell forward onto the damp ground. Knoblauch tumbled out of his saddle, rolled once, and came to rest on the ground beside the dense bushes on the edge of the road.

The other spawn jumped at Liam.

Bringing his long sword around with both hands, Liam caught the attacking undead in the chest, slashing it open and knocking it back to the ground. The beast let out a hiss, leaped to its feet, and bounded back at Liam, moving with amazing speed.

Pushing the horse with just his knees, Liam turned his mount so that the barding on its left side was between the vampire spawn's teeth and the horse's flesh.

"Bite down on that," he shouted.

The spawn slammed its fists against the horse's side, and the mount stumbled sideways from the blow. Liam was jostled around in the saddle, but he managed to stay on top of the horse as it caught itself and regained its balance.

The undead creature pressed on, following up its slam by jumping onto the horse's hindquarters. It crouched and balanced behind Liam. Hissing, it grabbed hold of his shoulders.

Liam tried to swivel in his seat to attack the creature, but it dodged his every blow. With no other option, he let go of his sword with one hand and grabbed hold of the reins. Yanking and kicking, he pulled his horse off its front legs. The mount whinnied and reared. The vampire spawn lost its balance and fell backward. But it had a good grip on Liam's shoulders, and as it toppled off the horse it pulled Liam right out of his saddle. The live man and the undead man fell to the ground, Liam landing on top of the spawn.

As they came to rest, Liam could feel the vampire's foul breath on his neck. He struggled to get out of the creature's grip, but it was tremendously strong. He could feel it lift its head to bite down on his neck. Liam sat up as far as he could, straining, and slammed his head backward, smashing the back of his helmet into the spawn's face. The creature let out a hiss, and its grip temporarily loosened.

"No one bites me." Liam tumbled away, jumping to his feet and bringing his sword around in a single fluid motion. The pale blue-white runes on the edge of the blade flashed lightly as the weapon connected with the side of the spawn's neck and cut its head clean from its body.

The headless carcass fell back to the damp ground, twitched once and lay motionless.

Turning away from the ruined body, Liam looked out at the biggest, most frantic fight he'd ever seen. Horses littered the ground, their riders on foot and fighting for their lives. Vampires dropped from the forest canopy on top of unsuspecting elite guardsmen. And in the middle of it all, he could see Captain Beetlestone, his armor splattered with black blood and gore, his lip curled up to one side as he swung his twin blades, cutting the head off another vampire spawn. Two others lay at his feet, but so too did the bodies of three guardsmen.

Liam looked along the road they had come down. It led back to Big Blue and away from all the vampires. His horse stood patiently beside him, ready to be ridden away from the carnage. The vampires who had guarded the path were now both dead, and Liam could make a clean getaway, leaving the elite guard far behind.

Then he turned to look for Knoblauch. The veteran lay on the ground beside the edge of the road. He was slowly getting to his feet, but it was clear by the look on his face and the way he moved that the fall from his horse had done some damage to his shoulder and hip.

Knoblauch got to his knees with the help of his long sword, its tip stuck deep in the ground beside him. He started to rise to his feet when something fell out of the canopy on top of him. The veteran was knocked back to the ground, and his blade was sent flying into the bushes.

A vampire—who appeared to have been a female elf in life—sat on Knoblauch's chest. She moved her head side to side, like a snake preparing to strike, as she sized up the potential meal pinned beneath her.

Liam's horse stomped on the road beside him, whinnied, and pushed its nose against his back. On the ground, the veteran soldier grimaced, obviously in pain. He opened his eyes and looked at Liam. Their eyes met, and Liam tightened his grip on the hilt of his sword.

Turning around, he put his hand on the horse's muzzle.

"Wait for me," he said, then Liam pushed off, spinning as he came around and threw himself at the vampire on Knoblauch's chest.

The blade whistled as it sliced through the air, headed right for the vampire's neck. But the undead creature was quick, and she ducked the attack, rolling away and scrambling up the closest tree.

Liam had overextended himself, and as his blade came around, he came around with it. He moved his feet as quickly as he could to catch himself, but he still wasn't used to fighting in full armor, and he had to lower his blade to regain his balance. He came up right in front of Knoblauch, looking down on the wounded veteran.

Something hit Liam hard in the back. He was lifted off his feet and thrown into the trees. Branches thrashed at his face and arms as he whipped through the foliage. Liam flailed his legs as he flew.

Liam's forward momentum slowed as he smashed through the trees. He lost his grip on his enchanted blade as he crashed to the ground on a pile of broken branches. The impact knocked the wind out of his lungs, and he struggled to draw a breath.

Behind him, he could hear the rustling of footsteps through the bushes.

Every fiber of Liam's body ached. With much effort, he flopped over onto his back to look up at the elf vampire. In her hand she gripped the collar of Knoblauch's armor, dragging the veteran's partially limp body behind her as she methodically paced through the underbrush toward Liam.

Her words hissed from between her lips. "Looks like you both belong to me."

CHAPTER 16

Nazeem stood concealed in the shadows. He had watched Ryder pull the statue down on top of the undead giant leader and had seen him foolishly try to trip the beast with only the strength of his arms. That man was going to get them both killed. Damn Erlkazaran.

No one in Chult was that bold or that stupid. That included Nazeem. If Ryder wanted to get himself smashed into bits, then that was his business. There were limits to a man's loyalty.

"You wouldn't ask Nazeem to walk off a cliff, so why get him into this?" he whispered.

He liked Ryder. He seemed like a good man. A man a criminal like Nazeem could use to his advantage. A man like that could likely accomplish anything as long as it were in the name of justice or fairness or whatever cause those revolutionary types seemed to use to justify their existence.

Nazeem's lack of riches seemed like a pretty good cause to him. And he had intended to find a way for Ryder to help him correct this injustice.

But judging from his heroics in the plaza before Fairhaven, Ryder was not only driven to fight inequality, he was also crazy. Nazeem liked to think of himself as a brave man, a man willing to take risks—an entrepreneur. But looking out at the two undead giants, he felt this venture was taking a turn for the worst.

Perhaps it was time to cut his losses.

Taking one last look at Fairhaven and Ryder, Nazeem skirted down the shadows on the edge of the rock wall toward the giant-sized stairs. "Goodbye, Ryder of Duhlnarim," he said as he slipped over the edge of the first step and into the darkness beyond.

❧   ❧   ❧   ❧   ❧

"I need a weapon." Ryder crouched beside the open gate to Fairhaven.

"I told you," said Giselle, "there's nothing here that we haven't already put to use."

"No one here has a second? Not even a dagger?" Ryder threw his hands in the air. "How do you intend to—"

"I ... I have something," said Jase timidly.

Both Ryder and Giselle turned to the young man.

"I didn't think it was much of a weapon until I saw you fight the giants with your shackles, but ..."

"Great," said Ryder. "Whatever it is, I'll take it."

"It's in my footlocker," said the young Broken Spear.

"Well go get it then," spat Giselle. "And be quick about it."

Jase nodded his head then took off running into the courtyard.

The undead giants had finished with Curtis's illusion and were making their way toward the open gate.

"All right. Everyone stay calm," whispered Giselle. "We wait until they cross the threshold, then we pull the rope tight. As soon as that smelly bastard hits the ground, we jump on him."

The Broken Spear nodded their understanding.

The moments that followed seemed to take an eternity. The shuffling footfalls of the giants could be heard outside the gate, and no one inside moved a muscle. Ryder looked out at all the waiting warriors. He hadn't studied them all that closely before. The few standing here were young, and they all looked completely terrified. All of them, that is, except Giselle.

Their leader had a grim glint in her eye, a look of complete determination, as if her will alone could carry the day and deliver these young men and women to safety. Ryder nodded. Perhaps it could.

Ryder could smell the first of the giants before it stepped through the gate. Its foul stench burned his nostrils, and he began breathing through his mouth.

The lumbering undead appeared inside the threshold. It took two steps more.

"Now," shouted Giselle, standing up from the shadows and pulling on the rope as hard as she could. The fine muscles in her arms lifted to the surface, and Ryder could see her straining.

The other Broken Spear warriors did the same, and the rope snapped taut. The giant obliged and moved forward, entangling itself in the trap.

"Pull," shouted Giselle. She redoubled her efforts.

The giant took another step. But instead of falling, it dragged the rope and the Broken Spear warriors with it. All eleven of them slid forward a step, their feet slipping on the dry, dusty ground.

"I can't get a grip on the ground," shouted one of the warriors.

The giant took a second step, and the group slid several more feet. A few of them even lost their grip, and the rope came free of their hands.

The second giant came through the gate. The Broken Spear warriors still clinging to the rope had all been pulled out of the protection of the shadows and into the middle of the path that led through the front gate.

"Look out," shouted Ryder.

The gigantic undead growled and brought its club down on the closest Broken Spear warrior it could find. The man was focusing so hard on keeping hold of the rope that he never even saw it coming. The club smashed the man's head down through his shoulders and into his own chest. Blood splashed across the ground, looking like specks of black rain in the pale moonlight.

"Let go," shouted Ryder. "Scatter. Fight for your lives."

Giselle looked back from where she held the rope, then echoed Ryder's warning. "Run for the shadows."

Just then Ryder felt someone tug on his elbow. It was Jase.

"Here," he said, holding out a length of steel chain.

Ryder took the weapon from the young man with a smile. He never thought he would be so happy to see a simple length of chain, but under the circumstances, he'd take it. "Thanks." He slapped Jase on the shoulder. "Now scatter."

Jase nodded and bolted for the dark edges of the courtyard.

Ryder did the same, skidding to a stop behind a broken section of rock that had fallen down from the wall high above. Dropping into a crouch he quickly examined the weapon young Jase had given him. It was beautiful. It was made of fine blue steel. Unlike the regular chain that Ryder had used hundreds of times on the farm to hitch carts to oxen, the links on this one were rectangular. In the middle of each was a thick, sharpened spike attached to the rest of the chain on a hinge. The point could swing one way or the other, supposedly depending on how the wielder swung it. Along the edge of each link there were tiny sigils—what looked like a pair of triangles with their tips attached and an extended **S** running through from the middle of the base of one to the base of the other.

The spikes were absent on each end and along a stretch in the middle of the chain. These spikeless links were a darker color than the others. It was hard to see in the gloom, but when Ryder grabbed hold of the end, he could feel that the darkened sections were wrapped in some sort of leather or hide. This wasn't just a chain; it was a masterly crafted weapon.

"That's more like it," said Ryder. He lifted his gaze to find the giants in the middle of the courtyard.

The pair of them had their backs to Ryder. They stood before the wall on the opposite side of the courtyard, bent forward, looking down at something. Though he couldn't see for sure, Ryder thought it looked as if they had someone cornered.

He gave his new chain a quick tug. "Time to give you a test run."

Charging across the open space, Ryder brought the chain around in a long loop, letting it pick up momentum. At a full run, he skipped twice and brought the flailing spiked chain over his head as he closed on the first undead giant.

The chain whistled as it whipped through the air, and it lit up with crackling purplish energy. Ryder brought it down on the giant's back, and it sizzled as it struck, discharging the built up energy into the undead creature. The beast's hide lit up with arcane energy, and the spiked chain tore a huge gash across its back.

The giant let out a tremendous roar, stomping its foot and shaking the ground. It spun around and slapped at the crackling energy that played across its body. As it did, Ryder could see Giselle and two of her Broken Spear warriors with their backs against the wall.

Giselle stood bravely before the other two warriors, holding them back with one arm and menacing the giant with her long sword.

Then Ryder heard Curtis's voice. "Excuse me."

Ryder felt something brush by him, and a string of footprints appeared in the dusty ground accompanied by the sound of running. The prints led right up to the cornered trio then they stopped.

Ryder heard Curtis's voice once more. "*Visi indisi vaso.*" And right before his eyes, Giselle and the Broken Spear warriors disappeared.

The giant looked down, then to both sides, obviously confused.

"Psst," whispered Curtis. His voice sounded as if it were coming from somewhere in the middle of the courtyard. "Ryder. Draw them away."

Ryder nodded, not knowing where Curtis was, but assuming the illusionist could see him.

Taking two large steps backward, Ryder twirled his spiked chain over his head. It lit up again, and when he brought it down on the ground the energy dissipated across the stones and through the dirt.

"Hey," he shouted. "Over here."

Both undead giants turned and took a step toward the master of chains. And Ryder in response took ten large steps back. As he hoped, the giants followed. Their legs were larger than his, and they covered more ground. Eventually, he was going to run out of room.

"All right," he said to himself, "now what?"

Nazeem lowered himself down and dropped from the end of the last stair. Turning around, he bumped right into the returning Broken Spear raiding party.

"Where do you think you're going?" said a tall, robed warrior.

Nazeem looked out over nearly three dozen Broken Spear.

"Fairhaven is under attack," he blurted, pointing back up the steps. "Giants. Undead giants. Giselle and the others are in terrible danger. We must hurry, there isn't much time."

The warrior nodded then looked back over his shoulder. "To Giselle," he shouted. In a single bound he leaped to the top of the first stair and turned around to offer Nazeem his hand. "Come, it's faster this way."

Nazeem looked once at the path that led away from the stairs to the Giant's Plain. Then he nodded and grabbed hold of the hand. The man pulled, and Nazeem climbed up the edge of the stair with ease.

The others followed suit, headed up the steep path toward Fairhaven.

❧ ❧ ❧ ❧ ❧

Ryder scrambled up the ladder that led up the steps to the top of the wall. The undead giants followed close behind him. They had an advantage. The steps in Fairhaven had been made for creatures of their size. For every four steps Ryder took, the giants took one, and they gained on him as he climbed.

At the top of the stairs he bolted down the walkway. He didn't know where he was going to go, only that he wanted to draw the creatures away from Giselle and the others. But now that he'd done that, he had no more plans, no more surprises or easy escapes.

On the flat ground, Ryder tried to put some room between him and his pursuers. But on top of the wall he quickly ran out of room. His path was blocked by a pile of rocks—debris from the top of the crenellations being smashed in. Ryder tried to climb up it and over to the other side, but as he put a foot on the pile, it shifted and tumbled into the courtyard far below, bouncing off a large dead tree and nearly taking him with it.

Jumping back to avoid falling off the edge, Ryder turned to face the oncoming giants. With his back against the wall, he had no choice but to try to fight them. And judging from his last encounter, this wasn't a fight he could win.

Whipping the enchanted spiked chain over his head, Ryder steeled himself for the fight. The giants closed the distance quickly and bore down on him.

"Forgive me, Samira," he said as he prepared to strike at an oncoming giant. "I did not mean to leave you like this."

The first giant hefted the bolder it had been carrying and hurled it at the cornered fighter. Ryder expected to have to deal with the creature's club, but not this, and his reaction to the flying stone was slow. He jumped to his right, away from the projectile and off into the thin air above the courtyard.

Behind him, the bolder connected with the defensive structures on top of the wall and shattered in a shower of sharp stones. In front of him, the darkness of the courtyard opened up, and the ground rushed toward him. Flailing as he fell, Ryder didn't think, he reacted. Flinging the chain out, it wrapped around the narrow trunk of the same dead tree the stones had bounced off.

Catching on itself, the chain pulled tight, and Ryder's arm was nearly yanked out of its socket as he held on for dear life. He swung out and around the tree, circling the trunk. It wasn't the most graceful move, but it saved his life, and Ryder thanked the gods that it had been a chain Jase had given him rather than a sword.

As he came to rest against the tree, Ryder grabbed hold of the trunk with his legs, dislodged the chain, and slid all the way to the ground. The moment his feet landed on the paving stones, he felt someone touch his shoulder, and he spun, prepared to fight another undead giant.

Instead he turned to see Nazeem smiling at him. "That was a pretty good trick," he said, pointing to the tree.

"Nazeem, you're alive."

The Chultan nodded. "I am a very hard man to kill," he said. He hitched his thumb over his shoulder. "Look what I found."

Through the gate came what looked like the rest of the Broken Spear.

They sprinted into the center of the courtyard, many of them with bows in hand. Dropping to one knee, they nocked arrows and let them fly at the top of the wall.

"Look out," Nazeem grabbed Ryder by the arm and yanked him away from the dead tree.

A heartbeat later, the first of the two remaining undead giants fell from above, landing atop the skinny tree and crushing it utterly. The second followed shortly thereafter.

With the immediate threats gone, Ryder slumped to the ground.

"I need a bath," he said.

Nazeem sniffed the air. "You aren't kidding."

CHAPTER 17

The Royal Herald of Erlkazar opened the double doors with a practiced flair. In the center of the throne room, he dropped to one knee, bending at the waist to perform an elaborate bow in the middle of the huge, woven Zakaharn rug. Standing again, he cleared his throat and looked up at the dais and the throne where King Korox of Erlkazar sat.

"My lord, King of all five baronies and the kingdom of Erlkazar," said the herald, "I present to you Master Montauk of Ahlarkham."

The double doors swung open again, and Montauk stepped into the throne room.

As he expected, it was an opulent affair. The circular room was broken into two discrete sections by a ring of pillars halfway between the wall and the center of the room. They created a reception area in the center and a long, curved walkway on the outside edge.

On the other side of the pillars was an open area. High above, on a huge ceiling dome, was an elaborate painted representation of the Black Days of Eleint. It depicted the secession of Elestam and the slaying of the counts and barons who conspired with the Duchy of Dusk to overthrown the Morkann family—a reminder of how Erlkazar came to be an independent country, separate and autonomous from Tethyr.

On the outside of the pillars were the king's dais and throne and more than two dozen heavily armed guardsmen. The pillars served to keep the soldiers hidden from the view of visiting dignitaries—present but unobtrusive was the king's policy. In addition to the bodyguards, the outer ring also held the king's personal art collection. Paintings and sculptures from all over Faerûn were displayed in recessed alcoves along the curved wall. King Korox's collection was thought to be one of the best and most valuable collections in all Faerûn. The king's favorite story to tell foreign monarchs was about several well-known historical texts in Cormyr. Each of them included descriptions of the destruction and loss of a particular statue of Ondeth Obarskyr that was now in the king's own possession. He would say even the sands of time couldn't detract from his collection.

Montauk admired the room as he strode through. Someday, he thought, the Twisted Rune would hold a meeting here. When the country fell to civil war, the capitol would be easy pickings.

He smiled and bowed as he approached the throne. "My lord."

The king sat atop his gilded throne, a goblet of wine in one hand and an ornate pearl-hilted dagger in the other. He regarded the bowed man with heavy eyes.

"Rise, my subject," said the king, lifting his goblet off his knee to take a drink of the blood-red wine inside.

Montauk got to his feet, placed his hands together, and bowed his head once more. "Thank you, my lord."

The king took a large breath, his chest heaving inside his golden breastplate. "You have petitioned my council for what you have called a grave and urgent matter regarding Ahlarkham."

"That is correct, my lord." Montauk kept his head slightly bowed, never making eye contact with the monarch.

"Well, out with it, man," said the king, leaning forward in his throne. "For I much desire to hear news from the realm of my sister, Princess Dijara."

"The people, my lord," replied Montauk, "the good farmers, merchants, and fishermen of Ahlarkham are up in arms."

This got the king's full attention. "Up in arms? Over what?"

"Over unnecessary taxation, my lord."

The king waved his hand. "Bah. Taxation is never popular, but it is a necessity. The people will grumble, but they will never revolt over it."

Montauk raised his eyes. "You don't think so?"

The king shook his head. "They know that without the baron and the taxes they pay to him they would not have the protection of his army. They would be forced to defend themselves against the dangers that run wild in the countryside." He waved the pearl-hilted dagger in his hand. "The trolls, goblins, and drow are far worse than any tax. The people know this."

"This is precisely my point," said Montauk. He took a step closer to the throne.

The king bristled a little at the move, but he allowed Montauk to stay where he was.

"The people know what it is they are supposed to get for their taxes," Montauk said. "But they aren't getting it."

"Baron Purdun employs a full-time army. He has some of the best soldiers and equipment in all of Erlkazar." King Korox turned sideways in his throne, shifting his weight onto his hip. "Besides, if he were having trouble keeping the peace he would have sent a message to me or one of the other barons." He took another sip of his wine. "I have heard of no such communications."

Montauk took another step forward. "My lord, the vampires have returned."

The king sat up straight. "The vampires?"

Montauk wrinkled his brow. "Yes, my lord. They have returned, and the people fear for their lives."

"Why have I not heard of this before?"

"Pride, my lord," said Montauk. "Perhaps Lord Purdun doesn't want his king to think he cannot handle this problem."

The king shook his head. "Purdun is not that sort of man. It's been only a handful of years since the old kingdom fell. He knows the stories. He was there—he was a Crusader, for gods' sake."

"True, true," said Montauk. "But things have been quiet in Erlkazar for some time. Despite the growing threat, Purdun feels he can deal with the situation without outside help. His reputation as a hero and as a Crusader makes him stubborn and proud. The people know this, and they grow tired of the baron's attempts to regain his former glory."

The king placed his goblet on the arm of his throne and scratched his chin. A servant immediately jumped up onto the dais, grabbed the wine, and disappeared. The king sat silently on his throne for several moments, then looked up at the painting in the dome above. He pointed to it.

"The Black Days of Eleint were a direct result of the barons failing to please the whims of the people." He shook his head. "Morkann failed to see how deeply the dissent of the people ran, and it nearly cost him his life." He slammed the hilt of his dagger down on the arm of his throne. "That was how Erlkazar came to be a country independent from Tethyr."

Montauk nodded his agreement. "This is why I bring this problem to you now, my lord, before it is too late."

The king looked down on Montauk from his dais. "Tell me more."

"Nightly the town of Duhlnarim comes under attack by the undead. The people have organized a rebellious group called the Crimson Awl. They work to install a real leader in Zerith Hold, one who will protect them and keep their families and farms safe from the vampires."

The king stood up from his throne, gripping his dagger tightly in one hand. "And I suppose you are that man."

Montauk bowed. "At your service, my lord."

"And what would you have me do with Baron Purdun?"

Montauk took another step forward.

The king put his hand up. "That will be quite far enough."

Montauk nodded. "My sincere pardon, my lord." He took a step back. "I would suggest you do to Lord Purdun what King Morkann did when faced with the same situation."

"Place him in irons?" The king scoffed. "You forget, Master Montauk, Baron Purdun is married to my sister. He is part of my own family."

"Yes, my lord, but the history books are full of stories about monarchs losing power because of the machinations of a greedy relative."

"Are you suggesting that Lord Purdun is after my throne?"

Montauk shook his head. "No, my lord. Only that to overlook the obvious simply because of family ties is a mistake made frequently by the dispossessed and the dead."

King Korox sat down on his throne, a look of deep contemplation on his face. He snapped his fingers. In an instant, a servant was at his side, placing a full goblet of wine in his empty hand.

"I will give this matter my utmost consideration, Master Montauk," said the king. "I thank you for bringing it to my attention."

Montauk bowed again. "Of course, my lord. I do what I can to serve my country and my king."

The king waved his hand, and with that, Montauk turned and exited the double doors, the concerned look on his face replaced with a wide smile.

Ryder sat in a ceilingless room—illuminated by starlight—high in the spiraling tower of Fairhaven. He let one leg dangle over the edge of a huge tub of hot water—an extravagance to say the least. The Broken Spear had boiled the water over the fire and carried it in buckets all the way up the stairs to this chamber. Giselle had ordered the water be drawn and had given Ryder the privilege of the first bath.

The tub itself was huge—easily as big as the public baths in Duhlnarim. When he was younger and had thought he could make a life somewhere off the farm, Ryder had taken a job in the nobles' quarter, cleaning up after the rich people. Scrubbing out the bath basins had been the last straw. The wealthy people of Duhlnarim were far filthier than even the pigs on the farm. He had decided, then and there, knee-deep in a dirty public bath, that he would far rather slop the filth of the animals than the filth of Duhlnarim's upper class.

His experience made him appreciate just how much work had gone into preparing the bath before him. Somehow, the absurdity of his location and the extra effort required to produce such a lavish thing made it feel that much better. He lowered himself fully into the water, closed his eyes, and took in a deep lungful of warm, humid air.

As the warm water relaxed his muscles, he let his

thoughts drift back to Samira. She had always loved baths. She would certainly enjoy this one. When he got back, the first thing he was going to do was take a long bath with her.

He imagined her with him in the giant tub. He though back on baths he had taken with her before. The memories were so vivid he could almost feel her skin on his.

A hand caressed his shoulder and ran up the side of his neck. The sensation sent a warm tingle down his spine. It had been so long since he'd been with a woman, even his fantasies felt real.

The hand massaged the sore muscles on the back of his neck, and Ryder let out a sigh.

"If only," he said.

"Are you enjoying this?"

Ryder's eyes shot open. He spun around in the water.

On the floor beside the huge basin sat Giselle. She was wearing only a woven shirt, loose at the neck, that stopped just at the top of her naked thighs.

"Uh . . ." Ryder said, trying not to linger on the smooth arch of her hip, "hi."

Giselle smiled and raised an eyebrow. "Hi." She stood up.

Ryder looked up. She was stunning. With his eyes he traced up her long, soft legs—from her bare feet crossed on the stone edge of the basin, all the way to the edge of her shirt. Above that, the loose neck of the garment was open to the middle of her chest, exposing the subtle curve of her breasts.

Her hair was tied into a knot behind her head, and as she reached up to untie it, the bottom of her shirt lifted up even higher. "Do you mind if I get in?" She let her long black hair fall down over her shoulders.

Ryder felt the same warm tingle run up his spine and spread out across his arms and chest. "Uh . . . uh . . ."

Giselle laughed. "I'll take that as a no." She lifted her shirt up over her head and let it fall to the floor. She dipped her foot into the warm bath, making little circles in the water with her big toe. Then she crouched at the edge of the gigantic basin and lowered herself in.

Fully submerged to her neck, Giselle splashed the warm water, circling around Ryder as she did. She kept her eyes locked on him the whole time.

"You showed courage out there," she said, slowly moving her arms back and forth under the water.

Ryder could feel her movements. The waves pressed up against his chest and moved the tiny hairs on his legs. It was as if her hands extended through the water, reaching out to caress his skin.

He looked away from her eyes. "I would say the same about you."

Giselle moved back into his field of view. "I'm glad you were with us." She moved closer, putting her hand on his arm.

Ryder looked down at where she was touching him. "You are?"

"Uh-huh." Giselle slid her fingers down his arm and took his hand. "Come here," she said, pulling him toward her and placing his hand on her hip.

Ryder felt the urge to pull away, but Giselle stepped in closer, pressing her chest to his. The hairs on the back of his neck stood on end, and he could feel his heart quicken.

She ran her hands along his back, pushing him against the edge of the tub. Leaning in, she pressed her lips against his. They were soft and warm, and they felt so good. He stood there, letting her kiss him, not knowing exactly what he should do.

She must have sensed his hesitancy because she pulled away.

She looked disappointed. "What is it?"

"It's just . . ." He looked into her eyes. In the flickering candlelight the dark brown appeared almost black. They were so deep. "I could get lost in those eyes."

Ryder reached around her hip and wrapped her up in his arms, pulling her back to him and plunging into a deep kiss. Giselle pressed herself against him, seeming to almost melt in the warm water into his skin.

She placed her head on his shoulder. "What are you thinking?" she asked.

"I'm thinking," replied Ryder looking once again into her eyes, "that I am a weak, weak man."

Then, grabbing her with one arm, he lifted the two of them out of the tub and gently pushed Giselle down on top of the warm stone. Starting at her lips, he kissed her skin, following down the arch of her neck.

Giselle closed her eyes and leaned her head back, moaning softly.

"A weak, weak man," repeated Ryder, as he continued across her belly.

CHAPTER 18

Liam looked down at himself. There were leaves and splinters of wood sticking out of his armor at odd angles. He shook himself and scanned the ground for his sword. It was nowhere to be found.

The elf vampire stepped up beside Liam, dropping Knoblauch on the ground. The veteran groaned and shifted, but he was obviously in worse shape than Liam.

"I think I'll start with you," she said to Liam. "I prefer fresher, younger blood."

Dropping to her knees, the vampire straddled his chest and leaned down close to his neck. Under different circumstances, a woman pressing herself against his chest might have been nice. As it was, he struggled to get free.

"Hold still," hissed the vampire into his ear,

"and this will only hurt a little."

Liam could hear a pop as the vampire opened her jaw. His hands probed the ground, searching frantically for the hilt of his sword. As the warm, damp air from the elf's breath hit his neck, Liam's fingers closed around something. It wasn't his blade, but he'd use anything he could get.

Lifting his makeshift weapon in the air, Liam jammed it down as if stabbing himself in the stomach. Whatever he had grabbed impaled the vampire in the back, and she let out an otherworldly howl.

The creature spun away and off of Liam, flailing around on the ground as if she were a stuck pig.

Liam struggled to his feet, ready to beat the undead elf to a second death with his fists if necessary. But as he got up he saw what it was he had stabbed the vampire with—a shattered tree branch. Its tip plunged deep into the creature's back, right between the shoulder blades. Liam realized his luck and, as the creature squirmed, he jumped on her, slamming his boot into the makeshift wooden spike and pushing it through the elf's chest.

The vampire hissed one last time then slumped to the ground motionless.

Liam took a deep breath. His hands were shaking, and his brain was buzzing with adrenaline.

"I told you," he shouted at the finally dead vampire, "nobody bites me."

Knoblauch groaned and pushed himself up onto an elbow. Having partially regained his composure, Liam went to the veteran's side.

"You showed her," said the older soldier.

"That was a nasty spill you took," said Liam, grabbing Knoblauch's arm and helping him to his feet.

The veteran drew air in through his teeth, obviously in pain. "Not the most graceful way to get off a horse."

The bushes rustled, and Liam stepped in front of

Knoblauch, putting himself between the veteran and whatever it was that was coming after them.

"If you two lovers are done," said Captain Beetlestone stepping into view, his armor and face smeared with splotches of blood, "then I suggest you help us cut the heads off of those we felled, so we can get out of here before those that got away come back with friends."

Liam never thought he would be so glad to see the inside of Zerith Hold. He wearily tromped down the long stone hall that wound through the keep from the stable to the barracks on the other side. His body ached from the fighting, and the thought of his own room and a private bed was delicious.

Traversing the entire length of Zerith Hold, he finally crossed the threshold into the barracks. Voices wafted down the hall, and as Liam got closer, he could hear the conversation from around the corner.

"No, I'm telling you, he was great," said the first voice.

"Come on," argued another. "Everyone knows the Awl aren't anything more than a bunch of angry thugs. He's never even had any training."

"Hey, I don't know, but I saw him out on the parade grounds," said a third. "He looked pretty good to me." The man laughed. "I'll tell you what. I'm glad he's on our side now."

"So's Knoblauch," said the first voice. "Liam saved his life."

Liam came around the corner to see a group of four elite guardsmen leaning on their doorframes, talking. He hadn't seen many of them without their helmets on, but he did recognize a man with a goatee—the only one beside himself who still wore his armor.

"There he is," said the man, "the hero of the day."

Liam looked at the other three men then back to the speaker. "You're in my unit."

The man with the goatee nodded. "I sure am." He put his hand out. "The name's Claudius." He glanced at the other three men. "These men are in Captain Phinneous's unit, so they're completely unimportant."

The three guardsmen grumbled, one chuckling at the jibe.

He shook the man's hand. "Liam." And nodded to the others.

Claudius's face broke out into a huge grin. "Well, well, Liam. More than three months in the unit and finally you're one of us." He stood up from the wall and grabbed Liam by the shoulder. "Come on, friend. There is beer to be drunk and songs about your bravery to be sung." He turned Liam around and ushered him back down the hall.

Liam partially resisted. "But I still have my armor on."

"Me too, lad. Me too." Claudius slapped him on the back. "Believe me, it's safer that way."

The other men fell into step behind Liam and Claudius, and they marched together to a pair of plain wooden doors at the end of the hall.

Two of Phinneous's men stepped in front of Liam and pushed the doors open. Before them was a large room, filled with wooden tables, flagons of ale, and a whole mess of drunken guardsmen.

Still carrying his helm under one arm, Liam stepped through the door, and a cry went up.

"Three cheers for Liam."

The room exploded in noise.

"Huzzah! Huzzah! Huzzah!"

The next moment, Liam was surrounded by other soldiers slapping him on the shoulders and back (and even a time or two on the rear). Someone grabbed his helm, but before he could reach for it someone else replaced it with a large stone flagon.

Claudius appeared at his side. "Drink up," he said, lifting a flagon himself. "All of this is for you."

"For me?" Someone pushed the bottom of Liam's flagon toward him. Faced with the choice of drinking the golden liquid or letting it slop wastefully to the floor, Liam chose to take a huge quaff.

It was both sweet and bitter at the same time. Liam recognized it immediately. "Honey mead," he said, taking a breath followed by another drink. He looked at Claudius, a big smile on his face. "My favorite."

Claudius lifted his flagon, clinking it against Liam's. "I knew I liked you, lad." He took a drink. "Yes sir, I knew I liked you."

The mead flowed all night. Songs were sung and stories were told. Soldiers climbed on the tables and did little dances. As the night drew on, the crowd of drunken soldiers got rowdier and rowdier, and from time to time, chunks of bread and even an empty flagon or two flew through the air.

All the while, the accounting of the fight with the undead and of Liam's bravery grew larger. Pretty soon there was an army of vampires, each standing as tall as the highest tower of Zerith Hold. And Liam cut them down two at a time.

Liam's head spun. He wobbled unsteadily, a smile plastered to his face. This wasn't such a bad thing. These men liked him. They threw parties in his honor.

He raised the flagon to his lips again. He smiled even wider.

They had an endless supply of honey mead. What more could a man ask for?

He spotted Knoblauch in the corner seated against the wall, a sling over his arm. Liam wandered over and sat down next to him.

"How you feeling?" he said as he plopped down.

Knoblauch laughed. "Not as good as you, I'm afraid."

Liam lifted his flagon. "I'll drink to that."

Knoblauch lifted his empty hand and nodded his head.

"What? Don't you like honey mead?" asked Liam.

The veteran shook his head. "I like it plenty," he said. "It's the torment I endure the morning after that I don't like so much."

"Ah," said Liam, pointing his finger at Knoblauch, "but no one said you had to have too much." He brought his thumb and forefinger almost together, leaving only a pebble's space between them. "Only a little." Liam squinted for emphasis.

"Thank you Liam. I've already had my fill," said the veteran.

"Already?"

Knoblauch shrugged. "I'm an old man now, Liam. That stuff hits me a little harder than it used to." He leaned forward and grabbed hold of an empty flagon on the table, turning it over and letting the last few drops of mead drip out. "When I was a young man like you, I could drink all day and all night and never feel the wrath of the mead." He righted the flagon and put it back down on the table. "But then I got old, and the stuff caught up with me." He shook his head then laughed. "It's just not worth the pain anymore."

Liam sighed. "Suit yourself." He took another swig.

Knoblauch pointed across the room. "Look who came to your party."

Liam followed the veteran's finger. Beside the door, looking on with a rather disapproving frown, stood Captain Phinneous.

"Bah," said Liam, "what does he want?"

Knoblauch leaned back against the wall. "I don't know. That one's a real manure bag—always steaming and never pleasant to be around."

Liam nearly blew mead out of his nose. "You should—" He coughed, spitting a little errant mead onto the table— "You should warn me when you're going to do that."

"That wouldn't be any fun, now would it?" Knoblauch placed his hands behind his head.

"Yes. Yes it would," said Liam, putting his flagon down and wiping splattered mead off his face.

The room went silent, and Knoblauch jumped to his feet. "Purdun's here."

Liam coughed once, trying to clear his throat. Then he got to his feet and stood beside the veteran just as the baron approached their table.

Knoblauch bowed. "My lord."

Liam watched the veteran out of the corner of his eye and scowled. He didn't know how he felt about the bowing thing. Not that long ago he hadn't felt the need to show Lord Purdun any respect or even acknowledge his authority.

Now though, something had changed. He kind of liked being part of the elite guard. That gave him something to lose, something that could be taken from him.

Liam bowed as well. "Lord Purdun."

"Please, gentlemen, no need for ceremony here," said the baron, lifting a full flagon of mead from the table and taking a large swig. "I've only come to tell you how relieved I am that you made it back safely."

"Thank you, sir," said Knoblauch. "It's really only because of Liam that I made it back today at all."

Purdun nodded, looking directly at Liam. "So I have heard. So I have heard."

Liam was a little uncomfortable. He'd saved the lives of many men before. It was an almost daily occurrence in the Awl. But he'd never received so much attention for it. He stood silently, not knowing what to say, trying to avoid eye contact with the baron.

"Well," said Purdun after a long awkward moment of silence, "I don't want to derail everyone's well-deserved fun." He turned to the room. "Please, everyone, carry on."

A few of the men started to drink their mead, but for the most part the room stayed quiet. Only Captain

Phinneous, lurking near the door, seemed to be enjoying himself.

The baron turned back to Liam and Knoblauch. "Liam, may I have a word with you in private?" he asked in a hushed voice.

Liam looked to Knoblauch. The veteran soldier nodded his head and gave Liam a little shove.

"Uh, all right," said Liam.

"Excellent," replied Lord Purdun, then he headed across the room and out the double doors.

Liam put his mead down on the table and did his best to look sober as he followed the baron out of the room.

Once they were outside, Liam could hear the soldiers begin to laugh and talk again. Purdun walked on in silence, waiting until he was halfway down the hall before speaking again.

"You've done well, Liam," he said, slowing his pace.

"Thank you."

"Far better than I ever imagined."

Liam shrugged. "Guess you underestimated me," he said.

Purdun smiled. "Indeed. And that is precisely what I wanted to talk to you about." Purdun stopped only a few steps from the door to Liam's room.

Liam stood at attention, his hands behind his back.

"I think your talents aren't being fully used," continued the baron. "I want to offer you a promotion."

Liam's head swam. "A promotion? What . . . what exactly does that mean?"

Purdun put his hand on Liam's shoulder. "It means that with the undead incursions into Ahlarkham on the rise, the threat to my personal safety has increased as well. I'm going to be adding more men to my personal bodyguard, and I want you to be one of them."

Liam shook his head, trying to clear the fuzzy haze of mead covering the inside of his skull. This was happening so fast. It wasn't that long ago that he was fighting against this man, and now Liam was being offered a job as his personal bodyguard. Was this really happening?

"I ... I don't know what to say," he said. It was one thing to take refuge in the elite guard, but protecting the life of the man he had worked so long to kill ...

Liam shook his head. "I ... don't think—"

Purdun put up his hands, interrupting Liam. "Wait," said the baron, reaching over and grabbing hold of the door to Liam's private room. "I have a surprise for you." Tugging it open, Purdun waved his arm as if he were a herald presenting a visiting dignitary.

"Listen," said Liam, gathering his will to turn down the offer. "I—"

A slippered foot appeared first, followed by the rest of a beautiful woman. Out of his room stepped Samira, and Liam's jaw dropped.

She looked like an angel descending into Zerith Hold. She wore a flowing white silk gown with ornate lace sleeves that flared at her hands, hiding them from view. Her long black hair had been lifted into an exquisite pile on top of her head, adorned with wildflowers and a handful of tiny sparkling jewels. She seemed to float as she moved, the smooth fabric of the gown trailing behind her.

Looking at her made Liam feel warm all over.

"Hello, Liam," she said.

"Uh." Liam did a once-over of his own appearance. He was still wearing most of his armor and was covered in tiny bits of leaves and wood. "Hi," he said.

Liam looked into Samira's eyes. She smiled, and the rest of the world seemed to disappear.

"I don't want to keep you two any longer than I have to," interrupted Purdun.

Liam tried to break eye contact with Samira, but he simply couldn't. She was entrancing, and he was helpless.

"Liam," continued Purdun, "don't give me your answer

now. But let me leave you with this one thought. The position I am offering you would come with a considerable raise in pay. Enough to, say, keep a lovely young woman in the custom she deserves."

Liam and Samira continued to stare into each other's eyes.

Lord Purdun bowed to the two of them. "I take my leave." Then he turned and hurried down the hall.

Samira reached up and pulled out one of the torn leaves stuck in Liam's armor. "What happened to you?"

Liam looked down at himself again. "Got in a fight," he said.

"I heard," she said. "Baron Purdun told me you saved a man's life."

Liam nodded. "I guess I did."

The two of them stood in the doorway for a moment longer, looking at each other. Then Samira grabbed his hand.

"Come on. Let's get that dirty armor off you."

Liam followed her inside his room and closed the door behind him.

CHAPTER 19

Ryder lay on the warm stone floor, Giselle's head on his chest, his fingers dangling in the quickly cooling water, staring at the stars.

The muscles in his back that had relaxed from the warm water and Giselle's caresses were once again knotted and tense. His head hurt, and it took tremendous effort to simply lie still. He laughed at the absurdity. This was a fantasy come true—he was on top of a tower inside a splendid palace with a beautiful, exotic woman lounging naked beside him. Things like this didn't happen to people like Ryder. They happened to the rich and powerful, not the poor farmer or the revolutionary. Yet, he couldn't enjoy it.

The moment they had finished, Ryder was struck right smack in the middle of his chest with a tremendous wave of guilt.

Samira.

How could he have done that to her? She would never forgive him, and he wouldn't blame her. She would never do something like that to him. Had he been killed, she would have likely spent the rest of her life celibate, grieving over him.

But not him. He had always thought of himself as a good man. But right now, he didn't feel like one.

Giselle stirred, stretching her arms and turning to look up at Ryder.

"Hi," she said, smiling.

He looked at her but couldn't keep eye contact. "Hi," he said, trying to put a smile on his face.

Giselle rolled over and got to her knees, then climbed up to straddle Ryder, looking down into his face.

"That was nice," she said.

"Uh-huh," he said, looking off over the tub.

Giselle grabbed his chin and forced him to look at her. She was frowning. "What's wrong?"

Ryder shook his head.

Giselle shook hers as well. "No. I mean it. What's wrong?"

Ryder took a deep breath and let it out. He was nervous about how she would react to the truth, but if he didn't tell her ... well, he didn't know what would happen, but he was sure it wouldn't be good.

"I ... I don't know what to say," he said. He sat silently for a moment, trying to build up the courage to say what he needed to say. Finally he blurted, "Giselle, I'm a married man."

"Well," she said, leaning back a bit but not getting off his chest, "that doesn't seem like you don't know what to say."

Ryder looked up at her. Instead of being angry, as he had expected she would be, she smiled and touched the edge of his face.

"You're feeling guilty," she said, not a question, just a matter-of-fact statement.

Ryder swallowed. "Yes."

"That's understandable." She paused. "Thank you."

"For what?"

"For your honesty," she said. Then she leaned down and kissed him. "And for not turning me down."

Ryder blushed. He'd never been in this situation before, but he felt tremendous relief. Much of his guilt was simply concern over what this attractive woman would think of him when she found out the truth.

"Listen, this life is very short," she said. "I learned a long time ago that every moment I waste regretting something I did or didn't do is another moment I don't spend actually living my life."

"Spoken like a true farmer," said Ryder.

"What is that supposed to mean?" Giselle frowned.

"Just that before you can truly move forward, you have to be willing to live with the consequences."

Giselle looked puzzled. "And what does that mean?"

"It's something an old farmer in Furrowsrich used to say. To him it was a bit of wisdom about how and where to plow a piece of land into a new field. I've always thought it had a larger meaning."

"All right, philosopher. How?"

Ryder lifted himself up onto his elbows. "Living your life is a scary proposition. The more you gain, the more you have to lose. The more you have to lose, the harder it becomes to live with the consequences. But that shouldn't stop you from living the life you think you should live." He looked into Giselle's beautiful brown eyes. Then he touched her face. "You and I aren't that different."

Giselle leaned into his touch. "No?"

Ryder shook his head. "No."

There was a long silence with both of them just gazing at each other.

After a long while, Giselle broke the silence. "So, this

wife of yours must be the reason you've been so eager to leave Fairhaven."

A sudden chill ran down Ryder's spine. "You're not going to have me locked up again, are you?" He didn't struggle or try to get away. Whatever she wanted to do to him, he was going to let it happen.

Giselle laughed. "Oh," she said, "what a good idea. I could keep you here as my personal love slave." She smiled then lay down on him, pressing her breasts against his chest. "Then you couldn't feel guilty. It wouldn't be your choice."

"Would I have to live in that dirty, rusted cage? I don't think I would like that very much."

Giselle shook her head. "No. You could stay up here. Of course, I'd have to make you work for your keep."

"I have one question." He sat up and, in one fluid motion, turned to his side, lifting Giselle off the ground and into the air as he got to his feet. Holding her in his arms, he stepped forward until her back was pressed against the stone wall. "Would this work—" He interrupted himself by kissing Giselle— "require any heavy lifting?"

Giselle's face was flushed. Ryder could feel her heart pounding through her chest as he pressed his skin against hers. "I think it might," she said.

Ryder nodded, kissing her neck. "Just checking."

Inside the closed, private room, Samira helped Liam unbuckle his armor, placing it piece by piece back on the rack in the corner. Underneath, his long woven shirt was stained in places with blotches of blood and sweat.

"Oh, Liam," said Samira, taking off his ruined undershirt to reveal several recently scabbed wounds and a pair of massive bruises on his shoulder and chest. She cringed as she ran the tips of her fingers over the blackened skin. "Do they hurt?"

All Liam could feel was the soft caress of her fingers. He shook his head. "No."

Going to the chest of drawers, Samira retrieved a wet cloth from the washbasin. "Lie down on the bed," she said.

Liam did as he was told. As he lay down on the soft linen, he realized how exhausted he was.

Samira stood with her back to him now, dipping the cloth in the washbasin. The back of her gown came down low, exposing everything from her shoulder blades to the small of her back.

She wrung out the cloth and came back, smiling when she saw that his eyes were open. Sitting down beside him, she ran the cool cloth over his wounds. Liam closed his eyes and followed her motions over his body.

"So what are you going to do about Purdun's offer?" asked Samira after a short silence.

Liam shrugged. "I just can't help thinking that Purdun might be right."

"Right about what?" asked Samira.

Liam sat up a little. "When I talked to him the first time, he told me that the Crimson Awl were being manipulated by an outside source. He said that we were being used to a greater end."

"Used? By whom?"

A bolt of realization struck Liam. "By a vampire."

"A vampire?" Samira laughed, running the cloth down his arm. "The vampires haven't been seen in Erlkazar for years. The Crusaders dealt with them during the revolution."

"We fought vampires today."

Samira dropped the cloth, gripping Liam's hand.

"There's something else too, something that has been bothering me."

She gave his hand a squeeze. "What?"

"Do you remember when Montauk and his thugs came by the field to take me to talk to the Council?"

"Yes," she said. "I was so worried about you."

"They took me to the old druid's circle. But when I got there, there was a group of strangers there. Most of them were wearing cloaks. I couldn't see their faces, but I'm pretty sure I had never seen them before."

Samira frowned. "But I thought you knew everyone in the Awl."

Liam nodded. "Me too. I mean, I do. And that's what bothers me." He shook his head, remembering back to that day. "When Purdun's troops arrived, things got pretty crazy. Still, I could see the strangers leaving the druid's circle." His eyes met Samira's. "As they walked away, I could have sworn several of them transformed into wolves."

"Wolves?"

Liam nodded. "I know it sounds strange, but ... I saw it. With my own eyes."

Samira ran her hand along his arm. "But what does it mean?"

Liam took a deep breath. "I think it means Purdun was right. Someone has infiltrated the Awl and is manipulating the Council."

"What are you going to do?"

"I don't know," said Liam. He turned away from her for a moment, then turned back. "What do you think?"

Samira smiled at him. "Well, I don't think you need to solve all of Ahlarkham's problems tonight." She reached up and pulled out the sticks holding her hair in a pile atop her head, letting it fall down over her shoulders. Several of the flowers and tiny gemstones toppled out onto the floor.

Then she stood up and slipped the gown off her shoulders, letting it slide to the floor as well. Samira stood before Liam. The candle on the chest of drawers behind her lit Samira's naked body in a soft orange-yellow outline.

Liam admired the exquisite woman before him, a warm sensation spreading up his spine. It had been a long time. He had always wanted this, but Samira was his brother's wife.

Samira knelt on the edge of the bed and leaned over him.

Liam placed his calloused hand along the side of her face. He felt like such a brute, his rough, broken hide alongside Samira's smooth, soft skin. He pulled the hand away, but she reached out and pulled it back, placing it again where it had been.

Liam looked away, but Samira grabbed his chin and turned him to face her.

"Ryder is gone," said Samira. "Nothing either of us can do will bring him back."

"I know that," replied Liam.

"It's time we started living our lives for ourselves," she said.

"But . . ."

Samira moved his hand down her shoulder and across her chest.

"But nothing, Liam," she said. She leaned down and kissed him.

The aches and pains in his battered body were instantly replaced with a feeling of euphoria.

"I've seen how you've looked at me, Liam," said Samira, pulling away slightly. "I've secretly looked at you too."

Whatever worries Liam had in the world were swept away by those few words. He wrapped his arms around her, pulling her down on top of him and squeezing her to him.

"I've always loved you," he said, somehow now not afraid to tell her about the feelings he had been holding back for so many years.

"I know," she said as she moved her hand along the side of his body and down his leg. "I know."

Ryder stood beside the giant basin, slipping his shirt back over his head.

Giselle was also getting dressed. She watched Ryder as he put his clothes back on. "If you didn't have a wife back in Duhlnarim, would you stay here?"

Ryder took a deep breath and shook his head. "There are other things in Duhlnarim that I must attend to."

"What is so important in that backwater village of yours? The farm?"

"No," said Ryder. "I have unfinished business with the Baron Purdun," he said.

"The man who put you in chains?"

Ryder nodded. "The man who holds all of Duhlnarim in chains."

"So you wish to return to get your revenge?" asked Giselle.

"No," said Ryder. "I return to free the people from the tyranny of a cruel and evil man."

A sad smile came across Giselle's face. "Well, Ryder of Duhlnarim, I can't let you leave the Broken Spear."

"But—"

She cut his objection off short. "So I guess the Broken Spear will have to go with you."

She turned and headed out of the tower. "Get a good night's sleep. We'll leave in the morning."

CHAPTER 20

The baron's personal herald burst into the sitting room, obviously upset. Lord Purdun looked up from the map he was studying.

"My lord," blurted the herald, not waiting to be acknowledged by the baron—an obvious breach of courtly etiquette, "there are men here looking for you."

Lord Purdun stood up, calmly adjusting his shirt and pantaloons. "There is no need to be so excited, Master Beverly," said the baron. "As you are aware, there are visitors to Zerith Hold every day."

The herald continued to barge into the room, coming right up to the baron, causing Liam to step in front of the lord. The half-giant guards came out of their corners as well, but Purdun raised his hand, and everyone stopped in their place.

"My lord," continued the frantic herald, "these men are from Klarsamryn. These are the King's Magistrates." Master Beverly swallowed. "They are here to put you in chains."

"What?" shouted Purdun. Then he quickly composed himself. "Well, good. Finally we will be able to communicate directly with Llorbauth."

He smiled and nodded as he looked at Liam, but the baron's newest bodyguard thought he could see significant worry in the man's eyes.

"Master Beverly, show the King's Magistrates in, won't you?"

The herald looked from the baron to Liam, then back to the baron. "But, my lord, they are here to imprison you. You must flee."

Purdun placed his hands behind his back, and nodded. "I thank you for your concern, Master Beverly, but I assure you there is no reason to be alarmed. Now please, let them in."

The herald was slow in backing up. He grabbed the baron's hand and kissed it several times. "It has been a pleasure to serve you, my lord." Then he turned around and, taking a look back, hesitantly walked out of the room.

When the herald was gone, the half-giant guards returned to their spots in the corners of the room.

The baron took a deep breath. "Liam," he said, "stay close. I don't know what all of this is about, but I do not intend to be taken from Zerith Hold in chains."

The grim possibilities of what might happen in the next few moments gripped Liam. He nodded, touching the hilt of his enchanted long sword, just to remind himself that it was there, waiting for him if need be.

The two men stood in silence for what seemed a very long time. Liam could feel his heart beat in his chest. He didn't know what was going to happen. The uncertainty unnerved him. He'd rather know he was about to fight an entire tribe of goblins with only a rolling pin and a rock than face the unknowable next few moments.

When the herald finally knocked on the door, the sound startled Liam, sending a shot of adrenaline through his veins.

"My most excellent Lord Purdun, Baron of Ahlarkham, Ruler of Duhlnarim, and purveyor of all that can be seen from the Deepwash to the borders of Tanistan . . ."

Liam had heard the herald present visitors to Lord Purdun before, but never had he been so elaborate or long-winded.

"I present to you King Korox's Magistrates," finished Master Beverly.

Through the door came six highly polished soldiers. Each of them wore a helm and heavy plate mail, painted white, with the red entwined twin-wyvern crest of King Korox on their chests.

Typically, as Liam had learned not only as a guard but also as an invited guest, visitors to the baron's private sitting room were not allowed to carry weapons. The King's Magistrates were an exception to this rule. They were the strong right arm of Llorbauth, the policing force for the entire kingdom of Erlkazar. The Magistrates could be judge, jury, and executioner. They were the enforcers of the kingdom's laws, and they answered to the king alone.

From what Liam understood, there were almost as many Magistrates as there were soldiers in the King's army. The fact that Korox had sent only six to talk to Purdun meant either that he didn't expect any trouble, or that these were extremely dangerous men.

"Welcome to Zerith Hold," said Lord Purdun. "To what do I owe the pleasure of having six of the King's Magistrates in my personal chambers?"

A man on the end stepped forward and doffed his helm. He was a rugged-looking man with a jet black goatee and long black hair pulled back in a ponytail.

"Lord Purdun, I am Magistrate Olivio." He put his helm under his arm and bowed. "We are here under order of the king to take you back to Llorbauth."

Baron Purdun stood up straight. "And may I ask why the king would need to send the Magistrates to collect me?"

"The king has heard that the good people of Ahlarkham are up in arms. He has sent us to collect you so that he may avoid another Elestam," explained the Magistrate.

"Another Elestam? The king is worried that the people hate me so much that they will revolt and eventually secede from the country?"

Olivio nodded. "Yes. That is what the king would like to avoid."

"That's preposterous," said Purdun. "The king should know that the situation in Ahlarkham is nothing like it was in Elestam."

"I beg the baron's pardon," argued the Magistrate, "but the king understands that the vampires have returned."

This gave Purdun pause. "Yes," he said after a moment, "we have seen vampires recently, but—" He placed his hand on Liam's shoulder—"my men have them and the local rabble under control."

Magistrate Olivio bowed again. "While I'm sure your men are quite capable of taking care of any threat that plagues your barony," he looked Liam up and down, "that does not change the fact that the king wants us to bring you to him." The Magistrate took a step forward. "So you can come with us peacefully, or we can use other means."

Purdun shook his head. "This must be part of her plan."

"Excuse me?" said the Magistrate.

"Nothing." Lord Purdun shook him off. "With all due respect, Magistrate, you don't understand. If you remove me from the barony, then there will be no one here to lead the fight against the vampires. If the king is truly worried about the reappearance of the undead causing a major peasant uprising and a secession of the barony from Erlkazar, then surely he wants me here to direct the effort to fight them off."

"Your logic is impeccable, my lord," said Olivio, a twinge of impatience entering his voice, "but I'm afraid I have my orders."

Purdun walked back and forth across the floor, shaking his head. The tension in the room grew as the man pondered the situation.

Stay calm, Liam, he said to himself. Wait for the baron's orders. The conflict was nearly unbearable.

Finally Purdun stopped his pacing, and he turned on Magistrate Olivio. "You go back to Llorbauth and tell my brother-in-law that instead of sending his Magistrates, he should be sending his army to help me defend my barony against an outside threat."

Magistrate Olivio visibly bristled. "I'm afraid I can't do that." Placing his helm back on his head, he said, "This is your last chance to come peacefully. If you refuse, we will have no choice but to use force."

All six Magistrates drew their swords at the same time, filling the room with the high-pitched ring of steel sliding against steel.

In a flash, the four half-giant guards were standing in a circle around Purdun. Just as fast, Liam had his weapon in hand.

"You're making a huge mistake," said the baron. He waved his hands before him, and the air began to crackle with arcane energy.

"No," said Olivio, "it is you who is making the mistake."

Montauk breezed down the staircase leading deep into Shyressa's tomb. The thick dust that had covered the stone steps was no longer present—it had been carried away by the feet of vampire spawn over the past few months.

At the bottom, he stepped through the archway and into the vampire's den. The sarcophagi that had dominated the room were gone, replaced with row upon row of kneeling spawn, their heads bowed in supplication to the glorious vision before them. On the dais in the middle of the room stood Shyressa. She was glamoured in her favorite image—one of a striking young woman with long dark hair and porcelain skin.

Shyressa stood before the kneeling throng, her hands raised in the air. Between them, over her head, floated a large box. Beams of pale white energy radiated out from the box, reaching out to touch each and every one of the kneeling vampire spawn.

Carved in the middle of the box were the twin entwined figures—the twisted runes—that Montauk had come to adore since his induction into the secretive organization. The man stood looking on, enjoying the sight before him. So many unsuspecting people worked for the Twisted Rune. Only a few had the privilege of knowing what sort of work they were doing. Many died for the cause never understanding their larger purpose in the puzzle. Not Montauk. He had been kept in the know from the very beginning. Shyressa was good to him, and he felt he had served her well.

It had all been worth it, of course. He was now the head of the Crimson Awl. Soon he would be the baron of Ahlarkham. He smiled. Some time after that he may even be King of Erlkazar. And after that, Shyressa had promised to help him achieve immortality. The thought brought a smile to his lips.

It was glorious to be a part of something so powerful.

The box Shyressa held over her head stopped glowing,

and she lowered it. The vampire spawn kneeling on the floor began to stir, and the Rune Mistress lowered her eyes to the human waiting in the archway.

"Montauk," she said, her voice sounding sleepy and lethargic. "Come to me, my pet." She waved for him to approach her on the dais.

The vampire spawn hissed as they parted before Montauk. The floor cleared quickly, allowing the human passage through the crowded room. Approaching the dais, he climbed up the steps and knelt before his mistress.

She offered him her hand, and he kissed the back of it. Though it appeared to be the soft, supple skin of a beautiful young woman, against his lips it felt like cold, lifeless flesh.

"What news, Montauk?" asked Shyressa, pulling back her hand.

"Everything goes as planned," said the human, getting up from his knees. "Lord Purdun has backed himself into a corner, and the king's enforcers are in Duhlnarim as we speak."

Montauk rubbed his hands together, excited at the proposition of his plans all falling into place. "The King's Magistrates will put Purdun in chains and take control of Zerith Hold. They'll see for themselves how your vampires attack the peasants, and the king will have no choice but to side with the Crimson Awl. Wanting to avoid the same fate as Elestam, which he himself helped to topple, Korox will lock Purdun away for good and institute me as the Baron of Ahlarkham."

"The pieces are in motion. Soon the entire country of Erlkazar will be ours to command," purred the vampire. "You've done well."

Montauk swelled inside. "Thank you, mistress."

Shyressa opened her arms. "Come to me, Montauk. Let me embrace you."

Montauk paused. "Embrace me?" A chill wind blew

through the chamber, and Montauk pulled his cloak tighter.

The vampire smiled. "Is it not the custom of humans to embrace when they are pleased?"

"Well . . ." said Montauk hesitantly. This didn't feel right. "Yes. It is."

"Then come to me. Let me embrace you. For I am pleased." Shyressa spread her arms wider.

Montauk took a step back, but he slammed into something that stopped him from moving. Looking over his shoulder, he could see the worshipful vampire spawn closing down on the dais. They hissed at him, blocking his path to the archway.

A cold sweat beaded on his forehead. "What's . . . What's this all about?"

Without moving her feet, Shyressa, her arms still out wide, slipped across the dais toward Montauk. "Will you not indulge your mistress?"

Montauk felt ill. His knees went weak under him and Shyressa's shadow loomed over his head. "But . . . but who will replace Lord Purdun?"

Shyressa wrapped her arms around Montauk. The glamour that covered her faded, revealing her long sharp fangs and the pressed, withered skin of her advanced age. She opened her mouth wide and bit down on the shivering human's neck.

Montauk sobbed. "But . . . I don't understand."

Shyressa took a long slurp of Montauk's fresh, live blood. Then she released him. Taking a step back, a shimmering glow encased her entire body. The air around her frame began to waver and shake, and the vampire Rune Mistress transformed into the perfect replica of a human male.

Montauk, holding the wound in his throat, looked up in horror at an exact copy of his own face.

Shyressa cleared her throat. "I won't be having any further need for you, Montauk," she said, her voice the same pitch and tenor as Montauk's own. "I shall be assuming the duties of the barony myself."

The vampire placed her foot on the real, kneeling Montauk and kicked him backward off the dais into the waiting hands of her vampires.

"Please, mistress, no," shouted Montauk as the spawn tore at his flesh. "I've served you well."

"Yes, Montauk," agreed the glamoured vampire. "Until the very end."

$\mathbf{I}$ ask you this one last time, Magistrate," said Lord Purdun, his hands beginning to glow with a blue-white light, "return to Llorbauth with my request for the king's aid in defeating the vampires."

Magistrate Olivio pulled a glass flask from a small pouch on his hip. It had a yellowish liquid in it. "Your request has been denied." He hurled the flask at the floor near the baron's feet.

In a flash, one of the half-giants reached out and snatched it from the air with its meaty palm. The vial never hit the floor, but it shattered against the guardian's skin, sending up a vaporous gas.

Another of the half-giants grabbed Purdun around the waist and pulled him back two large steps. The remaining two followed, stepping in front of the baron, forming a wall of flesh between the Magistrates and Lord Purdun.

The yellow gas wafted into the air, surrounding the guardian who had intercepted it. The half-giant let out a choking cough, then slumped to the floor.

In the next instant, all nine hells broke loose inside Zerith Hold.

The King's Magistrates rushed forward as a line.

Liam felt his stomach knot, then the rest of the world dropped away. He could hear his blood pump though his ears as he charged the closest Magistrate. He shouted like he had never shouted before as he brought his blade down. The enchanted metal cleaved through the soldier's gauntlet and his flesh and bone beneath, taking off the Magistrate's hand at the wrist. The severed appendage fell to the ground still gripping the hilt of his long sword.

The man wailed as blood pumped from his ruined arm, and he clamped down on the wound with his other hand, trying to stop the flow. Liam slapped the helmet off the man's head and brought the hilt of his sword down on his skull with a heavy thud. The Magistrate slumped to the floor beside the half-giant. His blood pooled beside them.

"Take the human first," shouted Olivio, and the other five Magistrates changed direction, surrounding Liam in a ring.

They closed in, cutting down Liam's ability to move or dodge their attacks. Then they struck. Their blades flashed in at him, all moving in unison.

Liam caught the first one, parrying it harmlessly to one side. His armor deflected another. But he didn't have enough room or speed to get to the other three, and each of them struck home. He was speared through the ribs and hip on his left side. The third blade slashed a deep cut along his right forearm.

The pain momentarily froze Liam in place. It seemed his whole body exploded with sensory overload. At first he couldn't tell where each of the wounds was. The searing pain jumped out, taking hold of every inch of him. It was a thumping wave that spread out farther and farther until finally it dragged him under.

He stood there unable to move for what seemed an unbearably long time. Then the pain receded, and the world came back. The fight before him took shape, and Liam regained control of his body. He held his left arm close to his ribs. Anything other than having it pressed tightly against his side brought complete agony. He glared at the Magistrates as they readied themselves for another attack. They were like separate parts of the same machine. They moved together, struck together, and for all Liam knew, they thought together.

Liam had on several occasions taken more than one soldier at a time—but not soldiers like these. One Magistrate was easily worth three elite guardsmen. And as Liam sized up the group around him, he started to feel the futility of his situation.

He might die here.

In that moment, Liam could see Samira's face. He finally had her, and he might lose her again. Anger rose inside Liam. These men were here to take away from him the one thing he had longed for, the one thing he had been unable to have until now. They ceased to be authority figures. They were no longer the king's messengers. They were here to destroy all that Liam held dear, and he wasn't going to allow that.

The pain in his ribs and hip was flushed out by a burning hatred for the Magistrates, and Liam saw red. He struck back, raising his sword to eye level and spinning in a quick circle. His blade struck each of the soldiers in turn. Two of them managed to defend themselves against the sudden, whirlwind attack, bring their blades up fast enough to make Liam's glance away. But despite their good steel and quick reactions, they couldn't deter his furious swing.

He scored direct hits on each of the other three Magistrates, cutting one across the neck and catching the other two across their shoulders. The move was so sudden and unexpected that the circle of Magistrates surrounding Liam grew wider. Each of the soldiers took a step back, giving Liam more room to move. He had taken away one of their advantages, and the odds didn't seem so hopeless.

Liam watched the Magistrates regroup. The fact that he was still alive at this point seemed to perplex them. They were obviously not used to drawn-out fights.

Out of nowhere, four spiraling magical blue-white orbs crashed into Magistrate Olivio, and he was thrown farther back, taking two steps before he regained his footing. Two more of the King's Magistrates sprang into the air. Behind them, Liam could see two of Purdun's half-giant guardians. They lifted the Magistrates off the ground and over their heads. With a heavy grunt—the only sound Liam had ever heard any of them make—both threw their captives at Magistrate Olivio.

The three heavily armored men crashed into a heap on the ground, clanging and banging as they tumbled around on the floor. Liam couldn't be certain, but he could have sworn he heard bones breaking mixed in with the rest of the cacophony.

A third half-giant guardian appeared in the hole left by the tossed Magistrates. It reached into the middle of the fray, grabbing Liam with a single hand. It seemed every time he was in this room he was being lifted off his feet by one of Lord Purdun's bodyguards. This time, however, he didn't really mind.

The half-giant took a step away and put Liam down near a bookshelf on the edge of the room. Though the creature had likely saved his life, the ride was less than comfortable. The wounds in Liam's side and hip flared again as he was set down. Liam wasn't able to keep his feet, and he crumpled into a ball as he came to the floor.

He cringed against the pain. He'd never been hurt so badly in his entire life.

Prying his eyes open, Liam forced himself to look out at the melee in the middle of Lord Purdun's sitting room. Only two Magistrates remained on their feet. Each now stood face to face with one of Purdun's half-giant guards. Olivio and the other two conscious Magistrates were disentangling themselves from each other on the opposite side of the room. Behind it all stood Lord Purdun, his hands alight with a fiery orange-yellow glow.

"Magistrate Olivio," shouted the baron, "I'll give you another chance," he said, lifting his hands over his head, a magical flame flickering between them. "Leave here now with your lives. Don't force me to kill you."

Just then the double doors blew open, and in charged Captain Beetlestone and the rest of Liam's old unit. The room filled with elite guardsmen, and they surrounded the Magistrates. Lord Purdun's troops outnumbered Olivio and his men more than five to one.

Magistrate Olivio dropped his long sword and rose to his feet. "All right, Lord Purdun," he said. "We will do as you ask."

The other Magistrates lowered their blades.

Purdun lowered his hands, letting the magical energies he held dissipate harmlessly into the air.

"Captain Beetlestone, please escort these men out of Zerith Hold. You can return their weapons when they are safely outside."

"Yes, my lord," said Beetlestone. He and his men collected the Magistrates' swords and began shuffling them out of the room.

As he left, Magistrate Olivio turned over his shoulder to look at the baron. "I hope for your sake that you are right about this."

"That makes two of us," said Purdun.

An army of servants ran around the baron's sitting room, repairing tables and uprighting chairs. Liam lay on a long, richly appointed couch. Lord Purdun's personal healer hovered over him, poking at the wounds in his side.

Every time the pudgy, robed man pressed on a wound, Liam drew breath in through his teeth.

Lord Purdun paced along the wall, deep in thought.

The healer poked Liam one last time, then pressed both his hands against his side. Closing his eyes, the cleric whispered some words to himself. Divine energy flowed through the healer's hand, and Liam let out a huge sigh. The pain in his side slipped away, and Liam was filled with relief.

Getting up off the couch, Liam lifted his arm. There was no pain. And where there had been weeping wounds in his hip, ribs, and forearm, there were now just tiny, pink scars.

"Thank you," he said.

The healer bowed, then turned and waddled his portly girth over to the half-giant who had succumbed to the strange yellow liquid. Shortly after the fight had ended, the guardian had awoken, getting back to his feet without a single word and returning to his place in the corner.

The healer examined him as Lord Purdun looked on.

After a moment the cleric shrugged. "He appears to be in fine shape. It was probably nothing more than an alchemical sleeping draught." The portly man turned to the baron. "If I had to guess, I would say it's a common tool of the Magistrates. Much easier to subdue criminals if they are dead asleep."

Purdun grunted his understanding then turned and walked over to Liam.

"You all right?" he asked.

Liam nodded. "I think so."

"Good." He looked Liam in the eye and he cracked a smile. "You know, I've never seen a man take on six

Magistrates by himself before." He started to laugh. "Either that was the bravest thing I've ever witnessed—or the stupidest. I'm not sure which."

Liam performed a shallow bow. "At your service."

Purdun smiled and slapped Liam on the arm.

"My lord," said Liam. "Do you think the king will do as you've asked? Even after we sent his Magistrates home in such poor shape?"

"Well," said the baron, pondering for a long moment. "I don't honestly know. I probably wouldn't believe me. This whole story is starting to sound too unimaginable." Purdun shrugged. "But no matter what, we're under a lot more pressure now. Shyressa has put her plan in motion. The appearance of the vampires just before a visit from the King's Magistrates is no coincidence. We must be vigilant. If we are not, it will likely cost all of us our lives."

CHAPTER 22

The Royal Herald of Erlkazar pushed open the double doors to King Korox's throne room. When he reached the middle of the round woven Zakharan rug that dominated the center of the room, he bowed as he had thousands of times before.

"My lord, King of all five baronies and the Kingdom of Erlkazar," said the herald, "I present to you Magistrate Olivio."

King Korox lowered his goblet of wine to the table beside his throne and sat up straight. Olivio had returned early. This matter was going to require a smooth and diplomatic hand. His sister was going to be none too happy with him for having apprehended her husband.

Korox grunted. Purdun was going to be none too happy with him for apprehending him. But they were old friends. They had been in the Crusaders together. Surely he would indulge his king and close friend.

Through the door Magistrate Olivio entered. He walked across the round room, bowing in the center of the rug as was customary, then continued to approach the throne. Officers in the King's Magistrates were the only soldiers in the kingdom allowed to approach the throne without first being given permission. It was they who were charged with keeping the laws of the land. It was their steel that kept the king safe from assassins and power-hungry nobles from other lands. If he couldn't trust them, who could he trust?

As Olivio came near, King Korox noticed that the man's face was battered and bruised. He also appeared to be walking with a slight limp.

The king stood up. "What happened to you? Were you ambushed? Where's Purdun?"

Magistrate Olivio shook his head. "No, my lord, we were not ambushed. We were bested by Lord Purdun and his guardsmen. The baron did not accompany us back. He is holed up inside Zerith Hold."

"What!" shouted the king. He was fuming. "He disobeyed a direct order from my Magistrates?"

Olivio nodded. "Yes, my lord. He did."

"Did he deny the accusations?"

Magistrate Olivio shook his head. "No, my lord. Baron Purdun acknowledged that the vampires had indeed returned, and that they were causing problems in Ahlarkham. He further acknowledged that there was a group of revolutionaries stirring up the locals."

"And he still refused to be escorted to Llorbauth?"

"Yes, my lord. He said that if your highness was indeed worried about the reappearance of the undead causing a peasant uprising then you should be sending troops to aid him, not to bring him in."

King Korox scratched his chin. "I see. Did he say anything else?"

"Yes, my lord. He said that taking him out of Ahlarkham was an attempt by the vampires to get him out of the way so that Ahlarkham would be leaderless during an all-out assault."

"What is your opinion of all this, Olivio?"

The Magistrate thought for a moment. "My lord, his story is far-fetched."

"Yes it is. But Purdun is not the type to exaggerate or to make things up."

"That is my opinion of Baron Purdun as well, my lord," replied the Magistrate.

King Korox turned around and lifted his still-full goblet of wine off the table. Lifting it to his lips, he downed the entire thing in one large gulp. Wiping his face with the sleeve of his robes he turned back to Olivio.

"All right. Prepare the rest of the Magistrates," he ordered. "And bring me my armor. We march to Ahlarkham."

❧ ❧ ❧ ❧ ❧

The trip back to Duhlnarim was long. The Broken Spear was in the habit of traveling discreetly, which suited Ryder's purposes. He was close to returning. The journey had begun. He had waited this long; he could wait a few days longer.

Giselle led the group through land that Ryder never would have guessed was passable. They must have traversed every possible hidden route and passage between the Giant's Plain and the Deepwash. Twice, while traveling past the borders of Impresk—and once again in the foothills outside of Carrelath—they effortlessly bypassed armed patrols of King Korox's soldiers without causing so much as a raised eyebrow. The soldiers of the Broken Spear were ghosts passing through the mortal realm, visiting but not leaving a trace.

As they crossed over from the hills of Carrelath and into the familiar borders of Ahlarkham, Ryder felt a tremendous joy fill him. Soon he would be embracing his mother. Soon he would be seeing his younger brother.

And soon he would gaze once again upon Samira.

The thought of his wife brought with it as much sadness as it did joy. He had missed her so. But he didn't know what he was going to tell her about Giselle. He didn't know how she would react. She might not want him back if he told her the truth, but he couldn't think of resuming his life with her without being honest.

Then there was Giselle. She was even more of an unknown. How would she react to seeing Ryder with Samira? Ryder didn't know which he feared more, having to fight Lord Purdun's elite guard or having to face the two women in his life.

"Now that you are home again," said Nazeem, interrupting Ryder's introspection somewhere in Tanistan, north of Five Spears Hold, "what will you do first? Kiss your beautiful wife?" The Chultan raised his eyebrows.

Ryder shook his head, glad for the intrusion. "I have unfinished business with Baron Purdun."

"You will go risk your life for your cause before you will go tell your family you are alive?"

"Believe me, if I could, I'd go to them straight away," said Ryder, "but then I would have to leave them again." Ryder could see that Nazeem didn't understand, so he continued. "If Purdun found out I had returned, there would be a huge price on my head. Every bounty hunter and guardsman in the barony would be after me." He shook his head. "Until the baron is dead, I will never be at peace. Besides, the fewer people who know I have returned, the easier it will be."

"The easier what will be?" asked Nazeem.

Ryder smiled. "Sneaking into Zerith Hold and killing Lord Purdun."

Nazeem craned his neck to look back at the men and women of the Broken Spear. "How do you intend to sneak all of us into the baron's stronghold?"

"I don't," said Ryder. "I'm going in by myself."

Nazeem lowered his voice to a whisper. "Then why did you bring the Broken Spear with you?"

"To get me back out."

Giselle stepped up next to Ryder, interrupting the conversation. "The sun is going down. It will be dark soon. We should be thinking about making camp."

Ryder nodded. "We need to be within a half-day's walk from Zerith Hold," he said. "I want to be within striking distance for tomorrow night."

"What does that mean?" asked Giselle.

"We should march on until dark and sleep into the day," said Ryder. "We'll need to be rested for a night raid." He rubbed his hands together. "Purdun has strangled the good people of Ahlarkham for too long. His reign of tyranny ends tomorrow night."

Nazeem stared up at the stars in the clear night sky. But he wasn't really looking at them. He was listening.

The Broken Spear had marched on until it had grown very late. They had made camp a morning's walk away from Zerith Hold. All the plans were laid and all the preparations were done. All that was left was to go through with them.

That, thought Nazeem, and collect the bounty for Ryder of Duhlnarim.

It was the deepest part of the night. Everyone around him was asleep, except for two Broken Spear sentries. But it had been a long, tiring haul from Fairhaven to Duhlnarim over the past two tendays. They were exhausted and nearly asleep themselves.

Quietly slipping out from under his blanket, Nazeem

rolled away from the others who slept near him. Then, as quietly as he could, he placed his hands on the ground and lifted himself up enough to get his feet under him in a crouch. In the shadows on the edge of the Broken Spear camp, Nazeem watched the sentries.

When he was sure they hadn't heard him, he backed farther into the darkness and stood up. It would be a long night for him. Ryder had said the trip to Zerith Hold would take them from sunrise to mid-morning walking. It was already very late at night, and he was going to have to make a round trip before dawn.

Nazeem began to jog. He had always been a good runner, especially when he was properly motivated. If his life or a large pile of gold was on the line, Nazeem could run forever.

The night wore on. Nazeem stopped only a handful of times to drink some water and rest. Eventually, he came upon a main road. He could hear in the distance the lapping waters of the Deepwash. And in front of them, in what remained of the pale moonlight, he could just make out the silhouette of Zerith Hold.

He would go around behind, to where they had taken him out of the Hold in chains several months ago. There would be soldiers there—men who would likely pay well for the information Nazeem had.

Staying in the shadows, Nazeem made his way to the other side of Zerith Hold. As he had suspected, there was a buzz of activity. He crouched in the low bushes along the side of the well-kept gravel road. Guardsmen on horses were coming and going through the heavily guarded entrance. And as he watched, a pair of riders came down the road toward him.

Now for the hard part. Nazeem took a deep breath and stepped out into the middle of the gravel, his hands in the air.

The guardsmen immediately pulled up and pulled their swords.

"Who goes there?"

"My name is not important," said Nazeem. "What is important is the information I have and just how much you are willing to pay for it."

❀ ❀ ❀ ❀ ❀

"Why should I believe you?" asked Captain Phinneous.

"Can you afford not to?" replied Nazeem.

The two riders he had approached on the road had taken him back to Zerith Hold. Nazeem sat at a wooden table, a flagon of water before him and a half-dozen armed guards around him.

The bald captain scratched his face, looking skeptically at the tattooed Chultan.

Nazeem took another drink of his water, then placed the mug back down on the table. "What have you got to lose?" he asked. "If I'm lying, you're out a few coins. But if I'm not—" he raised a long, skinny finger in the air— "and you disregard what I have said, then you will be blamed for any ill that happens here."

Captain Phinneous put his boot on the low bench beside Nazeem. "And what if I don't pay you and throw you in the dungeon instead?"

Nazeem shrugged. "When they wake up and I am gone, they will know something has happened and will likely change their plans," explained the Chultan. He looked up, staring into the bald captain's eyes. "You will be blamed for letting Ryder of Duhlnarim get away when you had him in your grasp."

The two men stared at each other for a long while without blinking. Then a grin broke out over Phinneous's scarred face. He took his boot off the stool, unhitched a sack from his belt, and tossed it on the table beside Nazeem.

"If what you have said is true," said the big captain, "there will be more—much more."

Captain Phinneous turned and walked out of the room. "Now get out of here, Chultan. Come find me after Ryder is dead."

Captain Beetlestone barged into Lord Purdun's sitting room, a pile of notes in his arms.

Liam stood behind Lord Purdun, who sat looking over a series of maps of Ahlarkham with his two military advisors. The baron looked up when the captain entered and waved him over to the table.

"What do you have for me?" asked Purdun, dispensing with the pleasantries.

Beetlestone nodded his head in place of a formal bow and got to the point. "We have word in from three scouting parties and have reason to believe that the undead will be making a move on Zerith Hold within the next day or two. There are also reports that the Crimson Awl are active and could be a factor."

Purdun nodded, looking back down at his maps, tracing his fingers along the shore of the Deepwash. "Anything else?"

"My lord," Beetlestone's face grew grim, "the King's Magistrates are on the march."

Purdun looked up from the map, his finger slipping from its place.

Beetlestone swallowed then continued. "The king himself leads them."

"How long?" asked the lord, his voice thin and quiet.

"They are within a day's march, my lord."

Purdun sat back in his chair and steepled his fingers. "How did it come to this?"

There was silence in the room for several heartbeats. Liam didn't know what to make of it all. Had things gone differently for him, he might have been overjoyed that Zerith Hold was about to be the center point of one of the largest battles in the history of Erlkazar. But things hadn't gone differently for him, and despite his earlier convictions, he believed Lord Purdun to be a good man. He didn't deserve all this. He didn't deserve the reputation that had been created for him.

Captain Beetlestone cleared his throat. "Lord Purdun," he started. "Things are going to get … chaotic in the next day. It is entirely possible that my men won't be available to come to your aid if one of these groups manages to breach Zerith Hold."

"What are you suggesting?" asked Purdun.

"I think it would be wise if you were to start wearing your armor inside the Hold."

Purdun nodded.

"And I would like to assign to you another bodyguard," Beetlestone looked up at Liam. "Someone to watch Liam's back the next time he decides to take on six Magistrates by himself."

Liam thought he detected a hint of a smile on the captain's face.

"Who did you have in mind?" asked the baron.

"Guardsman Knoblauch, sir," said Beetlestone.

Lord Purdun nodded, obviously weighing the suggestion in his mind. "You know my reservations," he said finally.

Beetlestone nodded. "Yes, but he is the best man I have. And if I may be frank—" He stopped, looking to the baron for approval.

Purdun nodded. "Of course."

"If Knoblauch had been accompanied by a second man, one to watch his back as I am suggesting for Liam, then the unfortunate events of several years ago may never have happened."

Purdun took a deep breath and rubbed his hand over his face. "All right, Beetlestone. Send him up." He turned to look at Liam. "We can use all the help we can get."

CHAPTER 23

Ryder woke late in the day. The sun was high in the sky, and the soldiers of the Broken Spear were quietly preparing themselves. All of the plans had been laid out the previous night. They all knew what they were supposed to do.

Ryder too knew what he had to do. He had to end this thing. He had to take the head from the serpent before it could strike at him. Once he had killed Purdun, he would locate Liam and the rest of the Crimson Awl. With the baron dead, they would have a real shot at taking Zerith Hold.

Tonight would be the spark that ignited the fire. It would be the break the Awl had always waited for.

He looked out over the men and women around him. With the addition of the Broken Spear, the

Awl would be twice as strong. His gaze searched the group and fell upon Giselle.

She was a fine leader. It would be nice to have someone to fall back on. The Awl had always lacked strong leaders. He hoped that Liam had risen to his expectations and been able to keep the momentum in his absence. He would soon find out.

Then there was Nazeem. The Chultan sat calmly on the edge of camp, his legs crossed, his eyes closed, meditating. Ryder wasn't sure where this man would fit into the overall plans. But somehow he knew that Nazeem would play a vital role. The tattooed man always seemed to be in the right place at the right time. He had a knack for showing up when he could do the most good. Ryder smiled to himself. He supposed those were skills one had to hone if one wanted to become a successful criminal. However he had come by them, Nazeem's ability to seemingly appear and disappear at will would be useful tools moving forward.

Giselle touched Ryder's arm. "Are you ready?"

He nodded. "You?"

Giselle smiled. "We will be waiting for your signal," she said. "You just stay alive long enough for us to have something to do. I would hate to have come all this way for nothing."

"I would hate that too," he replied.

Giselle placed her hand on his chest, her eyes lingering on his for a long moment. Then she reached up and gave him a kiss.

Ryder felt a wave of sadness fill him. "Giselle—"

"For luck," she said. Then she pushed him away. "Now take Curtis and go. We will see you before sunrise."

Ryder placed a hand to his lips, the soft wetness of her kiss still lingering. Then he turned and walked away.

"All right, listen up," said Captain Phinneous. He had his entire unit assembled in the common room of the barracks inside Zerith Hold. "I have volunteered all of you for late-night guard duty tonight."

This brought a few moans and groans from the men.

Under other circumstances, Phinneous might have been angry. But not today. Today he was going to get a little revenge. Nothing could spoil his good mood.

"All right, quiet down," he said. "I know none of you like that too much, but I have a little surprise for you."

The men quieted down.

"I have word that Ryder of Duhlnarim has found his way back to Ahlarkham."

"I thought he'd been shipped off to Westgate," shouted a soldier.

"Aye, lad," said Captain Phinneous. "Somehow the bastard has earned his freedom, and he's come back to finish what he started."

Phinneous looked at each of the men, making sure his words sank in. "I have it on good authority that he's going to try to infiltrate Zerith Hold tonight."

"Ah," shouted the same guard. "And we're going to be there to catch him." He slapped the guard next to him on the arm in celebration. "We'll all be heroes."

The men let out a huzzah!

Captain Phinneous shook his head. "No, lads," he said. "I've got an even better idea." The men grew quiet again as Phinneous leaned in, talking just above a whisper. "We're gonna let the man in and let him get all the way to the baron's sitting room."

"Why would we do that?"

Captain Phinneous smiled a huge bucktoothed grin. "Because, boys, we'll have a surprise waiting for our guest when he arrives. Stay sharp tonight. I've got hunch we'll be in for a spectacular show."

It was the darkest part of the night. The moon had yet to rise over the Deepwash as Ryder and Curtis inched their way closer to Zerith Hold.

There were only two ways into the fortress. The most accessible was the same way Ryder had been taken out—through the stables and barracks in the back where all of Purdun's elite guardsmen lived and slept. Even with Curtis's illusions, Ryder doubted there was much of a chance of his making it in through there undetected.

The other way was through the front gate. Though it, too, was heavily watched, there were far fewer guardsmen around and not nearly as much traffic. The back of the Hold was where all the real business—the comings and goings of merchants and soldiers—took place. The front was more for diplomatic purposes, and it didn't see as much use.

That night, Ryder was going to be a visiting foreign dignitary—an uninvited ambassador from Fairhaven.

Though the portcullis and double doors that blocked entry to Zerith Hold were down and closed, the drawbridge had not been raised. A person so inclined could walk right up to the front door of Zerith Hold and knock on the heavy wood. That wouldn't be the way Ryder chose to enter.

The huge chains that lifted the bridge back up against the doors of the Hold hung slack from the top of the wall. They attached to the wooden drawbridge by two large cast-iron hooks that were forged directly into the bridge. The links of the chain rose into the air, sagging as they climbed toward the top of the wall and through two large holes in the stone. Ryder had never seen the other side of the door, but he assumed the rest of the chains were connected to a wheel or a pulley, some mechanism that allowed a handful of guardsmen to open and close the drawbridge as the need arose.

Ryder watched the guards on top of the wall. From what he could tell, there were only a handful of them up there. They were paired off, and they marched from one end of the wall on a strict rotation. In the time it took Ryder to count to three hundred, one patrol had covered the entire length of the wall and had moved out of sight.

As they patrolled, the guards hardly even turned their attention away from their conversations. Only once did Ryder see a soldier actually look out off the wall through the crenellations. They really weren't paying any attention to the ground in front of the Hold, seemingly convinced that the doors, the portcullis, and their presence would make anyone wanting to get in think twice.

They were wrong.

"Are you ready?" asked Ryder.

Curtis nodded. "Yes. I think so."

Ryder frowned at the illusionist. "What do you mean, 'I think so?' "

Curtis shrugged. "I mean I think I'm ready. I won't really know if I'm ready until I actually try to be ready. Judging from every other experience I have, all signs point to me being ready." He held a finger in the air. "But you never know. I provide no assurances."

Ryder shook his head. "Get on with it."

"Right," said Curtis, and he began to cast a spell. Waving his hands over Ryder's head, the illusionist spoke two quiet words then snapped his fingers.

Ryder looked down at his hands. All he could see was the dirt and stones on the ground below. His body was completely invisible.

"Guess I was ready," said Curtis.

"Good work," said Ryder. "Now head back and meet up with the others. You know what to do, don't you?"

Curtis nodded. "I think so."

Ryder sighed. "Well, I guess that will have to do."

"All right," said Curtis, and without another word he turned and walked back toward where the Broken Spear would be waiting for Ryder's signal.

Ryder watched the wall. When the first guards came into sight, he started counting. When the same guards had moved out of view, he crept closer to the drawbridge. Darting under the huge links, he jumped, grabbed hold of the massive chain, and clung to its underside. Then he waited, finishing the count he started when the guards had moved out of sight. From where he was, he couldn't see the patrolling guardsmen. He smiled. Even if he could, they certainly couldn't see him.

Hanging there, upside down, Ryder counted. When he reached three hundred he began to climb. Hand over hand, he pulled himself up the chain. He moved cautiously, not wanting to rattle the links or to call any attention to himself. He was invisible, but not silent.

The going was slow, but soon he was close to the top. The chain entered the wall just below the bottom of the crenellations. As he got close, Ryder could hear the guards conversing.

"Do you think there is any truth to the rumors that the Crimson Awl are planning a raid on Zerith Hold?" asked one man.

Ryder stopped climbing to listen.

"No," said another. "Haven't heard much out of them for awhile."

Ryder smiled. By morning, they will have heard something out of the Awl.

He continued to climb until he got to the edge of the stone. The voices of the two guards grew softer as they moved on. When Ryder could no longer hear them, he hoisted himself up on top of the chain and through the hole in the wall.

Slipping inside, Ryder let himself down onto the darkened floor. As he had suspected, the chains ran through the wall and down into a torchlit courtyard beyond. About a man's height above ground level there was a raised platform that ran the entire circumference of the courtyard. In the middle of the platform, the iron links of the chains connected to a circular contraption that was covered with gears and had a large crank attached to one side.

Though the chain was the way Ryder had intended to enter the Hold, the platform below was not empty. Archers patrolled along the edge, looking down toward the wooden doors and iron portcullis, ready to pincushion anyone who set foot inside. If he climbed down the chain, he'd likely be heard.

Guess I underestimated this entrance, thought Ryder.

Though it was a clear night, a slight breeze blew through the openings in the wall. Turning away from the courtyard, Ryder scanned the space around him. Up here, where the chains ran through the stone, there was a narrow room. Only a small amount of light came in through the slits from the courtyard below, but it was enough for Ryder to see a ladder leading through the floor.

Better than taking the chain, he thought.

Placing his foot on the top rung, Ryder lowered himself one foot at a time into the shaft.

The ladder ended maybe fifty rungs below and left off hanging in midair above a stone floor. Ryder stopped on the second to last rung, keeping himself entirely concealed inside the shaft. Below he could see only a small square of the stone floor, lit by a sickly orange-yellow glow. From the ladder he couldn't tell what, or who, might be down there.

Closing his eyes, Ryder tried to listen. The wind coming in through the passage above him whistled lightly as it came through the rungs, making it impossible for him to hear anything.

Knowing that he didn't have any other choice, Ryder let go of the ladder and dropped into the passage below, grabbing the end of his enchanted chain as he came down in a crouch on the flagstones.

"Who goes there? Show yourself—"

Ryder's falling from the ceiling had startled an unarmed man wearing an apron. He was holding a large wheel of cheese in both arms. He cast his gaze back and forth in Ryder's general direction, but it was clear the man didn't see him.

Creeping quietly to his left, Ryder pulled his chain off his hip. The scared servant paced sideways, turning his head this way and that trying to follow the sounds.

"Show yourself," the man shouted again.

It was dark in the passage. The walls were lined with wooden shelves stacked high with mold-covered cheese and big slabs of salted beef.

Stepping behind the confused servant, Ryder flipped his wrist, flinging the end of his chain. The links of the enchanted weapon wrapped around the man's legs, and Ryder yanked it back just as he turned visible again.

The apron-wearing man yowled in surprise and tumbled flat onto his chest, the wheel of cheese breaking his fall.

Ryder took a step forward, and with the slack in the chain he hurled the handle of the weapon at the man's head. The enchanted links slammed into the downed servant's skull, knocking him out cold.

"Sorry about that," said Ryder, frowning. He looked down at the growing red lump on the man's head. "Nothing a little rest won't fix."

Unhitching his chain from the man's leg, Ryder scanned the hallway. Lit by two small torches, the stone passage led off in both directions. This was likely a service corridor, used by servants to travel across the Hold without getting in the way of the guards.

Ryder listened down both ways, hoping that no one heard the yelp the man had let out. Then, convinced as he could be that he hadn't abandoned his stealth, he turned to his left, grabbed a torch from a sconce in the wall, and set off down the hall.

The passage led down and around the corner. There were no windows or doors, only long, narrow brick walls lined with foodstuffs and old pots. Ryder traveled on for some time, encountering no one on his way.

Eventually he came to a set of wooden stairs, leading down into a wider, well-lit hallway. From up above, it looked like the floor was covered in a fancy, woven rug.

He'd found his way in.

Extinguishing the torch, Ryder quietly made his way down the stairs. This hallway was much larger than the one he'd just come from. The walls were covered with oil-painting portraits of preposterously dressed men and women. Each one was illuminated by a softly glowing mage-lit stone that cast a warm glow over the rather stark, uninterested faces of those in the pictures.

On his left, a wooden rail guarded the edge of the floor that dropped off into darkness below. Ryder moved over to look three flights down into what appeared to be an entry hall. There were empty suits of armor, artwork, and statues all over the place. Above him there were two more floors.

Turning away from the edge, Ryder quietly made his way down the deserted hall and around the corner to a set of stairs leading up to the next level.

"If I were a baron, I'd live on the top floor," he said, and he headed up.

CHAPTER 24

At the top of the final flight of stairs, Ryder encountered a set of double doors. The dark wood was polished to a high shine, and the ornate brass doorknobs sparkled dimly in the low magelight. A pair of halberd-toting guards stood at attention beside them, one on each side.

It had taken him the better part of the night to sneak through Zerith Hold to this point. Other than one oblivious random patrol, there had been no sign of guards on any of the doors. Whatever was behind that door was more important than anything in the other rooms. Ryder was betting it was the baron.

Gripping the end of his chain, Ryder readied himself, then charged out of the shadows. The spikes of his chain lit up as he brought it down around one of the surprised guards' hands.

Pulling the chain tight, Ryder ripped the halberd from the soldier's grip and sent it clattering down the stairs.

The guard's eyes went wide, and he started fishing around on his belt for his sword. The other guard managed to get his halberd pointed at Ryder, but that was all. The spiked chain slammed into the soldier's face, discharging its electrical fire and sending a tremendous jolt through the man's body. Before the man could recover, Ryder was on him again. He pulled the guard's legs out from under him and smashed the other end of the chain into his chest. The soldier's body jumped from the impact. He let out a muffled cry and slumped back.

Ryder turned his attention back to the disarmed guard. He was visibly frightened, trying to get his blade out of its sheath but having a hard time because his hands were shaking.

"Intruder!" shouted the man, his voice wobbling.

The end of Ryder's spiked chain clocked the man in the head and wrapped itself around his neck. With a quick flick of Ryder's wrist, the guard was pulled from his feet and sent tumbling down the stairs.

With stealth no longer an option, Ryder grabbed hold of the knob and shoved his shoulder against the door. It opened, and the master of chains stepped though to the other side.

Even lit as dimly as it was, Ryder could tell right away that he'd come to the right place. The room was opulently decorated. Bookshelves lined the walls, and the center of the room was dominated by little clusters of chairs, couches, and tables. It looked like the kind of place a baron would count his money and plot how he was going to get more.

On the far side were a series of medium windows that looked out on the harbor and the Deepwash. In the low light, Ryder could just make out two figures standing beside a closed door on the other side of the room—more guards. They already had their swords drawn, no doubt alerted by the shouting outside.

Ryder swung his chain at his side. It glowed purple and blue, painting everything in the room the color of bruised flesh.

The guards split up, swinging around to try to flank Ryder.

"Drop your weapon and stay still, or we will use deadly force," said one of the men.

"I wish I could give you the same option," said Ryder, "but in the name of the Crimson Awl, your lives are forfeit." Taking two steps, he lunged at the guard closest to him, extending his crackling chain to its full length and reaching over a couch to strike at the man's helmet.

The guard's blade intercepted the chain, batting it harmlessly to one side. "Dear Ilmater," said the man. "Ryder. Is that you?"

The low mage stones in the room flared, banishing the shadows and bringing the guards into stark view.

Ryder felt the pit of his stomach drop to the floor. "Liam."

◉ ◉ ◉ ◉ ◉

Liam stared across the room at his dead brother. "I watched you die," he said, not lowering his sword. "You're dead. I saw it with my own eyes."

"Liam, what are you doing here? Are you lying in wait for Purdun?" He pointed at Knoblauch. "Is this man also with the Awl?"

Liam took a deep breath. "Not exactly." Behind Ryder he could see Knoblauch still creeping around to flank his brother. "What . . . ? How . . . ?" He didn't even know what questions to ask.

Images flashed through his head. The day of the ambush. His meetings with Purdun. The events that had lead him to the moment where he stood on guard against his own brother.

"Liam," said Ryder, keeping one eye on Knoblauch, "I'm here to assassinate Purdun. Help me get in, and let's get out of here."

Knoblauch launched himself over a chair at Ryder's back. But the master of chains was fast. Dodging the oncoming blade, Ryder brought his chain up in time to catch the guardsman on the back of his leg, tearing several of the metal plates out of his splint mail and sending the veteran sprawling against the couch.

"Stop!" shouted Liam. "Just stop, everyone." He needed a moment to get everything clear in his head.

Ryder took a step back, his eyes darting back and forth between Knoblauch and Liam. "What's going on here?" he glared at his brother. "Liam! It's me, Ryder. Your brother."

"This is your brother?" said Knoblauch as he got to his feet.

Liam nodded, holding his hand up to stay Knoblauch while he got everything straight in his head. He couldn't believe what he was seeing. "Yes."

"Liam, we don't have much time. There will be guardsmen here any moment."

Liam lowered his sword. "There are guardsmen here already."

Ryder looked at Knoblauch. "But there are two of us. Surely we can take this one."

Liam shook his head. "I'm also in Purdun's elite guard."

Ryder's face dropped. "What?"

"I am an elite guard," repeated Liam, not able to look at his brother.

Ryder's eyes narrowed. "You sold out?" He shook his head. "How could you?"

"It's not what you think," pleaded Liam. But even as he said it, the words felt hollow on his tongue.

"No?" said Ryder, making a show out of looking around the room. "So you're working both sides?" He made a move toward Knoblauch, launching his spiked chain at the veteran.

"Stop," shouted Liam, reacting to his brother attacking his friend.

Knoblauch batted it aside with seemingly little effort. But Liam could tell by the look on Ryder's face that his brother hadn't really tried to hit the veteran. It had been a test—just like when they were young.

Ryder glared at Liam. "How could you do this? The moment I'm gone, you go running to the baron."

Liam felt his face get red. "It didn't happen that way."

"Oh no?" Ryder stepped sideways, pacing around Liam like a threatening snake, gathering his chain to him. With a smooth overhand motion, he brought it over his shoulder, striking at Liam.

Liam jerked back, but he was too slow. Ryder's chain caught his long sword on the hand guard. Liam tried to keep hold of it, but Ryder was stronger, and sword went tumbling to the floor.

Liam sidestepped away from Ryder, shaking his tingling hand. He matched his brother's steps, and the two men circled, facing each other. If this were another man—any other man—Liam would already have his short sword in hand.

"I suppose you've betrayed the rest of the family as well," spat Ryder, his face growing angrier.

The center of Liam's stomach grew a heavy lump—Samira.

"Ryder, I'm sorry." He held his empty hands up in front of him. "I thought you were dead."

"That's no excuse."

Liam averted his eyes, his chest nearly caving in on itself with guilt. "I know."

"I was counting on you."

He nodded again, almost able to feel Samira's touch on his skin. "I know."

"You should have continued where I left off," chided Ryder.

"What?" The images in Liam's head scattered, and he finally looked up at his brother.

"You should have led the Awl—not abandoned them." Ryder glared. "If you really thought I was dead, then you should have taken my place."

"What happened that day, Ryder?" blurted Liam. "I watched you fall. I went back to tell our family that you died. But you didn't. And you didn't let us know. What were we supposed to think?" Liam could feel the guilt in his stomach being replaced with righteous anger. "If you didn't die, why didn't you come back?"

"Because he'd been sent to Westgate," came a voice from the double doors.

Ryder spun around.

Captain Phinneous, backed by what appeared to be his entire unit, stepped through the doors. "Welcome back, Ryder," said the captain. "I see you've grown accustomed to your chains."

❖　❖　❖　❖　❖

"We wait for his signal," said Giselle. The Broken Spear had been waiting in the wooded plain outside Zerith Hold for a full day. The sun was setting, and soon it would grow dark again. Still no signal.

"There is no use waiting," said Nazeem. "He has been captured."

"Then we go in and get him out," replied the leader of the Broken Spear.

Nazeem just shook his head. "I have seen the inside. There is no way we will get in, or him back out."

Giselle looked again at the tattoos on Nazeem's forehead. Up until now she'd taken the Chultan at his word. He was Ryder's friend, and that was good enough for her. But something about this didn't smell right.

"If you thought Ryder's plan wouldn't work, then why didn't you say so before he went in?"

"He is a grown man," said Nazeem without skipping a beat. "He makes his own choices, his own mistakes." The Chultan uncrossed his legs and stood up from the ground. "We should learn from his error and move on." He turned and walked out of the clearing deeper into the forest.

Giselle watched him disappear amidst the trees. What was it Ryder saw in this man to put so much trust in him? Whatever it was, she didn't see it.

She grabbed Jase by the arm, startling the young man. "Come on," she said as she headed into the woods.

"Where are we going?" asked the Broken Spear warrior, hurrying to catch up.

"We're going to follow this Chultan and find out once and for all if he can be trusted."

The two of them slipped quietly into the woods, close on Nazeem's heels.

Giselle had to stop several times to find the Chultan's trail. He was being very careful. Twice he had changed direction, climbing on top of fallen logs to try to mask his footsteps. But both times, Giselle found his trail again. The tattooed man was heading out to the main road—toward Zerith Hold.

As they continued to follow, the sun dipped completely below the horizon, and the sky grew dark. Giselle and Jase skirted the edge of the forest, staying in the shadows as they followed the road. In the distance, Giselle could hear the soft splashing of waves against the shore, and Zerith Hold came into view.

"There he is," whispered Giselle, dropping into a crouch and pointing.

Jase followed suit, and the two of them stood in the shadows watching as Nazeem stepped out into the road and into the light. As they watched, a pair of soldiers on horseback came riding up to the Chultan.

"He's going to give us away," said Jase.

"Not if you do it first," said Giselle, quieting the young man.

Nazeem held up his hands, and one of the soldiers lowered himself from his saddle while the other held a crossbow trained on the tattooed man.

The soldier on the ground took his helmet off as he approached, exposing a bald head and a scarred face. He spoke to the Chultan for a moment. They appeared to be having an argument. One moment, the soldier was shouting something into Nazeem's face. In the next, he was laughing.

For his part, Nazeem seemed to be calmly negotiating, though he never took his hands down, and the other soldier never lowered his crossbow.

The bald soldier looked down the road, seeming to squint as his gaze passed over where the two Broken Spear were hiding.

"Don't move," said Giselle.

Then his eyes moved on, and he focused his attention back on Nazeem. He said something, laughed, and drew his sword. Nazeem turned and started to run, but he stumbled to his knees when a crossbow bolt struck him in the leg. The bald man nodded to the other soldier and turned the point of his sword toward the ground and stabbed Nazeem in the back three times.

"Come on," whispered Giselle, backing slowly into the forest and heading toward where the rest of the Broken Spear were waiting. "Ryder's in trouble. We gotta get him out of there."

Jase followed. "But how are we going to get in?"

Giselle turned and glared at the young warrior. "We're going to bust down the doors if we have to."

Ryder hung from the ceiling.

There were chains on his arms and legs. The room

was full of them. They draped down from above like long drops of metallic rain. They flooded down from the ceiling, a torrential downpour in the middle of Baron Purdun's dungeon.

And in the middle of it stood Ryder. He could just touch the ground if he stood on the very tips of his toes. But he'd been here for the better part of a day, and he'd given up trying to stand. The effort it took made his legs shake like they were made of jelly.

Instead, he let the links hold his weight, choosing to hang from the ceiling as he thought about Liam's betrayal.

The door to the cell creaked open.

"I won't tell you anything," said Ryder, not looking up.

"Not even where you've been?"

Ryder lifted himself to his tiptoes and raised his eyes. "Samira." His chest constricted. He'd been dying to see her. He'd dreamed about her nightly. It had been her who had kept him going when he was imprisoned in Fairhaven.

He had desired this moment for so many months—but he had also dreaded it. Samira would know what had happened with Giselle. She would sense it. He knew the moment she laid eyes on him, he would be exposed, and he was terrified.

"I thought you died," she said, stopping just inside the door.

He shook his head. His heart filled with both joy and guilt at seeing his beloved wife. "I didn't."

A tear slipped down Samira's cheek. "I cried for days," she said, wiping the tear off with the sleeve of her dress.

Ryder felt as if his belly had once again been sliced open. "I tried to come back sooner," he said, adding, "I came as soon as I could."

"Where were you? What happened?"

Ryder took a deep breath. "It's a very long story," he said finally, not knowing where to begin.

Samira bit down on her lower lip, nodding.

Ryder smiled, looking at his beautiful wife. Of all the times he had imagined this moment, of all the nights he had spent thinking about how it would be, never had he dreamed it could be like this. He opened his arms.

"Come to me."

Samira looked to the ground and shook her head. "Ryder, there is something I have to tell you."

Ryder dropped his arms. "Yes?"

Samira stood quietly for a moment, opening her mouth to start several times but never uttering anything. Finally, she took a deep breath and looked up at her husband. "I thought you were dead," she said.

Ryder smiled. "But I'm not."

"I know that," said Samira, "now. But until this morning, I thought you were dead." She took a step away from the door. "When I found out, something inside of me died right along with you. I can't explain it, but things changed when I knew my world wouldn't have you in it." Samira sobbed.

Ryder wished he could reach out and comfort her, wished he could take away her pain. But he was stuck— both by the chains on his arms and the knowledge that he had caused that pain.

"For the past several months, I've been trying to come to grips with the fact that you were dead," continued Samira between sobs. "For the longest time I didn't even want to believe it was true. I hoped that someday I was just going to wake up and you'd be at home with me, and everything would be the way it used to be. I wished for that every night. And every morning I woke up alone in our bed." She stopped and swallowed. "Then one morning I woke up, and it finally dawned on me that you weren't coming back. That I was never going to see you again. And as much as that hurt, it was also a relief. It meant that I no longer had to torture myself over losing you. It meant that I could move on to the next part of my life. It meant that I could start living again."

Ryder could feel his heart breaking inside his chest. "But now that I'm back, you can start living again. Both of us can. Together."

Samira shook her head. "No, Ryder we can't."

Ryder frowned. "Why not?"

Samira closed her eyes. "Because," she said, "I'm in love with another man."

Ryder felt all of the blood in his body turn cold. "Who?"

"Your brother," admitted Samira. "I'm in love with Liam."

Ryder had thought he might lose Samira when she found out about Giselle. Never had he thought he would lose her to his own brother.

Ryder looked down at the floor. "I don't know what to say." He felt hollow and numb. It was like he was stuck in time. All that had been seemed irrelevant now. His life to this point seemed a waste. The future looked just as bleak—nothing to look forward to, nothing more for him in life. No reason to move forward.

"I'm sorry, Ryder."

He just hung there, letting the chains hold his weight. He didn't feel anything and he didn't think anything. There was nothing left to feel, nothing left to think.

After a long silence he looked up. "Me too," he said. But Samira was not there. He was alone, the door to his cell wide open.

"Good-bye," he said. Lifting his hand to his lips, he kissed his fingers and blew it out to where his wife had been standing.

Suddenly the nothingness inside him was filled with sorrow. Samira was gone. In one beat of his heart, he lost both his wife and his brother. No, it was worse than that. He hadn't lost them; they had chosen to leave him. They had chosen to betray him. They had purposely taken from him everything he had and left him with nothing.

The sorrow inside his chest slowly began to boil, changing from a slow sadness into a roiling fury. This wasn't his fault. They had done this to him. The more he thought about it the more his anger grew. It filled him to capacity, threatening to burst.

His muscles tensed, and Ryder shook the chains. He opened his mouth and let out a terrible shout—a yell at the top of his lungs, a mix of anguish and fury.

Then, when he had squeezed all the air from his lungs and his voice was hoarse, Ryder let go. He hung again from the chains, letting them hold his weight and admitting for the first time in his life that it was not him but the world around him that controlled his fate.

"Hello again, Ryder," came a man's voice from the door.

Ryder didn't bother to look up or even to respond. They could do to him whatever they wanted. He didn't care anymore.

"What?" asked the sarcastic voice, "no greeting for your old friend?"

Ryder heard footsteps, and four feet appeared on the floor below him—soldiers' boots.

One of the men punched Ryder in the side, sending him swaying, suspended as he was by the chains. His ribs throbbed from the blow, but Ryder didn't make a sound.

"Oh, come now," said the voice. "This isn't going to be any fun at all if you don't at least talk back. Don't you remember last time? How much fun we had?"

Ryder recognized the voice—Captain Phinneous.

Another blow landed on Ryder's back. This time he grunted a little as the pain flooded through his body.

"That's a start," said Phinneous. "But I know you can do better."

Ryder stood up. "You're right."

Captain Phinneous loomed before him, a huge grin on his bald, scarred face. He had only one guardsman with him.

"Such a good sport," said the captain, winding back for another blow.

Leaping, Ryder grabbed hold of the chain high above his head and lifted himself into the air. The chains went slack. Kicking out with his right leg, he looped the extra links around the guardsman's neck.

Holding himself sideways, parallel to the floor, he let his legs drop toward the ground, and the chain around the guard tightened. The entire weight of Ryder's body hung from his neck. There was a terrific popping sound, and the man managed to let out a low gurgle before his face turned purple and blood began to ooze from the corners of his eyes.

Not waiting for the guard to fully expire, Ryder lifted himself off the ground again.

Captain Phinneous, the grin gone from his ugly face, went for his sword, but Ryder was too fast. In one swift move, his right hand shot out, wrapped the chain around Phinneous's arm and knocked the long sword from his grip. It went clattering to the floor.

Twisting the captain's arm, Ryder turned the man sideways, giving Ryder enough room to reach the veteran guardsman's belt.

"I'll take those," said Ryder, grabbing the keys to unlock his chains.

"Help," shouted Phinneous. "Guards!"

Without letting up on Phinneous, Ryder released the locks on his right arm. Leaning forward, he spoke directly into the captain's ear.

"Time to pay for your crimes, Phinneous."

He unwrapped the chain from the captain's arm and looped it around the man's neck. Pulling it tight, he locked it down, leaving the guardsman gasping for air and standing on his tiptoes to keep the chain from strangling him.

Captain Phinneous's eyes grew wide, and he clawed at his neck, trying to get his fingers between his flesh and the steel of the chain. The more he struggled, the more panicked he looked. His face grew red, and every few breaths he let out a high-pitched whistling sound.

Ryder finished unlocking himself from the other chains and stepped up to stare into the face of the slowly suffocating Captain Phinneous.

"I'd love to hang around with you, Phinneous," said Ryder, "but I've still got to kill your boss."

Putting both of his hands on the captain's chest, Ryder shoved the man. Phinneous struggled to keep his footing, but his boots slipped on the slick stone floor. As the chain grew short, Ryder continued to push. Captain Phinneous kicked, but it was no use. He was lifted off the ground, hanging from his neck.

Ryder gave one last hard shove, and Phinneous swung once. When he came back down, his feet touched the ground. His head listed sideways on his shoulder, his neck broken and limp.

Turning away from the two dead men in his cell, Ryder crossed to a table near the windows where a large pile of chains and locks sat.

A pair of guards came running through the door and skidded to a stop. They took one look at the slowly swaying frame of Captain Phinneous and the bloodied guard at his feet and turned their attention to Ryder.

"Looking for me?" Ryder calmly selected a length of chain from the table. Turning, he walked toward the two stunned guardsmen. As he moved, he shook the chain, making the links rattle.

The guards looked at each other then back at Ryder, fear apparent in their eyes.

"That's right," he said, shaking the chains again. "I'm going to do to you what I did to them."

Both men turned and bolted back out the door.

Ryder sneered. "That's what I thought."

CHAPTER 25

In her glamoured disguise as Montauk, Shyressa stood before the Crimson Awl. She didn't maintain her enchantment for their benefit. It wouldn't have mattered to any of them. They all knew what she was. They all belonged to her now—every last one.

There were some things about her work that she truly enjoyed. Turning an entire band of gung-ho revolutionaries into her able-bodied spawn was one of them. Another was watching one of her long-term plans finally come to fruition. Today just happened to allow her the pleasure of both.

Behind the Awl, the rest of Shyressa's vampires and spawn waited for her orders. Tonight would be one of the largest blood baths in the history of Ahlarkham. The peasants would suffer. The royalty would suffer. The only ones who wouldn't suffer would be the vampires as they swooped in from the southern shores of the Deepwash.

When King Korox and his Magistrates arrived, the countryside would be crawling with undead. So too would Zerith Hold. But the king wouldn't see that part. All he would see would be Shyressa, appearing to be Montauk helping his majesty clean up the mess. Then he would be forced to put her in charge of the barony, and phase one would be complete.

Sure, some of her minions were going to be destroyed by the king's men. A paltry price. After she had control of Ahlarkham, she would put the next part of her plan into action. It wouldn't be long before she controlled all of Erlkazar.

She smiled. The thought of turning the King's Magistrates into her own personal spawn sounded absolutely delicious. She might have to make it last for a few days. No sense in shortening her fun. She could have them all locked up—and could feed on their iron-rich blood at her leisure.

Shyressa licked her lips.

Shaking herself out of her daydream, she looked out at her little army. With a wave of her arm, her older spawn took off into the night, spreading out to ravage Duhlnarim and the surrounding areas.

The converted Crimson Awl, however, stayed put. They were all from local stock, and their appearance wouldn't immediately give them away as outsiders or undead. That was the way Shyressa wanted it. There was still some value in this game for deception.

"To Zerith Hold," she said in Montauk's voice. "Time to pay Lord Purdun a visit."

"There is an entrance to the back of Zerith Hold that does not have the same protections as the front gate," explained Giselle. "But that does not mean that it is an easier way in." She looked out at the brave men and women of the Broken Spear. She had stories about each of them, many of them tales of heroics that had helped save her own life. "There will be at least a host of guardsmen, and perhaps more. We will without a doubt be outnumbered."

"That's never stopped us before," said a warrior in the back of the tightly grouped Broken Spear.

Everyone nodded.

Giselle smiled. "These are trained soldiers," continued the leader. "And the potential exists that many of us may not be coming back."

The Broken Spear nodded at this as well.

"I'm not going to lie to you," she said. "We're not doing this just for riches or glory. This time it's personal." She took a deep breath. "I'm not ordering you to do anything. I'm asking you, as a favor to me, to help me go in there and get Ryder back out. But if any one of you decide that you don't want to go, then ..." Her voice trailed off. "Then you are free to go your own way," she said finally. "There will be no shame, no ill will." She looked up at the people she had thought of as her family for the past several years. "You all know what this means. If we break up, it will be the end. The Broken Spear will be no more." She paused a moment to let what she had just said sink in. "All I ask is that if you want to go, that you go now. I do not want to part with any of you, in this life or in death, but if I must, please be merciful and make it swift."

Giselle stood silently, her speech given and her plea finished.

No one moved.

"This is your last chance," Giselle warned.

Jase stood up, glancing to his left and right, seeming to take in all of the members of the Broken Spear.

Giselle looked at the young man, sadness in her heart. She smiled and offered him her hand. "May the world treat you well," she said. "No matter where your travels take you."

But Jase waved her off. "We're going with you," he said. "All of us. So you can save your speeches for after the battle has been won."

Giselle pulled her hand back. "Fair enough." She scanned the group for a particular face. "Curtis," she called.

The skinny man's face popped up between a pair of warriors. "Yes? That's me."

"You think you can get us up to the gates without being seen?"

The illusionist put his hand to his face, grabbing hold of his chin and scanning the sky. He changed hands, continuing to think. He seemed to be looking for something among the stars.

Giselle looked up, following his gaze. She didn't see anything but the early evening sky.

Finally Curtis nodded. "Yes. I think I have just the thing," he said, taking his hand from his chin and putting it inside his shirt. When his hand came out again it clutched a wrinkled, folded piece of paper. "Might hurt a bit," he said. He reached up and grabbed hold of his eyelid. Yanking out several of his eyelashes, he squinted, his eye watering. "But it'll work."

Giselle cringed. "Well then," she said, addressing the whole group. "You all know I'm not much for long drawn-out plans. If the guards open the doors for any reason, we hit them hard and fast. Agreed?"

As a group the Broken Spear nodded.

"All right. Let's go." Giselle stood up and led her warriors off toward the back entrance to Zerith Hold.

As they had so many times in the past few days, the double doors to the baron's sitting room burst open. Captain Beetlestone, accompanied by four elite guardsmen, came running in.

Baron Purdun, who had been eating his supper, leaped to his feet.

Liam and Knoblauch were already standing.

"My lord," started Beetlestone. He was out of breath. "The Crimson Awl is attacking the front gate."

Liam was gripped with a sudden fear. He was going to have to face those men—many of whom he had grown up with—in battle.

"There are also reports," continued Beetlestone, "that the villages surrounding Duhlnarim are under attack as well."

"By the Awl?" blurted Liam out of turn.

Knoblauch put his hand on Liam's shoulder, trying to calm him.

If Baron Purdun was upset by the outburst, he didn't show it. "By whom?" he asked.

"Undead, my lord," said Beetlestone. "Vampires are attacking the citizens of Ahlarkham."

The baron turned to Liam and Knoblauch. "I'm about to put both of you in harm's way," he said very matter-of-factly. Then he turned and headed for the door. "Captain Beetlestone, collect your men. Take them out of the rear gate and circle around to the front of Zerith Hold. I want you and your men to flank the Awl."

"Yes, my lord." The captain and his entourage left the room.

When Lord Purdun got to the double doors, he drew his saber from his hip. "We're going to the aid of the citizens," he said, looking back at Liam and Knoblauch. Then he turned and headed down the stairs. "And we're going out the front gate."

The half-giant bodyguards leaped up from their positions in the corners, striding quickly across the room and down the stairs after their lord.

Liam looked to Knoblauch.

"Guess that's it," Liam said.

Knoblauch sighed. "Yeah."

Then both men took off after the baron.

Lord Purdun knew the corridors of Zerith Hold so well that Liam and Knoblauch didn't catch up with him until he was walking out into the open air of the courtyard.

Liam stopped and looked out on the chaos before him. Everywhere there was shouting. Hundreds of flaming arrows sat lodged in the gravel at extreme angles, their shafts still flickering. More came zipping over the stone wall.

On top, behind the crenellations, men ran back and forth, firing down on the drawbridge, trading arrows with the archers outside the Hold. But it was what Liam saw *inside* the wall that made his jaw drop.

On the raised archer platform above the courtyard walked a beast of a man. He strode not *around* the soldiers between him and the front gate, but *through* them. This creature was more than a mere man, he was a force of darkness, and his very presence cast a pall over Zerith Hold.

Though he was no taller than a regular man, he was nearly twice as wide. But it wasn't his flesh that gave him this girth. It was a collection of jangling chains. They hung from his head and shoulders like matted, tangled dreadlocks. They wound around his chest like a crossbowman's bandoleer. They dangled below his knees like an overlong chain mail tunic—but these were not links from an armorer's anvil. These were the chains meant to imprison criminals. And they were being used now to protect the man who had come to kill Baron Purdun.

"Ryder," whispered Liam, recognizing his brother.

As Liam, Knoblauch, and Baron Purdun watched, the chain-covered man rattled his way along the archer's platform, knocking soldiers off its edge with little more than the flick of his wrist.

Archers took aim at him and let fly, but their arrows seemed useless against such a man. The chains on his body danced and writhed like serpents. When an arrow approached, it was simply batted away or deflected by the shaking mass of dangling metal. Those men not defeated by the master of chains fled before him, as if they had seen an apparition or been ensorcelled with fear.

Ryder made his way to the mechanism that operated the portcullis and the big wooden door. Grabbing hold of the crank, he turned it. The portcullis began to lift, and the huge wooden doors swung partially open. The rain of flaming arrows showering the courtyard stopped, and from outside the men and women of the Crimson Awl squeezed through the now-breached front gate.

With the way open, Ryder turned from the crank and stood on the edge of the archer's platform, looking down into the courtyard. He raised his arms over his head, the links of his chains clanking together, seeming to move with his body as if they obeyed his thoughts.

"It is time the people got back that which has been taken from them," shouted Ryder. "In the name of the Crimson Awl and the innocent victims of Baron Purdun, I now claim Zerith Hold."

"The hell he does," said Purdun. "To the gate!"

A battle cry went up from the elite guards on the wall, and they followed their baron into the teeth of the monster.

Lord Purdun charged across the open ground, his hands lighting up like miniature balls of lightning. His half-giant guards paced right along beside him, silently following the baron into the fray.

Liam watched as one of them reached under its cloak and produced a pair of wicked-looking greataxes. The steel of their blades was so dark it looked black in the flickering glow of the torches and flaming arrows. Each axe would have easily taken a normal man both hands to handle, but the half-giant wielded one in each.

As they closed in on the first of the Crimson Awl, the other half-giants followed suit, pulling out axes of their own. The four of them shifted side to side, cutting down the incoming invaders as if they were shafts of wheat.

Liam took a deep breath, steeled himself, and charged into the fight as well, Knoblauch beside him. They came down the steps, only a step behind their lord. And in a moment they were embroiled in the largest battle ever to take place inside the walls of Zerith Hold.

The soldiers stationed on the wall and along the archers' perch dropped into the courtyard. The Crimson Awl filed in through the barely open gate, and the two sides clashed. Metal clanged on metal, axes split skulls, and the brutal sounds of men being torn apart echoed off the stone walls.

In the first few moments, it felt as if the Crimson Awl would fold. The elite guards had the rebels surrounded. The half-giants worked like clockwork golems, tirelessly chopping down those who ventured close enough to be reached by their blades. Archers shot into the group with deadly accuracy. And Lord Purdun filled the courtyard with crackling orange flames.

But every time it appeared as though one of the Awl had taken a mortal wound, he seemed to shrug it off, continuing to come on despite taking massive damage. The rush of adrenaline and the furious battle around him was enough to drive Liam to action despite his reservations. He stepped up and crossed blades with the first of the Crimson Awl.

Bashing aside the man's sword, he came up and across, catching his opponent across the shoulder and slicing a deep wound. Returning to his guard, Liam looked up into the face of his opponent—Kharl.

The young man whose life Liam had saved the day they had attacked Lord Purdun's carriage now stood across from him, hatred in his eyes. The look on his face chilled Liam to the bone. But there was something else there too. His flesh was pale and sickly, almost transparent, and the veins under his skin were plainly visible. They stuck out in stark contrast, a dark blue-purple against the clear white of the rest of his face.

Kharl didn't even bother to bring his sword up; he just reached out and punched Liam with his closed fist. Liam was knocked back a step. The young man who had nearly wet himself when they had ambushed the carriage had somehow gotten much, much stronger.

As Liam staggered back to his footing, Kharl opened his mouth, hissing and exposing a pair of long, thin fangs.

"Vampires," whispered Liam. Somehow speaking the word made the situation they faced that much more palpable.

The Crimson Awl had been taken over by vampires. Lord Purdun had been right. Shyressa had been manipulating them all along. Had Liam not gotten out when he did, he too would be among the walking dead.

Liam scanned the crowd and the swirling melee. He recognized the faces of everyone in the Crimson Awl. He had fought beside them. He had been to their homes for stew. But what he saw before him—the beasts that had burst into Zerith Hold—these were not his one-time friends. These creatures were no longer even human.

Kharl leaped, landing on Liam's chest and knocking him off his feet. The two men tumbled to the ground, rolling around on the flagstones. When they finally came to a stop, Liam found himself pinned down, looking up into Kharl's gaping mouth.

Liam struggled to get free, but the vampire spawn held him down. He had the strength of an elephant.

"I've come to pry your sword from your cold dead hand," hissed Kharl, and he lunged for Liam's neck.

Liam flinched, and in the next moment, his face was splashed with a thick liquid. Blinking it out of his eyes, Liam watched Kharl's head roll off his shoulders and fall to the bricks.

"Get up," said Knoblauch, kicking the headless body off Liam. "The baron needs our help."

CHAPTER 26

The smaller doors guarding the back entrance to Zerith Hold swung opened and a unit of elite guardsmen rode hard into the night.

Giselle stood right beside the open doors, her hand on Curtis's shoulder. Jase's hand was on her shoulder, and everyone else in the Broken Spear followed suit, forming a human chain. They did this to stay together. Thanks to Curtis, every last one of them was now invisible.

"Wait for it," whispered Giselle.

The last of the riders galloped off into the darkness, and the doors began to close again. The leader of the Broken Spear let go of Curtis's shoulder.

"Yie, yie, yie, yie!" she shouted, and she bolted through the open door, bringing her scimitar down on the first standing guard she encountered.

The rest of the Broken Spear followed her lead, flooding through the gate. The walls inside Zerith Hold echoed with the war cry of the Broken Spear.

Giselle's sword connected with the unsuspecting guard, and the blow severed the soft flesh of his exposed neck. The man dropped to the ground, dead before his head hit the flagstones, and the invisible Broken Spear warriors reappeared.

"Alarm! Alarm!" shouted someone in a guard tower. The tolling of a bell came shortly after, but it was too late. The Broken Spear was inside, and they spread out like a deadly cloud of poisonous gas.

Giselle dispatched two more guards in quick succession, then she spun to see if the riders were going to circle back and come to the aid of their comrades. They had taken off in a hurry, but the bell likely got their attention.

When she turned around, there wasn't a single rider to be seen. Returning her attention to the fight, Giselle took on two more guardsmen.

Lord Purdun gathered the energy to cast another spell. He'd sent enough electricity through the men he faced to kill them ten times over. They would fall, but they would not die. His half-giant bodyguards had delivered some blows that would have felled an ox. But somehow the Crimson Awl got back up and fought on.

Here in the Hold, he and his men easily outnumbered the invaders, maybe two to one. Regardless, they made no progress. In fact, they were losing ground, and with it, the hope that they would hold the courtyard. Soon he was going to have to make the decision. He was going to have to cut his losses and pull back inside the keep.

Rapier in one hand, Purdun hurled four swirling blue-white spheres at an oncoming invader with the other.

"Will they never stop?"

"No, my lord, they will not," hissed a voice.

The Baron of Ahlarkham turned to see a decrepit old man. His skin was brown and wrinkled. His eyes oozed with purplish liquid that looked as if it might drip down his face at any moment if it weren't so thick. And he wore the tattered old robes of a courtly mage.

A chill like the dying breath of a white dragon ran up Purdun's spine. "Menrick."

The old man placed his hands together and bowed. "At your service," he said.

"But . . ." Purdun stood in wonder. "I watched you die."

Menrick nodded. "Yes, you did," said the mage. "And I have come to you in unlife to return the favor." The old man lifted his staff and pointed it at Purdun, sending a blast of icy crystals smashing into the younger man's stomach.

The wind was knocked from the baron's lungs, and he gasped against the pain and lack of air.

"Does it hurt?" asked Menrick. "Dying, I mean. It's been so long since it happened to me, I don't quite remember." The undead mage sent another blast at Purdun.

This one struck him in the face, slicing his cheek and tearing a chunk from his ear.

Purdun put his hand to the side of his face. It was numb from the magical cold, but he could tell it was mangled.

"Menrick, this is madness," protested the baron. "There was nothing I could do."

The wrinkled pile of bones stepped closer. "You could have heeded my warnings. You could have walked away from the tomb." He lifted the staff for another blast. "If you had, I would still be alive."

Purdun cowered, casting a quick spell he had memorized for just such an emergency. A shimmering ball of opaque plasma surrounded his entire body, and the blast from Menrick's staff splashed harmlessly against its surface.

"I see you have learned much," said Menrick, circling around the glowing globe. "That old fool in his underwater tower taught you well."

Purdun nodded, looking out of his protective shell. "You should know," he said.

"Yes," purred the wizard vampire. "I imagine his teachings didn't change much from my time to yours." Menrick ran his finger along the edge of the magical sphere, the melee around them continuing to swirl and rage in the courtyard.

"You know, though," continued the old mage. "I suppose I should thank you."

Purdun didn't know what to make of this, so he kept quiet.

"There are a few advantages to being a vampire," he said, stopping in front of Purdun and glaring in at him from outside the sphere. "For instance. Magic is no longer my only weapon."

Menrick reached through the swirling plasma and grabbed Purdun by the throat. Taking a step back, he dragged the baron out of the protective bubble and bared his teeth.

"Now I will be the master." Menrick lifted Purdun toward his open mouth.

The baron felt his body shake. Menrick's grip on Purdun's tunic tightened and both men were lifted from the ground. The lord found himself hanging over the flagstones, the silk of his shirt gripped tightly in Menrick's clawed hands—the old vampire mage held in the air by two of Purdun's half-giant bodyguards.

Purdun put his boot on Menrick's chest and kicked off. The fabric of his tunic gave way, and the baron dropped to the ground, his chest bare.

Menrick thrashed against the bodyguards, flailing

his limbs with preternatural speed. The old man hissed and clawed at the two silent half-giants, but neither of them budged an inch.

Scrambling to his feet, Purdun took a step back and looked into the eyes of his one-time mentor and friend, the vampire who had just tried to kill him.

"I am sorry, Menrick," he said. "I was sad to see you die the first time, but I will be doubly so the second."

Lord Purdun's saber flashed in the flickering light. It slid quickly through the withered flesh and brittle bone that had been Menrick's neck, and the old mage's head toppled from his body. The arms twitched for a moment, then the corpse of Purdun's old servant went limp.

"Put that somewhere safe," Purdun said to his two bodyguards. "We'll need to dispose of it properly when all of this is over."

Ryder looked down on the raging fight in the court-yard below. He couldn't have asked for anything better. To come out of the dungeon to find the Crimson Awl waiting at the front gate was all the justice he would ever need. Finally Zerith Hold would fall.

His brother and his wife may have betrayed him, but he would regain his family—he would return to the Awl and be embraced by them as a savior.

Looking over the familiar faces, he wondered who had been the driving force while he was gone. Who had taken over the role he had hoped Liam would fill?

The rest of the Awl finished making their way through the partially opened gate and portcullis. The last group to enter didn't seem all that interested in getting inside and walked casually into the Hold.

That's when he spotted the person he'd been looking for.

"Montauk." The name rolled off Ryder's lips with a certain respect and admiration. Ryder had never thought much of Montauk. He had always been a selfish, petty man. But Ryder was willing to overlook his previous opinion. He had been wrong in his characterization, and he would admit that to Montauk when they met again.

In the meantime, however, there was the little matter of dealing with his brother.

Placing a hand on the ledge, Ryder leaped over the low wall and into the courtyard below, his chains clanking as he landed. At the back of the melee, standing valiantly beside his baron, Liam fought against the men who had at one time been his friends and neighbors.

They were allies once. Liam had made them into enemies.

Ryder crossed the courtyard toward his brother. "Liam of Duhlnarim," he said as he approached. "I call you out." He grabbed one of the chains dangling from his shoulder and set it in motion.

Liam finished off the opponent he was fighting and looked back at his brother.

Ryder didn't wait for him to acknowledge the challenge. Swinging his chain, he let it fly at Liam's head. His brother stepped back, dodging the links with a quick weave.

Ryder stepped forward, pressing his advantage and coming in closer to Liam. This time though, he swung a chain with each hand. Again his brother stepped back, dodging out of the way.

"Ryder, what are you doing?'

"I'm killing you."

Liam pointed to the fight raging beside them. "Don't you see? The people of the Awl aren't what they seem."

Ryder swung his chain again. This time Liam had to bring his sword up to block it from slamming into his face.

"Propaganda," Ryder shouted, striking out again.

Liam bashed aside another attack. "I don't want to fight you. Just look, will you? They're vampires!"

"All I need to know is that you stole Samira!" Ryder went low, catching Liam by the foot and sending him sprawling.

Liam clattered to the ground and scrambled back to his feet. "I thought you were dead," screamed the younger of the two brothers. "I watched you fall in battle. I didn't think you were coming back."

"Well, here I am." Ryder shook his chains. "And I'm going to take back that which belongs to me." Again he attacked Liam.

This time Liam fought back, smashing aside the chain and countering.

"That's more like it," said Ryder through gritted teeth. "Let's see what she's worth to you."

Liam's eyes narrowed. "She's worth dying for." He lunged, feinting to the right then changing back to the left—a move Ryder had taught him many years ago.

The blade spanked off of the links of Ryder's armor.

"Nice form," said Ryder. "But you'll have to do better than that if you intend to stop me from killing you."

Liam lunged again. This time, Ryder slapped the blade away harmlessly with a pair of chains and followed through with another that slammed into Liam's arm.

Liam winced from the blow and took a step back, rolling his shoulder.

"Hurts, don't it?"

Liam ignored him. "I never meant for any of this to happen," he said. "Can't you believe me?"

Ryder shook his head. "No. I can't." He stepped up to take another swing at his brother.

A dark shadow flashed in front of Ryder, and in the next moment, he found himself struggling to stay on his feet. Some foul-smelling creature now clung to his shoulders and neck, its feet pressed against his back as if it were using him like a perch.

Ryder couldn't see the beast, but he could see the one clinging to Liam. It looked so strange. About the size of a man, it stood atop Ryder's younger brother at an odd angle, clutching his back. Somehow the creature, whatever it was, looked familiar, as if it were someone he knew.

Then a terrible chill ran up his spine. He did know this creature—this man. He was a farmer who had lived in Furrowsrich. He was a member of the Crimson Awl. As Ryder watched, the man opened his mouth, revealing long sharp fangs, and he tried to bite down on Liam.

What was happening here? This wasn't right.

Liam had been telling the truth—the Awl *had* been infiltrated, or worse, sucked dry and turned into vampires. His brother had tried to tell him, but Ryder had been blinded by his jealousy and rage.

Sorrow filled Ryder's chest. He had let these people in here, had let the vampires into Zerith Hold. Many men were going to die because of this, including his brother.

Truly, that was what Ryder had wanted when he escaped his bonds. He had stepped out of the dungeon with every intention of ending Liam's life.

But he'd felt that way before, when they were children. He would get so mad at his younger brother that the urge to kill would well up inside him. It was the only power a younger brother had over his older sibling—the power to push him to the point of blinding rage faster than any other human could.

But every time, that rage passed. Ryder would always forgive Liam. This time was no exception. Liam was his younger brother, and if he was in trouble, it was Ryder who was going to get him out of it.

Gritting his teeth, Ryder charged forward, launching himself at Liam. With the vampire attached to his back, he crashed into his younger brother and the creature trying to bite his neck. Everyone tumbled, and for the next few instants, Liam, Ryder, and the two vampires were nothing more than a spinning pile of elbows, fangs, and chains.

When they came to a stop, Ryder leaped to his feet, grabbed Liam by the arm, and lifted him as well.

Liam had lost his long sword in the tumble, and he pulled a shorter blade from his belt and pointed it at his brother.

Ryder held up his hands. "I'm sorry, Liam," he said. "I don't want to kill you."

Liam grimaced. "Great," he said, pointing over Ryder's shoulder. "Because if you still did, the line forms over there."

Ryder turned around to see more than a dozen vampires charging at the two of them. "Just like back in the old days," he said as he slapped away the first attack with a chain. He could feel Liam's back against his. "I'm afraid this is where we left off last time."

The Crimson Awl surrounded Ryder and Liam, hissing as they closed the circle.

CHAPTER 27

Captain Beetlestone spurred his horse on. It wasn't far from the back entrance to the front gate of Zerith Hold, but the ride seemed to take an eternity.

Behind him, he heard the alarm bell toll. Under other circumstances, he would have turned back. But right now, there was nothing he could do to help those men. His baron was in jeopardy.

"Onward," he shouted, pointing toward the front gate just to make sure the rest of his men knew his intentions. He didn't look back. They would follow. They always did.

Reaching the northeast corner of the Hold, they made the turn around to the front of the fortress.

The Crimson Awl was nowhere to be seen.

Beetlestone relaxed. That's right, he thought.

They fled before the arrows of the elite guards on the wall. He looked up to salute the archers who regularly guarded the entrance to Zerith Hold.

They were nowhere to be seen.

Now it was time to panic. If the guards had abandoned their posts, it could mean only one thing.

The Awl was already inside.

Kicking his horse again, Beetlestone tried to make his mount run faster. He wasn't going to lose the baron, not this way. Reaching the drawbridge, he could see that the portcullis and the heavy wooden doors behind it were only partially open—just wide enough for them to sneak in single file. Pulling up on the reins, Beetlestone leaped from his horse.

"Dismount," he shouted. "We go in on foot."

The others soldiers in his unit followed his lead, unsheathing their swords as they hit the ground.

"That'll be far enough," came a voice.

Captain Beetlestone turned to look up at King Korox sitting on a magnificent black steed.

"Drop your weapons and give up your allegiance to Lord Purdun, and the Magistrates will go easy on you," demanded the king.

Beetlestone stood firm, torn between his obligations to his baron and his king. Beside him, his men stood their ground, waiting for his order.

"I will not tell you again," shouted the king. "Drop your weapons and bow before your king, or we will use force."

Captain Beetlestone lowered his head in a simple bow. His hands were shaking. "I apologize, my liege," he said. He could feel his palm sweat against the hilt of his sword as he thought on what he was about to do. "But I cannot abandon my baron in his time of need." Then he turned and ran toward the portcullis.

The twang of crossbow strings sang through the night air, and the drawbridge before him suddenly sprouted bolts. Beetlestone froze in place, turning to face King

Korox. He dropped his sword then dropped to one knee.

His men did the same.

"My king," he said, looking up into the eyes of King Korox, "please forgive my rash actions, but the baron's life is in mortal danger."

Giselle led the Broken Spear through the winding hallways of Zerith Hold. Neither she nor any of the men with her had ever been inside the building. They had no idea where they were going and even less of an idea where Ryder would be.

They had dealt quickly with the guards at the rear entrance. There were surprisingly few of them there, and Curtis's invisibility spell had given the Spear an advantage.

But as they worked their way through the stone corridors, Giselle began to grow nervous. This wasn't right. They hadn't encountered anyone. The halls were empty. The rooms were empty. There was no one home.

"This feels like a trap," she said to no one in particular.

"I don't think so," replied Curtis. "No. I really don't think so."

"Why not?"

"Well," said the illusionist, "they didn't know we were coming. How could they set a trap, if they didn't know we were coming?"

Giselle thought about this as they continued to run through the halls of the second floor. "Maybe they did," she said finally. "We don't know what Nazeem told them. He might have tipped them off about us."

"I doubt it," replied Curtis.

"How can you be so sure?" asked Giselle.

"I can't," replied the illusionist.

Giselle threw up her hands. "If this isn't a trap, then where is everyone?"

"Outside," said Curtis.

"What?" Giselle stopped running and looked the skinny man in the face.

Curtis smiled and pointed at the window in the far wall.

Giselle sprinted over to the edge and looked down through the warped glass at the huge battle raging below.

"When did you know they were out there?"

Curtis shrugged. "The first time we passed a window." He thought about it. "Yes, on the first floor, after we passed through the dining hall."

Giselle turned and took off toward the stairs. "Then why didn't you say something?"

"No one asked me," said Curtis.

"Come on," she growled at the rest of the Broken Spear. Then she bolted down the stairs.

Two flights later, Giselle found the entrance hall and the open front door that led out into the courtyard. She couldn't make heads or tails of any of it. Pockets of fighting were scattered all over the place. The bodies of dead men lay on the ground, their blood staining the flagstones. And though he looked far different than he had the last time they had been together, in the middle of the swirling madness, Giselle spotted what she was looking for.

"Ryder," she said, smiling. "He's alive." Lifting her sword high in the air, she shouted the Broken Spear's ululating war cry. "Yie, yie, yie, yie, yie!"

The other warriors behind her did the same, filling the entire courtyard with the bouncing sound.

Then they charged into the fray.

Ryder stood facing Montauk, a chain swinging in each hand. Behind him, Liam held off the vampires coming from the other direction.

"I never did like you," said the master of chains.

Montauk smiled. "That's funny," he said. "I thought I'd had you killed."

Ryder nodded. "I'll hand it to you. I never would have guessed it was you."

Ryder's chain lashed out, wrapping around Montauk's sword arm. He pulled, attempting to disarm the man before caving his head in. But Montauk proved to be much stronger than Ryder, and he pulled back on the chain with the force of an elephant. Ryder was jerked forward and sent sprawling onto his belly at Montauk's feet.

"How could you have guessed?" taunted Montauk. "You with your miserably short lifespan."

Ryder tried to get to his feet, but Montauk stepped on his back, holding him to the ground with one foot.

"But I suppose I should be thanking you for opening the gate." Montauk laughed. "Then again—" He stepped down hard, crushing Ryder's ribs against the flagstones— "It's far more enjoyable to kill you again."

Ryder struggled to get free, but Montauk was just too strong. His chest felt as if it were going to collapse, and his ears were ringing. The muscles along his ribcage burned from being stretched. The harder Montauk pushed, the louder the noise in Ryder's ears grew. The sounds of battle that had moments ago filled the courtyard were swallowed up by the whining.

Then his vision began to narrow. It was just at the periphery at first, but then the center began to go blank. He lost track of Liam. The world was disappearing. Soon it would all be gone.

Ryder turned his head, looking out over the courtyard. With his last sliver of vision, he could just make out a robed woman stepping up beside him. From what sounded like a great distance, he could barely make out her voice.

"Let go. He's mine," she said. Then she slashed down with a curved blade on something outside Ryder's limited vision.

Montauk's foot came off Ryder's back, and the world flooded back to him. The ringing in his ears was replaced by the thumping of his heart. His vision cleared, and he could breathe again.

Rolling to one side, Ryder struggled to his feet. Giselle had slashed a large wound in Montauk's neck, and the man held his bleeding throat with both hands.

Giselle pressed in with her attack, coming down—her scimitar in both hands—on Montauk's face.

"Enough," shouted Montauk, and he raised a bloody hand, catching Giselle's blade with his open palm.

He tore the blade from her grip. Not bothering to turn it around, he slammed the hilt into Giselle's chest, knocking the leader of the Broken Spear back into Ryder.

"I'm done toying with you," said Montauk, his voice gravelly and hoarse. He tossed Giselle's blade aside. As he did, Ryder could see the slashed flesh on his palm knitting itself back together, healing as if he'd just consumed a magic potion.

Stepping forward, Montauk grabbed both Ryder and Giselle by their throats. "Now you will die." He began to squeeze.

Ryder grabbed Montauk's hand with both of his own. He scratched and clawed, but he couldn't pry the man's fingers loose from his neck. Out of the corner of his eye, he could see Giselle trying to do the same thing. Her skin flushed, and there was panic on her face.

Then, as he watched, the leader of the Broken Spear stopped struggling. Her body didn't go limp, she just seemed to relax. Her eyes were still open, and hatred burned in them. Giselle hadn't given up, and she hadn't resigned herself to death. That was maybe the only thing this woman wasn't capable of.

Ryder felt Montauk flinch. The grip around his neck tightened, then dropped away, and Ryder was free. Behind Montauk, something shimmered into existence. It was a person. In the next moment, Curtis came into view. He had his hand up against Montauk. Gripping a dagger in his hands, he held the blade buried in the man's back.

Montauk let out an inhuman shriek. He was pinned like a bug by Curtis's dagger, and he thrashed about, trying desperately to get off the illusionist's blade. Then his skin began to stretch and melt. It wobbled and drooped, looking as if it would simply fall from his face and body.

Ryder got to his feet. Stumbling back, he grabbed hold of Giselle's shoulder, pulling her away from Montauk.

The new head of the Crimson Awl flailed for a moment longer. A scowl grew on his disfigured lips, and he stood up straight, shaking his fists in a triumphant gesture. There was a soft popping sound, and Montauk's melting flesh simply vanished, leaving in its place an ancient and withered visage. The creature that stood where Montauk had been seemed vaguely female. She had long, graying hair, an ornate dress, and fangs.

The creature raised her arms, and a deep shadow filled the courtyard. All fighting inside Zerith Hold came to a complete stop, and the air was filled with a collective hiss from the Crimson Awl.

"Submit now. Bow down before Shyressa," said the woman, her words echoing across the entire courtyard. With a casual flick of her wrist, she swatted Curtis away with as much effort as she would pay to a buzzing insect.

The skinny illusionist went flying, and his dagger clattered to the ground.

Ryder felt a chill wind blow in, and he shivered against it. He felt Giselle grip his arm. She was shaking. If these were to be their last moments, he was glad she was there with him.

A huge *boom* filled Zerith Hold as the heavy wooden doors and portcullis of the front gate exploded inward. Splinters of wood and shards of metal flew everywhere, and a huge cloud of dust and smoke erupted into the night sky.

Then a black horse and its rider appeared out of the swirling debris, trailing tendrils of smoke behind him as he rode into the courtyard, his sword drawn and raised over his head. Though Ryder had never seen him in the flesh before, he recognized the man from Erlkazar's golden coin—this was the Crusader King, King Korox.

"To the baron!" King Korox shouted.

More riders emerged from the smoke. They poured in, appearing as if by magic out of the mists. To Ryder it looked like an entire army—and then some.

The withered woman glared down at Ryder. She let out a deep, bone rattling growl.

"This is not over," she said. Then she wrapped the sleeves of her dress around her body and evaporated, leaving behind only a thin stream of translucent mist that lifted into the air and rose over the wall.

The rest of the Crimson Awl did the same, turning themselves into insubstantial clouds of gas and escaping into the night.

CHAPTER 28

Liam knelt beside Baron Purdun as the king lay into him.

"Of all the foolish things to do," chided Korox, "why did you have to disobey my summons?"

Lord Purdun, down on one knee, apologized. "Please forgive me, my liege, but there was no other way. Had I not been here when the vampires attacked Zerith Hold, it may have fallen." He looked up at the king. "I sent messengers, but they were intercepted."

Liam cringed.

"It was only by the might of your Magistrates that I managed to communicate with you. I have Magistrate Olivio to thank for that."

The king nodded. "Well, I want a full explanation of this matter."

"Yes, my liege," agreed Purdun. "But not now."

"What?" The king was obviously not in the mood to be told when or how things were going to be done.

"Zerith Hold was not the vampires' only target," Purdun explained. "All of Duhlnarim is under siege."

The king spun his horse. "Then get to your feet, man. We ride to their aid."

Lord Purdun jumped up. "An excellent idea, my king."

Liam got to his feet.

Lord Purdun began to issue orders. "Liam, Knoblauch, you're with me." Without a moment's hesitation, he walked across the courtyard to stand before Ryder, Giselle, and the rest of the Broken Spear.

Liam cringed again. He and his brother hadn't fully patched things up. The next few moments could destroy the delicate peace that had developed during the fighting.

The Baron of Ahlarkham looked Ryder up and down then shook his head. "I don't know what to make of you," he said of Liam's chain-covered brother.

Ryder opened his mouth as if to explain himself, but the baron cut him off.

"Captain Beetlestone," shouted Purdun over his shoulder.

Liam gripped the hilt of his long sword.

"Yes, my lord," replied Beetlestone.

The baron smiled. "Get these men horses." He looked back at Ryder. "And bring this man his weapon. We'll need all the help we can get."

Shyressa rematerialized in a graveyard just outside Furrowsrich village. The rest of her Crimson Awl minions did the same.

"Years of work," she spat. "All of that time, wasted."

Shyressa couldn't remember the last time one of her plans hadn't succeeded.

"There will be retribution for this." She stalked back and forth, tapping her fingers on top of the headstones. "I *will* take Ahlarkham tonight, even if I have to kill everyone in it."

Lifting her arms in the air, she spoke the words to an incantation. One that she dearly loved.

The ground around her shook and roiled. Headstones turned on their sides as the earth churned and pushed up from underneath. From out of the soil crawled the dead of Duhlnarim. Bony hands clawed at the dirt as every body in the graveyard pulled itself out of its supposedly final resting place.

"This will do fine," purred Shyressa, her mood improving. "Just fine."

At the head of the Broken Spear, Ryder and Giselle raced down the road from Zerith Hold toward Furrowsrich. As they got closer, Ryder felt it had been a lifetime since he'd last seen this familiar terrain. So much had happened, but he didn't have time to think about that now.

The undead were back in Duhlnarim. His mother, his father, and Samira were in danger.

Turning down the road into Furrowsrich, Ryder's breath caught in his lungs. The place was crawling with zombies. The creatures bashed at the locked doors of the village houses. With each thump, blood-curdling screams issued out into the night.

"This way," shouted Ryder, forcing his horse off the road and into the fields behind the village.

Over rows and rows of planted vegetables, the horses rode through Furrowsrich. Leaping the low fence behind the house Ryder had built with his own hands, he came around to the front. The door was wide open, and a row of zombies was making their way inside.

Not bothering to bring his horse to a stop, Ryder threw his legs over the edge of his saddle and came down at a full run, barging into the back of the zombies and bowling them over as he came through the front door at full speed.

Ryder collided with two zombies and continued on, running them into one of the support beams holding up the roof. The heavy chains hanging from his shoulders added their weight to his momentum, and in combination, he smashed the rotting creatures to something resembling horse manure. Their decayed flesh and brittle bones made for a soft cushion, and Ryder stepped away from the stout, wooden pole unharmed.

Inside the house, half a dozen zombies had Samira, Angeline, and Douglas backed into a corner. Douglas stood in front of the two women, a burning log from the fire in one hand. He tried to hold back the walking dead, swinging the flaming timber back and forth. But it wasn't doing much good. The zombies were still advancing.

"Ryder!" screamed Samira. There was real terror in her voice. "Ryder, help us! Please help us!"

Ryder unleashed his spiked chain, letting it fly at the back of the first zombie. The enchanted links crackled with purple energy as they came down around the head of its victim. The zombie's rotted flesh seared under the electrical assault, sending a plume of thick gray smoke into the air, and the end of the spiked chain encircled the creature's neck. Giving it a sharp pull, Ryder tore the creature's head from its shoulders.

The zombie took one more step, then fell over, dead again.

The rest of the group, now aware that they were under attack, turned around and came for Ryder.

"That's right," he said, gripping his chain in the middle and spinning it in a large circle before him. "Come to Ryder." He backed up as they advanced, drawing them away from his family.

A smile broke across Ryder's lips. He'd taken on three undead giants. He could handle five undead humans by himself.

The Broken Spear appeared in the doorway just then. They rushed into the small house, drawing their weapons and surrounding the zombies.

Ryder shrugged. Help was always good. He lunged at the first undead. His chain turned its brittle corpse into a pile of broken bones. The Broken Spear followed his lead, charging into the fray and cutting down the foul beasts in short order.

Douglas threw the flaming branch into the fire pit. "Where have you been, boy?"

Angeline brushed past the old man and folded her arms around Ryder despite his chain-wrapped appearance. "We thought you were dead," she said, squeezing him tight. "We thought you had left us."

"I'm sorry," he said. "I got a little sidetracked."

Over his mother's shoulder, Ryder stared down on Samira, sitting on her knees in the corner. She looked tired and scared. The last few months had taken their toll.

Disengaging from Angeline's embrace, Ryder went to Samira's side. "It's all right. You're safe now."

Samira looked up at Ryder. There was sadness in her eyes.

Giselle came to stand beside the two of them. "So," she said, "I take it this is your wife."

Ryder looked up and nodded. There were a lot of things that needed to be said, but right now he didn't know how to say them.

"Who is this?" asked Samira.

Ryder opened his mouth, not sure what was going to come out.

Giselle cut him off. "I'm just a friend. Ryder did me a big favor, so now I'm returning—"

Outside, the high pitch of a horse shrieking tore

through the night, accompanied by the sounds of battle.

Jase came bursting through the door, interrupting Giselle. "Ryder, it's your brother. He's in trouble."

Samira jumped to her feet. "Liam, no." She gathered her dress in her arms and went running into the night.

◉ ◉ ◉ ◉ ◉

Liam fought for his life—and the life of the baron.

They had ridden into Furrowsrich at Liam's insistence. The place was crawling with zombies. The elite guard had managed to dispatch most of the shambling dead in short order. But they had been merely a ruse.

The vampires had been lying in wait, and they pounced out of the treetops on Lord Purdun, Liam, and Knoblauch. The three men stood now with their backs together, surrounded by the hissing, shrieking undead. At the head of them all stood their mistress.

"If it isn't Lord Purdun," purred Shyressa.

"What is it you want, Shyressa?" Purdun didn't look at the vampire as he spoke, keeping his eyes on her threatening minions.

"Nothing much." There was a giddy edge to the vampire's words. "Just control of your barony."

"And you think if you kill me you'll get my throne?" Purdun shook his head. "It doesn't work that way."

"No?" toyed Shyressa. "We'll see about that."

Shyressa leaped forward wrapping her arms around the baron and biting down on his neck.

"Lord Purdun," shouted Liam. The vampire had moved so fast, he hadn't had time to react. He spun and stabbed at Shyressa, but the tip of his blade passed through the cloth of her gown and out the other side.

"Hold," shouted the baron. "Mind the others." He pointed out the advancing horde.

Liam did a double take. It wasn't the baron the vampire had wrapped in her embrace—it was Knoblauch. The veteran guardsman had been just fast enough to step in between the baron and his attacker. He'd been given the chance to atone for his sins, and he'd taken it. This was the price he paid.

Liam couldn't see Knoblauch's body, wrapped up as it was in the vampire's gown, but he could see the man struggle inside her embrace. It reminded Liam of watching a spider slowly devour its prey.

There was no more time to mourn. The vampires closed in on them, and Liam fought frantically. It was all he could do to keep their clutching, clawed hands from grasping his arms and legs. Liam felt the panic of desperation, and his sword moved faster than ever before. Still, with every passing moment, the undead closed down on him.

He was going to share the same fate as Knoblauch. He was going to be sucked dry.

A heavy rattling sound filled Liam's ears, and a pair of chains came whipping over his shoulder, knocking two vampires to the ground. Ryder appeared at Liam's side, chains flinging out from his body, slapping aside grasping claws. They laid low undead, and they forced the advancing vampires back, giving Liam back the slimmest glimmer of hope.

In the clearing space, Liam could see Shyressa again. She opened her arms, letting Knoblauch's body fall lifeless to the ground. Lifting a finger to her lips, she pushed a stray drop of the man's blood back into her mouth.

Ryder didn't hesitate. He ran right for her. His electrically charged chain circled over his head, lighting up the night with a purplish glow. Then it came down, discharging as it slapped against Shyressa's flesh and plunging the streets of Furrowsrich again into darkness.

The electrical energy played over the vampire's frame, but if it did her any harm, she didn't show it.

"Is that it?" taunted the vampire. She grabbed Ryder by the chains wrapped across his chest and pulled him close to her. "I told you this wasn't over."

Ryder ducked out of the metal links, sloughing off the chains and escaping the vampire's grip. His makeshift armor rattled to the ground.

"Come back here," shouted the Rune Mistress. She grabbed hold of Ryder's ducked head, one hand on each side of his face and lifted him onto his tiptoes. "Your blood will be the sweetest of all." Distending her mouth, she plunged her teeth into his exposed neck.

"Yie, yie, yie, yie, yie!" The ululating cry came from behind the ancient vampire, and the woman who had ridden out of Zerith Hold with Ryder sprang onto Shyressa's back.

She was smaller than the withered creature of the night, but she was fast, and her curved blade struck Shyressa hard, sliding lengthwise down her spine. The blow would have severed a normal woman in two. As it was, the vampire let out a terrific wail, pulling her teeth from Ryder's neck and letting go of his face. His body fell limply to the ground, and Shyressa's screeching turned into an ear-splitting howl.

The leaves on the trees shook, and the hairs on the back of Liam's neck stood on end. His skin felt cold, and the night seemed to grow darker.

Shyressa's body collapsed in on itself, and she leaned forward, putting her hands on the ground. Her gown changed into a thick coat of fur, and her face grew a long nose and two pointed ears.

The vampire had transformed herself into a dire wolf.

The creature growled, saliva dripping from its lips. Shyressa howled once again, a long spine-rattling sound that jangled the nerves. All around, the noise grew, filling the air. The Crimson Awl, every last one of them, paused amidst the fighting and howled along with their mistress.

When it had finished, the dire wolf turned toward Liam and leaped. He dropped to one knee, guarding his head with his arms. But it didn't matter. The creature was over him and gone, dashing off into the shadows, its spawn following right behind it.

It was a sad day.

"May he find rest in the afterlife..."

It was the day of Ryder's funeral.

"May we all find it in our hearts to forgive him for his mistakes..."

Liam stood with his head bowed, his arms around Samira. The rest of the village had come out. So too had a contingent from Zerith Hold. A unit of elite guardsmen stood at attention while Baron Purdun himself presided over the ritual.

"But most of all, may we always remember Ryder of Duhlnarim for his bravery, honor, and courage in Ahlarkham's greatest time of need."

The baron finished his speech, and the casket holding Ryder's body was lowered into the ground.

People formed a line and took turns putting shovels full of dirt on top of the casket, saying their final good-byes to a man they all knew and loved. It was a ritual Liam had never really understood until now. He was glad to be able to do one last favor for his brother, glad to be able to say good-bye even if Ryder couldn't hear him.

Once he had taken his turn, Liam grabbed hold of Samira's arm and the two of them began walking back toward the village.

Someone put a hand on Liam's shoulder.

"Excuse me," said a young woman.

Liam turned around to look into the beautiful brown eyes of the woman who had accompanied Ryder, the same woman who had mortally wounded Shyressa only two nights before.

"Your name is Liam, right?" she asked.

Liam nodded. "Yes."

The young woman smiled sadly. "My name is Giselle." She offered Liam her hand.

"You're Ryder's friend," said Samira.

Giselle nodded. "Was." She looked as if she might cry.

Liam pulled a handkerchief out of his pants and handed it to Giselle, but she shook her head.

"No, thank you," she said. "I'll be fine." She lifted her chin, gritted her teeth, and cleared the tears from her eyes. She smiled again. "But there *is* something you could do for me."

Liam looked at Samira, then back at Giselle. "Any friend of Ryder's is a friend of mine," he said. "What can I help you with?"

"I was thinking that I might like to stay around here, in Duhlnarim," explained Giselle. "And I thought maybe you could put in a good word for me with the baron. Thought maybe I could join up with the elite guard."

"What about your friends?" asked Samira. "The ones who came with you to our home?"

Giselle smiled. "They have their path, and I have mine," she said. "Most of them have returned north, to the Giant's Plain. Some will no doubt find trouble in other parts."

Liam put his hand on her shoulder. "I'm sure the baron would be happy to have you," he said. "Come. I'll introduce you to him right now."

❧ ❧ ❧ ❧ ❧

In the dark of the night, a lone figure walked into the graveyard outside of Furrowsrich. It didn't have a torch or a lantern. It didn't need one. All it carried was a length of rope and a shovel as it walked through the rows of tombstones, looking at each of the names.

The figure stopped over a fresh grave. This one didn't have a tombstone. It hadn't been placed yet. All there was to mark the location was a plank of wood with the name "Ryder" burned into it.

The figure smiled and dropped the rope on the ground. Then, placing the head of the shovel into the fresh dirt, the figure began to dig.

The figure stopping digging when it reached the wood of the casket. When it found the edges, it got down into the grave and finished the job with its bare hands, carefully removing the dirt little by little, uncovering the casket as if it were a priceless artifact.

Grabbing the rope, the figure attached it to the handles on the edge of the casket and climbed out of the hole. Then, with the free end, it began to pull, slowly, carefully dragging the coffin to the surface.

At the top, the figure lifted the lid and peered inside.

"Rise, child," the figure said in a hollow, wispy voice. "Your master awaits you."

Inside the coffin, Ryder's body sat up straight. He lifted himself to his feet. "Where am I to meet her?"

"In the tombs outside Dajaan. Near the Deepwash," said the figure. "Do not keep Shyressa waiting, or you will find that there are far worse things in this world than death."

In the far corner of the graveyard another man, this one invisible, turned and walked toward Zerith Hold. "Yes. Just as I thought," said Curtis to himself. "Yes, yes. This might be a problem."

DRAGONS ARE DESCENDING ON THE FORGOTTEN REALMS!

THE RAGE
The Year of Rogue Dragons, Book I

RICHARD LEE BYERS

Renegade dragon hunter Dorn hates dragons with a passion few can believe, let alone match. He has devoted his entire life to killing every dragon he can find, but as a feral madness begins to overtake the dragons of Faerûn, civilization's only hope may lie in the last alliance Dorn would ever accept.

THE RITE
The Year of Rogue Dragons, Book II

RICHARD LEE BYERS

Dragons war with dragons in the cold steppes of the Bloodstone Lands, and the secret of the ancient curse gives a small band of determined heroes hope that the madness might be brought to an end.

REALMS OF THE DRAGONS
Book I

EDITED BY PHILIP ATHANS

This anthology features all-new stories by R.A. Salvatore, Ed Greenwood, Elaine Cunningham, and the authors of the R.A. Salvatore's War of the Spider Queen series. It fleshes out many of the details from the current Year of Rogue Dragons trilogy by Richard Lee Byers and includes a short story by Byers.

REALMS OF THE DRAGONS
Book II

EDITED BY PHILIP ATHANS

A new breed of Forgotten Realms authors bring a fresh approach to new stories of mighty dragons and the unfortunate humans who cross their paths.

JOIN THE ADVENTURES IN THE FORGOTTEN REALMS WORLD WITH THESE NEW NOVELS HITTING STORES IN 2005!

QUEEN OF THE DEPTHS
The Priests, Book III

A valiant shalarin priestess braves the cruel waters of the Sea of Fallen
Stars to save her home and avenge the tragic death of her mother. But
will Umberlee herself stand in the young priestess's way?

MIDNIGHT'S MASK
Erevis Cale, Book III

PAUL S. KEMP

The author of *Resurrection* concludes the tale of the Realms' most
enigmatic hero, Erevis Cale. Drawn deeper and deeper into the
service of Mask, Cale may find himself so lost in the shadows that he can
never return.

WHISPER OF WAVES
The Watercourse Trilogy, Book I

PHILIP ATHANS

The New York Times best-selling author of *Annihilation* tells an epic tale of
intrigue, dreams, war, and love on the shores of the Lake of Steam. One
man struggles against deadly nagas, powerful men, seductive women, and
a Red Wizard bent on his destruction, all to realize a dream greater than
the Realms has ever known.